BEN BURTON

LECTOR HOUSE PUBLIC DOMAIN WORKS

This book is a result of an effort made by Lector House towards making a contribution to the preservation and repair of original classic literature. The original text is in the public domain in the United States of America, and possibly other countries depending upon their specific copyright laws.

In an attempt to preserve, improve and recreate the original content, certain conventional norms with regard to typographical mistakes, hyphenations, punctuations and/or other related subject matters, have been corrected upon our consideration. However, few such imperfections might not have been rectified as they were inherited and preserved from the original content to maintain the authenticity and construct, relevant to the work. The work might contain a few prior copyright references as well as page references which have been retained, wherever considered relevant to the part of the construct. We believe that this work holds historical, cultural and/or intellectual importance in the literary works community, therefore despite the oddities, we accounted the work for print as a part of our continuing effort towards preservation of literary work and our contribution towards the development of the society as a whole, driven by our beliefs.

We are grateful to our readers for putting their faith in us and accepting our imperfections with regard to preservation of the historical content. We shall strive hard to meet up to the expectations to improve further to provide an enriching reading experience.

Though, we conduct extensive research in ascertaining the status of copyright before redeveloping a version of the content, in rare cases, a classic work might be incorrectly marked as not-in-copyright. In such cases, if you are the copyright holder, then kindly contact us or write to us, and we shall get back to you with an immediate course of action.

HAPPY READING!

BEN BURTON

WILLIAM HENRY GILES KINGSTON

ISBN: 978-93-90314-26-3

Published: -

© 2020
LECTOR HOUSE LLP

LECTOR HOUSE LLP
E-MAIL: lectorpublishing@gmail.com

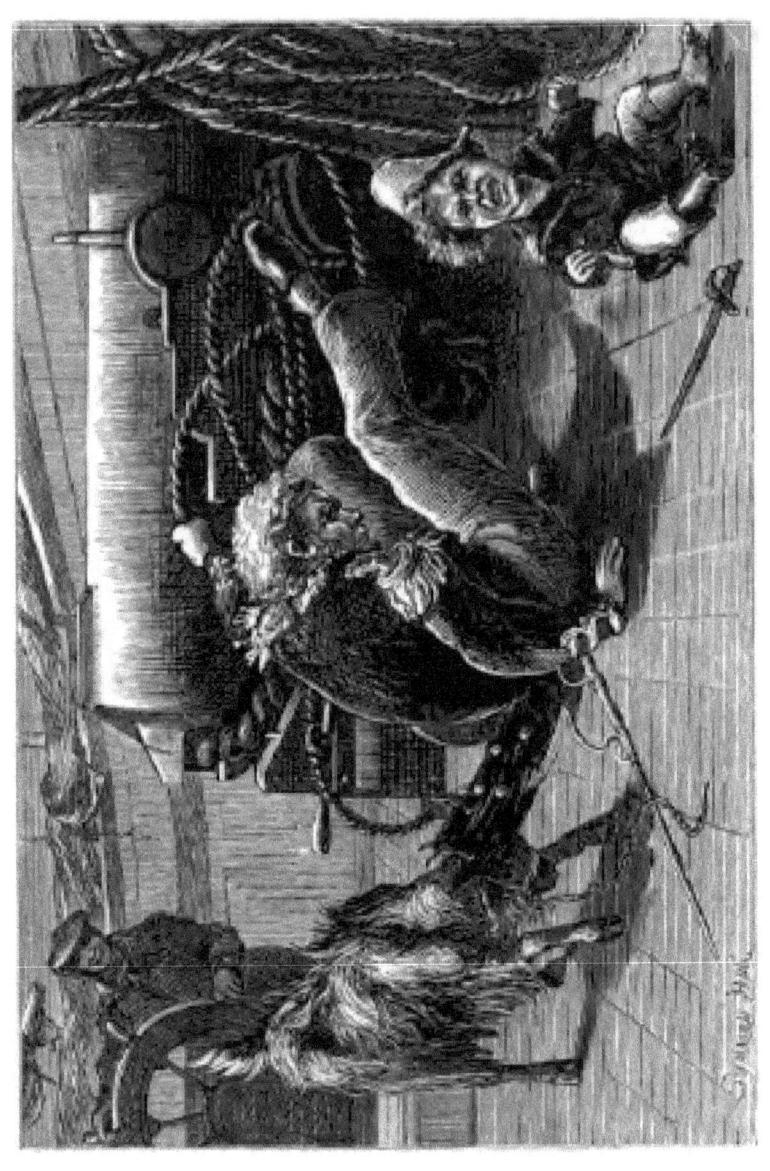

HER HORNS CATCHING IN HIS COAT-TAILS, HE AND SHE AND
I ALL WENT ROLLING OVER TOGETHER.

BEN BURTON;
OR,
BORN AND BRED AT SEA.

BY

W. H. G. KINGSTON

Author of "The Fire Ships," "Cruise of the Frolic,"
"Ernest Bracebridge," &c. &c.

CONTENTS

	Page
I. Chapter One	1
II. Chapter Two	6
III. Chapter Three	13
IV. Chapter Four	18
V. Chapter Five	23
VI. Chapter Six	29
VII. Chapter Seven	34
VIII. Chapter Eight	40
IX. Chapter Nine	45
X. Chapter Ten	50
XI. Chapter Eleven	56
XII. Chapter Twelve	61
XIII. Chapter Thirteen	66
XIV. Chapter Fourteen	72
XV. Chapter Fifteen	79
XVI. Chapter Sixteen	86
XVII. Chapter Seventeen	92
XVIII. Chapter Eighteen	98
XIX. Chapter Nineteen	102
XX. Chapter Twenty	107

CONTENTS

XXI. Chapter Twenty One	112
XXII. Chapter Twenty Two	118
XXIII. Chapter Twenty Three	123
XXIV. Chapter Twenty Four	128
XXV. Chapter Twenty Five	133

CHAPTER ONE.

"Dick Burton, you're a daddy! Polly's been and got a baby for you, old boy!" exclaimed several voices, as the said Dick mounted the side of the old "Boreas," on the books of which ship he was rated as a quarter-master, he having just then returned from a pleasant little cutting-out expedition, where he had obtained, besides honour and glory, a gash on the cheek, a bullet through the shoulder, and a prong from a pike in the side.

"Me a what?" he inquired, bending his head forward with a look of incredulity, and mechanically hitching up his trousers. "Me a daddy? On course it's a boy? Polly wouldn't go for to get a girl, a poor little helpless girl, out in these outlandish parts."

"On course, Dick, it's a boy, a fine big, walloping younker, too. Why bless ye, Quacko ain't no way to be compared to him, especially when he sings out, which he can do already, loud enough to drown the bo'sun's whistle, let me tell you," was the reply to Dick Burton's last question.

That baby was me. Quacko was the monkey of the ship. I might not have been flattered at being compared to him, though it must be owned that I stood very much in the light of his rival. I soon, however, cut him out completely. My mother was one of two women on board. The other was Susan King, wife of another quarter-master. The two men enjoyed a privilege denied to their captain, for they could take their wives to sea, which he could not. To be sure, Polly and Susan made themselves more generally useful than the captain's wife would probably have done had she lived on board, for they washed and mended the men's shirts, nursed them when sick or wounded, prepared lint and bandages for the surgeons, and performed many other offices such as generally fall to the lot of female hands. They had both endeared themselves to the men, by a thousand kind and gentle acts, but my mother was decidedly the favourite. This might have been because she was young and remarkably handsome, and at the same time as good and modest as a woman could be; and so discreet that she was never known to cause a quarrel among her shipmates, or a pang of jealousy to her husband; and that, under the circumstances of the case, is saying a great deal in her favour. Fancy two women among nearly four hundred men, and not one of the latter even thinking of infringing the last commandment of the Decalogue. What an amount of good sense, good-temper, and self-command must have been exercised on the part of the former.

Susan's qualifications for the position she held were very different to those of my mother. In appearance she was a very Gorgon, a veritable strong-minded, double-fisted female, tall, gaunt, and coarse-featured. A hoarse laugh, and a voice which vied with the boatswain's in stentorian powers, and yet withal she was a true woman, with a gentle, loving, tender heart. Bill King, her husband, knew her good qualities, and vowed that he would not swap her for Queen Charlotte, or any other lady in the land, not if the offer was made to him with a thousand gold guineas into the bargain.

I ought to be grateful to her, and do cherish her memory with affection, for she assisted to bring me into the world; attended my mother in her time of trial and trouble, and nursed me with the gentlest care. Yet Sue had a tongue, and could use it too when occasion, in her judgment, required its employment. But she always took the side of right and virtue against wrong and vice, and woe betided the luckless wight who fell under the ban of her just displeasure. She would belabour him, not with her hands, but by word, look, and gesture, till he shrieked out for mercy and promised never again to offend, or took to ignominious flight like a thief with a *posse* of constables at his heels. Bill King was a quiet-mannered little man with a huge pair of whiskers, like studden-sails rigged out on either side of his cheeks, and a mild expression of countenance which did not belie his calm good-temper and amiability of disposition. But though gentle in peace, he was as brave and daring a seaman as ever sprang, cutlass in hand, on an enemy's deck, or flew aloft to loose topsails when a prize had been cut out, amid showers of bullets and round-shot.

Of my father, I will only say that he was in no way behind his friend Bill King in bravery, and though he spoke the sailor's lingo like his shipmates, he was vastly his superior in manners and appearance. Indeed, he and my mother were a very handsome couple. They were also, I may say, deservedly looked upon with great respect by the officers, from the captain downwards, and regarded with affection by all the crew.

To go back to that insignificant little individual, myself, as I certainly was on the day I have mentioned, when I made my first appearance on board the HMS "Boreas". I came in for a large share of the regard entertained by the ship's company for my parents. My father was the first person introduced by Susan King into my presence.

"Well, he is a rum little youngster!" he exclaimed, taking me up in his open palms. "He is like Polly—that he is!" he added, as he gazed at me affectionately, the feelings of a father for the first time welling up in his bosom. "Yes, he is a sweet little cherub! Shouldn't wonder but he is like them as lives up aloft there to watch over us poor chaps at sea. Ay, that he must be. They can't beat him. Lord love ye, Sue, I am grateful to you for this here day's work."

I here interrupted my father's remarks by a loud cry, and other infantine operations, on which Sue insisted on having me back again to her safe keeping, while outside the screen several voices were heard entreating my father to bring me out for inspection, a request with which Mrs King had before steadily refused to comply.

"I say, Dick, just let's have a look at him. One squint, Burton, just to see what

CHAPTER ONE. 3

sort of a younker he may be. Come now, he ain't a chap to be ashamed of, I'm sure. There ain't none like him here aboard, I'll swear. He don't come up to Quacko anyhow. Come, Dick, show us him now, do, there's a good chap."

These and similar exclamations were sung out by various voices in different tones, to which my mother, as she lay in her cot, listened not unpleased, till at length my father having given her a kiss, and uttered a few words of congratulation and thanks to Heaven—sailors are not addicted to long prayers—again took me in his outstretched palms, and thus brought me forth to the admiring gaze of his shipmates. So eager were they to see me, that I ran no little risk of being knocked out of my father's hands, as they were shoving each other aside in their endeavours to get to the front rank. Then one and all wanted to have me to handle for a moment; but to this Susan King, who had followed my father from behind the screen, would on no account consent.

"Why, bless you, my lads, you would be wringing the little chap's neck off, if you were to attempt to take hold of him," said Susan.

"Oh! No, don't fear, we will handle him just as if he was made of sugar," was the reply.

"Oh! You don't know what delicate, weak little creatures these babies are when they are first born," observed Susan. "Just like jellyfish, they will not stand any rough handling."

Still in spite of my kind nurse's remarks, the bystanders continued to urge my father to let them have me.

"It is as much as my place is worth, mates," he answered at length; "I would not let him out of my hands on no account."

My new shipmates were, therefore, compelled to admire me at a respectful distance. I believe the remarks they made were generally complimentary, only they seemed to have arrived at the opinion that I was not at that time so fat or so fair as the cherubs they had heard of who live up aloft.

"And now, mates, I will just hand him back to Susan, and go and get the doctor to look at me, for I begin to feel pretty stiffish with the holes I got made in me just now," said my father.

And I was forthwith reconsigned to the charge of my mother and her attendant, while he went to the surgeon to get his wounds dressed. There were none of them, fortunately very serious, for the bullet had gone through the fleshy part of the arm, and the pike had missed the bone; the cut in the cheek, which at first appeared the most trifling, giving in the end more trouble and annoyance than either of the other hurts. The expedition in which he had been engaged was something out of the common way, though when I come to note down the numerous ones he has described to me, it is somewhat difficult not to mix them all up together.

The frigate, on board which I thus suddenly found myself, formed one of the East India Squadron, of which Admiral Peter Rainier was Commander-in-Chief.

The "Boreas" had a short time before this been despatched to Macao for the protection of the China trade. I speak of course from hearsay, as what I am about to relate occurred just before I came into existence; indeed, of many other subsequent events which I shall venture to describe I cannot be said to have any very vivid recollection, although present at the time. The frigate was standing to the eastward, some three or four leagues from the coast, when one of the topmen, Pat Brady, on the look-out at the mast-head, discovered a sail in shore to the northward. Pat was a relation of my mother—she was an Irishwoman, and, as Pat never failed to assert, a credit to her country. He would at all times have been ready to fight any man who ventured to hold a different opinion.

Our Captain, Christopher Cobb, was a brave man, but somewhat peppery, and very easily put out.

The wind had previously been light. It fell a dead calm soon after the stranger had been sighted. Our First-Lieutenant, Mr Schank, who, in spite of having a wooden leg, was as active as any man on board, having gone aloft himself to take a look at her, came to the opinion that she was a brig of war. From the way in which she increased her distance from the frigate after she was seen, it was very evident that she had her sweeps out, and there was every probability of her escaping.

"That must not be! That must not be!" muttered the Captain, as he paced the quarter-deck, fretting and fuming under the hot sun of the tropics. "Mr Schank, we must not let her go."

"No, sir," said the First-Lieutenant, "that would never do."

"We must take her with the boats if we cannot overtake her with the ship," said the Captain, with one of his quiet laughs.

"The very thing I was thinking of, sir," answered Mr Schank, who, I may observe, presented a great contrast to his excellent superior, the one being short and rotund, while in figure the Lieutenant was tall and gaunt.

"Then we will have the boats out and see what we can do," said the Captain.

"With all my heart, sir," answered the First-Lieutenant. "I will, if you please, take the command."

"Out boats!" was the order. The object was quickly known. In an instant the men who had till then been listlessly hanging about the decks in the few shady places they could find, for the sun was pretty nigh overhead, were instantly aroused into activity.

In a short time six boats were in the water manned and armed. In them went three lieutenants and the master, two master's mates, fifty seamen, and twenty marines. One of the gigs, the fastest boat, led the way, each boat taking the one next to her in tow. As they shoved off their shipmates cheered, and heartily wished them success. That they were determined to obtain, though they well knew that they had a pull before them of a good many hours under a burning sun, and probably some pretty sharp fighting at the end of it. After following her for an hour or more, Mr Schank perceived that they gained nothing on the brig. He therefore ordered the boats to cast off from each other, and to make the best of their way, provided no boat rowed ahead of the barge under his command. It was

CHAPTER ONE.

just two o'clock when the expedition left the frigate. My father was in the launch commanded by a master's mate, Mr Harry Oliver, a slight delicate youth who appeared utterly unfit for such work, but he had the heart of a lion, and daring unsurpassed by any officer in the service. For four long hours the chase continued, when, at about six in the evening, she was still four leagues ahead. Mr Schank now ordered the master to proceed in the gig as fast as he could pull, and by all means to keep sight of the brig, while in the event of darkness coming on he was to hoist a light to show her position. It had been arranged that the attack was to be made in two lines. The barge, pinnace, and gig were to board on the starboard quarter; and the other line, consisting of the three other boats, on the larboard quarter. For upwards of two hours longer the boats pulled on, the gloom of evening gradually closing over them. Still they could distinguish the dim outline of the brig ahead. The First-Lieutenant having got within musket-shot of the chase with Mr Oliver's boat, he directed his men to lie on to their oars that they might arm, and allow the sternmost boats to come up. Just then the master in the gig rejoined them.

"What is she?" asked Mr Schank.

"A French man-of-war brig of sixteen guns," was the answer. "She is under all sail with her sweeps out, and we shall find it pretty brisk work getting on board." The crews had of course been ordered to keep silence, or I rather think that they would have uttered a hearty shout at this announcement. In a few minutes more the sternmost boats got up, and their crews also armed and prepared for the attack. They were directed to steer one on each side of the brig, and to get in under the sweeps and close to her sides. In ten minutes they were within pistol-shot of the enemy, who was slipping along through the water, her sweeps being aided by the light wind off the land, at about two knots an hour.

And now the silence which had hitherto been kept was broken by the voice of their gallant leader shouting, "What vessel is that?"

There was no answer. Again he asked the same question in French. It was very bad French, and perhaps was not better understood than the previous question. At all events no reply was made.

"Then at her, lads!" cried Mr Schank; and the crews of the boats, uttering three hearty cheers, dashed up towards the brig's stern. As they got close up, however, a tremendous fire of heavy guns and musketry was opened on them, the bullets whizzing round them and wounding many, though fortunately none of the boats were struck by the round-shot, while, as they got up, pikes were thrust down at them and pistols fired in their faces. The bowmen in the leading boats which had got hold of the ship's sides were killed or wounded, and the boats dropped astern. Among those hit was their brave leader, but undaunted he shouted to his men to pull up again. Again as they did so they met with the same reception.

CHAPTER TWO.

The First-Lieutenant was not a man to be defeated. Wounded as he was, he still resolved to persevere.

"Never say die, lads!" he shouted, as they were driven back. "Give them a taste of our powder in return!"

On this, the boats poured a hot fire of musketoons and small-arms through the brig's stern and quarter-ports. It told with tremendous effect, for not a shot was now fired upon the boats.

"On, on, lads!" shouted the First-Lieutenant; and before the Frenchmen could recover, the boats were hanging on to her quarters, and the crews were climbing up on deck. The First-Lieutenant, in spite of his wooden leg and wound, was among the foremost. My father, though also hit, followed close behind the brave young mate—Harry Oliver. Scarcely had they gained the brig's deck, however, ere the Frenchmen rallied and opposed them with the most determined bravery. The English crew climbing up one after the other, quickly gained possession of the whole of the after part of the brig, not, however, without several being killed and wounded, the Second-Lieutenant being among the former. He was cut down, after being twice shot through the body. For a few minutes a most bloody and tremendous conflict ensued. A Frenchman thrust his pike through Mr Oliver's side, and another was following it up with his sword, and would certainly have put an end to the young officer, had not my father, just as he got an ugly prong in his side of the same description, with one sweep of his cutlass brought the man to the deck, never to move again. French crews can very seldom, if ever, stand against English boarders. The bravest of the enemy were cut down, or began to give way. My father, with Mr Oliver on one side and the First-Lieutenant and Master on the other, with the men at their backs, now made a clear path, strewing the decks with the bodies of those who attempted to oppose them. The remainder of the enemy fled; some leaped down the hatchways, others took shelter on the bowsprit and jib-boom, and the more nimble sprang up the shrouds, where, as my father declared, like so many monkeys, they hung chattering and asking for quarter.

"Of course, if they would but have been quiet and peaceable, we had no wish to kill them," he used to say, "and glad enough we were when we found ourselves in possession of the brig, just about five minutes from the time we had first stepped on her decks. It was about the hardest bit of work I ever was engaged in," he always averred. "We lost our Second-Lieutenant, five seamen and three marines killed, three officers and twenty-two men wounded. The Frenchman had a crew of one hundred and sixty men and boys, out of whom there were no less

CHAPTER TWO.   7

than fourteen killed and twenty wounded—pretty badly, too, for we were not apt to use our cutlasses over gently, you may suppose.

"We had still plenty of work to do, for, though cowed for the moment, the Frenchmen would not have made much ceremony in trying to turn the tables again upon us. We had barely fifty men fit for work, and they had still one hundred and twenty—considerable odds against us.

"Mr Schank, as soon as he saw that the deck was ours, directed one of the officers to hurry down into the cabin and secure the private signals, and ordered me, at the same time, to go with a couple of marines to take charge of the magazine, for one never knows what desperate fellows may do when they have lost their ship, and some mad chap or other might have set fire to it, and blown us and themselves up into the air. Such things have been done before now.

"The next thing we did was to carry the wounded below. Our own people and the enemy's were treated alike. Poor fellows! How some of them did groan when they were lifted up. Next, an order was given to heave the dead overboard, 'And look out, lads, that you don't send any with the breath in their bodies to feed the sharks,' said the First-Lieutenant. The caution did not come too soon. Two men, one of whom was Paddy Brady, were about shoving a big Frenchman through a port, when the poor fellow uttered a groan. 'What is that you say, monsieur? Just speak again. Are you alive or dead?' exclaimed Brady. No answer was returned, and Paddy began to drag the dead body nearer the port. Again a groan, considerably louder than the first was heard. 'Arrah, now,' said Paddy, 'I wish you would just make up your mind whether it is overboard you would wish to go, or be carried below. Speak, man; I ax ye again for the last time: are ye alive or dead?'

"The Frenchman, maybe, might not have understood exactly what Brady was saying, but he must have had a pretty horrible idea that he was about to be sent overboard. This time he not only groaned, but uttered some words, and endeavoured to drag himself along the deck. 'Arrah, now, that's like a dacent, sinsible man,' observed Pat. 'Anyhow, you deserve to have your hurts looked to, and so we will carry him below, Jim.'"

The truth was that the man had been only slightly wounded, and afterwards stunned by a blow. Had he not come to himself at that moment, his career would undoubtedly have been finished. Hands were now sent aloft, the studden-sails hauled down, and the brig brought on a wind. The sweeps, which had all this time remained run out, were taken in-board, and the boats were veered astern.

"We now stood in the direction we hoped to find the frigate, hoisting two lights at the mast-head, firing guns, and burning blue lights to show our position. It was an anxious time, however, and we had to keep a very watchful eye on the Frenchmen. They evidently were hatching mischief, for they must have known as well as we did that the frigate was still a long way off, and that if they could overcome us they might yet get away with their brig. She was called the 'Loup' (the Wolf), and a wolf she had proved herself among our merchantmen. I had been relieved at my station at the magazine, when Pat Brady came up to me. 'Burton,' he said, 'I wish you would just take a look at the wounded prisoners. There is one of them whom I thought dead, and there he is, sitting up and talking away as if there was nothing the matter with him. I cannot understand his lingo, but, by the way he moves his arms about, I think he means mischief!'

"I went below with Brady, and there, sure enough, was the man he had so nearly thrown overboard, apparently very little the worse for his hurt, and evidently, as it appeared to me, trying to persuade his countrymen to do something or other which he had proposed. Sentries had been placed over the other prisoners, of course, but desperate men might soon have overpowered them, especially if the prisoners knew that there would be a little diversion in their favour.

"Hurrying on deck, I reported what we had seen to Mr Schank, who immediately ordered the man to be brought on deck, and as his wound was dressed, there was no cruelty in that. He grumbled considerably; the more so, probably, because his plan had been defeated.

"We continued every now and then sending up blue lights, keeping a very watchful eye all the time on our prisoners. At length, far away on our weather-beam, a bright light suddenly burst forth as if out of the dark ocean. We tacked and stood towards it. However, as the wind was very light, the Third-Lieutenant was sent off in the gig with an account of our success. Two hours had still to pass away before we at length got up to the frigate, and pretty well-pleased we were when the cheer which our shipmates sent forth to congratulate us on our success reached our ears." Such was the substance of my father's account, often subsequently told.

I do not know whether the anxiety which Burton felt when she saw her husband setting out on what she knew must be a dangerous expedition had any peculiar effect on her, but certain it is, that while my father was slashing away at the Frenchmen, and the bullets were flying about his head, I was born into the world.

With regard to the prize, she was carried safely into Macao, in the expectation that she would be fitted out as a cruiser, and that Mr Schank would get the command of her. Her fate I shall have hereafter to relate.

I meantime grew apace, and speedily cut out Quacko in the estimation of our shipmates. He, however, had his friends and supporters; for some months, at all events, he afforded them more amusement than I could do. They could tease him and play him tricks, which my mother and Mrs King took very good care they should not do to me. I had no lack of nurses from the first, and highly honoured were those into whose hands my mother ventured to commit me.

Mrs King had enough to do for some time after the action, in attending both to my mother and the poor fellows who had been wounded, both English and French, the latter receiving as much care from her gentle hands as did our own people. The two chief rivals for the honour of looking after me were my cousin, Pat Brady, and Toby Kiddle, boatswain's mate. Although many of my old shipmates have passed away from my memory, Toby Kiddle made an impression which was never erased. Nature had not intended him for a topman, for though wonderfully muscular, his figure was like a tun. His legs were short, and his arms were unusually long. With them tucked akimbo, he could take up two of the heaviest men in

CHAPTER TWO.

the ship, and run along the deck with them as lightly as he would have done with a couple of young children. He had a generous, kind heart, could tell a good story, and troll forth a ditty with any man; and as to his bravery, where all were brave, I need scarcely mention it, except to say that I do no not think anyone beat him at that. Boatswain's mate though he was, Toby Kiddle had a heart as gentle as a lamb's. He scarcely seemed cut out for the post, and yet there was a rough crust over it which enabled him to do his duty, and when he had to lay on with the cat, to shut his eyes, and to hit as hard as he was ordered. And yet I always have pitied a kind-hearted boatswain's mate, though he is not after all worse off than the captain and officers, who have to stand by and see men punished. However, I will not say anything about that matter just now. Time went on, and I grew bigger, and began to chew beef and bacon with the rest of the ship's company becoming more and more independent of my mother in every way. Yet I loved her, as such a mother deserved to be loved. As I grew bigger I made more and more friends. The Captain himself very frequently took notice of me, and patted my head, which was beginning to get curls upon it, and often gave me cakes and other Chinese manufactured delicacies which he had got from the shore. Captain Cobb was a short man, and since he came out to China had grown very round and stout. His face, as a boy, had been probably pink and white, but it had now been burnt into a deep red copper colour. His eyes, which were small, were bloodshot, with a ferrety expression, and altogether his outward man was not attractive. His uniforms, which had hung loosely on him when he left home, had been, by the skill of the tailor, let out and out to meet the demands of his increasing corpulency; but no art or skill could do more for them; and as he was unwilling to procure others till those were worn out, he looked, when walking the quarter-deck, very much as if he had on a straight waistcoat.

Captain Cobb was not disregardful of his creature comforts, and in order to supply himself with milk for breakfast and tea, he had shipped on board, some time back, a she-goat, which fully answered his wishes. Seamen will make pets of everything—monkeys, babies, lions, pigs, bears, dogs, and cats. The goat had become a favourite, for she was a handsome creature, and very tame, but it was chiefly in connection with Quacko, who was soon taught to ride upon her. Quacko was certainly very well aware that he must never venture upon the quarter-deck, and before, therefore, he reached the sacred precincts on his daily rides, he always managed to wheel the goat about and retrace his steps forward. Quacko was a wonderfully sagacious monkey, and held his position in the good opinion of the crew in spite of my rival claims. Had I been thrown entirely upon their mercy as Quacko was, I might have completely cut him out; but having my mother and Mrs King, with two or three select friends to look after me, the remainder very naturally felt that they had not so much interest in the matter. On one occasion, when I was about three years old, the frigate was caught in a typhoon. I was safe below in my poor mother's arms, but Quacko remained on deck to see what was going forward. Nobody was thinking of him. The seamen, indeed, had to hold on with might and main to secure their own lives. Some preparation had been made, and fortunately it was so, for all the sails still set were blown out of the bolt ropes. The frigate was hove on her beam-ends. Where Quacko had come from nobody knew, when on a sudden he was seen hanging to the slack end of a rope. In vain one of the topmen made an attempt to grasp him. The rope swung away far over the foaming sea. He swung back, but it was to strike the side apparently, for the next instant the rope returned on board and no Quacko hanging to it. The ship righted without having suffered much damage; indeed, the loss of Quacko was our greatest misfortune.

After the sad event just mentioned, Quacko's friends made various attempts to appropriate me; indeed, Mrs King and Toby Kiddle had, in order to console them for their loss, to give me up to them occasionally.

"Here, Toby, let's have the little chap and learn him to ride," said Tom Trimmers, one of the topmen. "Why, Nanny will be forgetting how to carry a human being as she has been accustomed to do, and you will soon see what a capital horseman he will make, won't you, Ben?"

"Ay, ay," I answered, for though I could not say much I could say that, and so Nanny was brought forth, and I was placed on her back, Toby, however, remarking, that though some day I should have more sense than the defunct Quacko ever had, yet at present, as I had no experience in riding, he must decline allowing me to mount unless he held me up. "It will be time when the little chap has had some practice to let him go along by himself," he observed, looking round at our shipmates. "Now, you don't know what would become of him, for Nanny is more than likely to trot off on the quarter-deck and make herself disagreeable there, and maybe pitch Master Benjy down the main hatchway. No, no, I will stand by and hold him on till he is a bit older."

This resolution was certainly very prudent; but I very soon began to complain of it, and to assert, by signs rather than by words, that I was well able to take care of myself, and steer the goat as Quacko had done.

"And where is Quacko, Master Ben?" asked Toby, who understood me better than anyone else. "He thought he could take care of himself, but he could not do so, you see, nor can any of us, and that's my opinion. If there was not one better able to take care of us than we are of ourselves, we poor sea-going chaps would be in a bad way."

In spite, however, of Toby Kiddle, my other friends managed occasionally to let me have my own way; and with great pride they looked on while I, with the end of a mop stick in my hand, went galloping about the deck, belabouring the goat's hinder quarters, very much after the fashion of an Irishman riding a donkey at a race. The Sergeant of Marines, Julian Killock was his name, on seeing the use I made of my weapon, took it into his head to teach me the broadsword exercise, which I very soon learnt. The Jollies now began to contemplate appropriating me to themselves, and thus, as it may be supposed, made the Blue-jackets somewhat jealous.

"No, no, Tom Sawyer," I remember hearing one of the latter observe, "you shall not have little Ben to turn into a horse-marine on no account. He is our'n and cut out for a blue-jacket, and a blue-jacket he will be till the end of his days."

CHAPTER TWO.

Still the Jollies were in no way disposed to give up their share of me, to which they considered they had a right. I was very nearly the cause of a serious dispute between the two Services. A compromise was at length entered into by the suggestion of my father, who agreed that the Jollies might teach me the sword and platoon exercise, while the Blue-jackets might impart as much nautical knowledge as I was capable of taking in.

But I was speaking of the goat. I was especially fond of mounting Nanny's back, though she must have found me considerably heavier than Quacko. However, as I never played her any tricks, which he constantly had done, she had no objection to carry me. I consequently took my daily ride round and round the deck, sweeping close round the mainmast and forward again.

It is not surprising that people should lose their temper under such a climate as our ship's company was doomed for so many years to endure. One afternoon, just as the men had finished dinner, it being a dead calm, the ocean like a sheet of molten lead, smooth as a mirror, the sun's rays striking down with tremendous force on our decks, making the pitch hiss and bubble, while one of the midshipmen was frizzling a piece of beef on a metal plate, that he might declare when he got home, without injuring his conscience, that it was usual to cook dinners by the heat of the sun out in China, and the men lay about gasping for breath, I was brought up by Pat Brady, that, as he said, I might enjoy a breath of air, only there happened to be none at the moment, and while I, the least important personage on board thus made my appearance on the upper regions of our ocean world, so did the most important, the Captain, come up to look about him, and whistle for a breeze. It did not come however, although the Captain kept whistling and whistling away till his cheeks must have ached. Nanny had been let out of her pen to discuss the remains of an old straw hat, the other part of which had been given her for her supper the previous evening, when it came into Pat Brady's head to place me on her back; I, nothing loth, sung out for my broadsword, with which I began forthwith to whack the hinder quarters of my long-horned steed. Off she set, but instead of wheeling round the mainmast, on she galloped along the forbidden district of the quarter-deck. The Captain just at that moment, with a stamp of his foot, vexed at his not getting the wished-for wind, turned round, when Nanny and I, at a furious speed, dashed bolt against him; and the goat, catching him between the legs by the impetus she had obtained, sent him sprawling on the deck, and her horns catching in his coat-tails, he and she and I all went rolling over together. There we lay, the Captain spluttering and swearing incontinently, though scarcely able in his rage to utter a word clearly, the goat tugging away to get again on her legs, I all the time shrieking out lustily for help. The officers, who had been pacing the other side of the deck, could scarcely for laughter come to their chiefs assistance, nor could he, from the struggles of the goat, get again on his legs, for each time he made the attempt the terrified animal in her efforts to escape his fury once more pulled him down. I however, had managed to roll out of the way, while my cries, which did not cease, although I was clear of danger, caught the ears of Toby Kiddle, who was coming along the main-deck. He sprang up the main hatchway ladder, and rushing up seized me in his arms. Just then the purser and surgeon managed to raise up the Captain; not, however, till Nanny had almost torn off his coat-tails, and finding herself released was scampering back to the fore-part of the ship. The Captain's whole frame seemed bursting with indignation and rage. Just then his eye fell on Toby Kiddle and me in his arms.

"Who did it? Who did it?" he exclaimed. "Who set them on? You did, sirrah—you did. You shall have three dozen for your fun!"

"Please, sir, it was not me," answered Toby, "and it could not have been the poor innocent child. It was the goat, sir. What put it into her head to do it, is more than I can tell."

"Hang the goat!" exclaimed the Captain, who by this time had begun to feel that his anger was not very dignified; and turning round he went below to hide his annoyance, as well as to put on another coat, instead of the nankeen garment which Nanny had destroyed.

"Ay, ay, sir," answered Kiddle, as he turned forward. "I will take care the goat never plays such a trick again."

As Toby had always objected to my riding the goat, he now came triumphantly forward among those who had placed me on her back, telling them the orders he had received from the Captain.

"But the skipper will lose his milk if you hang his goat," observed one of them.

"Arrah, now, I suppose he is thinking it is time to wean himself," observed Paddy Brady, who had been the chief cause of the accident.

"At all events, his orders must be obeyed," observed Kiddle, "and so, mates, as it was an evident case of mutiny, we will run her up to the yard-arm at sunset. To my mind, if the goat was got rid of, we should have a quieter ship than we have now."

Fortunately, the preparations which the men were making for hanging the goat were observed, and reported to the Captain.

"Really, I do believe I did say so," he answered to the First-Lieutenant. "Just go and tell Kiddle and the rest, that, in consideration of her general good conduct, I purpose reprieving her. That will settle the matter, and show my leniency and consideration in favourable colours."

Thus our worthy Captain was in the habit of arranging even more weighty matters, by which mode of proceeding, in spite of his eccentricities, he warmly attached the ship's company to him.

CHAPTER THREE.

Time passed by, as it does in youth as well as in old age. The ship's company were looking forward to being relieved, for the frigate had already been the best part of five years on the station. I was learning to knot and splice, and could already perform a hornpipe, if not with much grace, at all events with an exhibition of considerable elastic power, and greatly to the admiration of Toby Kiddle, Pat Brady, and my other friends, as well as my father and mother and Mrs King. They would get round applauding me greatly, as I sprang up and down, shuffled round and round and snapped my fingers, kicking out my legs in every direction. Sometimes the officers would come forward to have a look at me, and on several occasions I was invited aft to exhibit before the Captain.

Several changes had taken place on board, one of the lieutenants having invalided home, while another had died, their places being filled by others whom I shall shortly have to describe. The brig we had captured was ultimately brought into the service, and she was about to be commissioned. She was fitting out at Macao, and it was understood that Mr Schank would take the command of her. He had long been expecting promotion, though frequently disappointed, and he now made sure that he should obtain it. He might also hope, in so fine a vessel, to make a fair amount of prize-money. He required it much, for he had an old mother and several maiden sisters at home to support, besides two or three younger brothers to educate and send out in the world. This was generally known among his brother officers, and, although the cut of his uniforms was somewhat antiquated, and his best coat was tolerably threadbare, even the most thoughtless never ventured to quiz him. Every sixpence he could save went to the cottage in Lincolnshire. There his father had been the incumbent of a living of under a hundred and fifty pounds a year, on which he had to bring up his family and pay certain college debts, which had hung like a millstone round his neck all his life. I mention these things now, although, of course, I did not hear them till many years afterwards. Mr Schank was still doing duty on board the frigate expecting to be superseded, that he might commence refitting the brig. It had just become dark. She was lying some distance inside of us. Happily for themselves several of the crew in charge had come on board the frigate. Suddenly a tremendous explosion was heard. Bright flames burst forth from the spot where the brig lay, and a huge pyramid of fire was seen to rush upward towards the sky, where it burst into a thousand fragments, which, scattering far and wide, came hissing back into the mirror-like ocean, reflecting, ere they reached it, a thousand bright lights on its tranquil bosom.

"What is that about?" exclaimed Captain Cobb, coming on deck.

"The brig has blown up, sir," was the answer.

"And so then are all my hopes!" exclaimed Mr Schank, who had followed him on deck. "Lower the boats though, and we will try and pick up any poor fellows who may have escaped."

Mr Schank leaped into the first boat which reached the water, and in his eagerness to save his fellow-creatures instantly forgot his own bitter disappointment. Three men only were picked up alive, floating on fragments of the wreck. It sank almost directly the boats got up to the spot. What had caused the catastrophe no one could tell, but the brig certainly must have had a larger amount of gunpowder on board her than was supposed. Mr Schank therefore, as before, continued to act as our First-Lieutenant. Once or twice we returned to the Hoogley to refit, and on one occasion we were sent round to Madras and Bombay on special service. We were running down the Coromandel coast; the wind fell, and we lay, rolling our lower yardarms under in a long heavy swell, which came moving onwards in giant undulations towards the coast. We had to get rolling tackles set up, for sometimes it seemed as if the frigate would shake the very masts out of her. The Captain was on deck whistling away as was his wont. I do not know whether he expected his whistling to produce a breeze, but certainly I observed that he never failed to whistle when there was a calm.

He was thus employed when Mr Schank, who had previously been on deck for some hours, and had gone below to rest, once more made his appearance. He cast a look round, and pointed out a dark spot in the horizon. The order was immediately given to furl sails and strike topgallant masts. The royal-masts had previously been sent down. It was a time when a careless hold was likely to cause the stoutest seaman a leap into eternity. Scarcely was the ship made snug when down came the blast upon her. The sky grew of a leaden hue, and the long swell was broken up into a thousand tossing seas, foaming and leaping, and crossing each other in a way trying even to a frigate, and fearfully dangerous to any smaller craft. We, having been prepared in good time, ran on before the wind, having, however, as it shifted, which it did suddenly several points at a time, to change our course. The gale was a violent one, and did, I believe, send more than one ill-found ship to the bottom, but it was fortunately short in its duration, and by daylight had greatly decreased. Pat Brady, who had as sharp a pair of eyes as anyone on board, being on the look-out, discovered an object floating far away on the lee-bow. Whether it was a rock or a vessel on her beam-ends it was difficult to say. The ship was, however, kept away towards it, and the master being consulted, declared that no rock was to be found thereabouts. As we approached nearer, there was no doubt that the object seen was a vessel, and probably capsized in the late hurricane. The sea was still running very high, and washing over the greater portion of it, almost hiding it from view. Still the after part was higher out of the water than the rest, and it was possible that some human beings might still be clinging to it. As we approached, the frigate was brought on a wind, and hove to, but lowering a boat was still an operation of danger. All glasses were turned towards the wreck.

"I cannot help thinking there may be somebody on board," exclaimed Mr Harry Oliver, the mate I have spoken of. "If you will let me go, sir, I will board her,"

CHAPTER THREE. 15

he added, turning to the Captain.

"As you like, Oliver," said Captain Cobb. "You know the risk; you can take a boat, but only volunteers must accompany you."

Mr Oliver smiled. He knew well there would be no lack of them. Pat Brady was the first to spring forward, and Bill King and my father both volunteered to go likewise. The crew was soon formed, and the boat safely reached the water. Away she went. No small skill was required to keep her afloat. My mother and Mrs King were looking on, and I have no doubt offering up prayers for the safety of their husbands. At length the boat got round to the lee side of the wreck. A cloth of shawl of some sort was seen to be fluttering from under the weather bulwarks.

The boat drew nearer. "There is somebody there, to a certainty," exclaimed Mr Oliver. "We may get up under her quarter, and an active man may then leap on board."

My father volunteered. The boat approached. Taking a line in his hand, he sprang on to the deck, half of which was under water. Supporting himself by the stump of the after-mast, and then catching hold of a portion of the weather-rigging, he hauled himself to the upper part of the wreck, where, secured to a stanchion, was what looked like a bundle of rags, out of the midst of which appeared a brown face, while his ear, at the same time, amidst the roaring of the sea, caught the sound of an infant's cry, to which, since I came into the world, his ears had been pretty well accustomed. Although Mr Oliver and the men in the boat gave him notice at that instant that the wreck was sinking, that cry had aroused all the father's feelings in his bosom. He sprang forward, and, as a seaman only could have done, cut away the lashings which secured a dark female, in whose grasp he then discovered a fair young infant. Seizing the woman and child in his arms, as the bow of the vessel was already sinking, he gave one spring aft, and struggled out of the vortex of the sinking vessel.

"Haul away!" he cried out, while he held the rope with one hand and kept his charges afloat with the other. A strong man alone could have saved them, and even a strong one, unless a truly brave fellow, would not have made the attempt. In a few seconds they were lifted safely into the boat. The infant breathed freely, and seemed not to have got any harm, but the poor black woman suffered greatly, and this further immersion had contributed still more to exhaust her. Yet she was perfectly conscious of what had occurred. Her lips moved, and a smile lighted up her countenance when she saw the infant lifted carefully in my father's arms. Unfortunately, there was no food in the boat, but just as Mr Oliver was stepping in, the surgeon had put a small brandy-flask in his pocket. This he produced, and attempted to pour a few drops down the throat of the poor woman, but the instant she tasted it she spat it forth as if it was poison, and showed signs of the evident disgust she felt at its being put into her mouth. All that those in the boat could do, therefore, was to make the best of their way back again to the frigate. There was not a sign of another human being on the wreck. As there were no boats, it was possible that the crew might have attempted to make their escape in them, but then surely they would not have left the woman and child behind. When the wreck went down, scarcely anything floated up by which any information could be gained as to what she was. From her appearance, Mr Oliver supposed that she was a snow, possibly belonging to one of the neighbouring ports. The black woman, from her dress and appearance, was at once known to be a native nurse—a class noted for their fidelity to those to whom they become attached. Not without great difficulty and danger, the boat at length reached the frigate's side, when a cradle was sent down into which the nurse was placed, and hoisted on board, my father following with the infant. I rather think it created far more sensation than I did when I came on board. In the first place, it made its appearance in a more public manner, and the Captain and officers crowded round to look at it and the poor nurse.

"Wonder whether it's a boy or a girl," said Toby Kiddle, who was amongst the foremost crowding round. "If it's a boy the younker will make a fine playmate for our Benjy. Let's have a squint at it, Dick. He won't cut our little chap out, anyhow; but we'll let the Jollies have him in keeping, and let them see what they can make on him. He'll help, at all events, to keep peace and quiet between us and them."

From the delicate features of the child, the officers seemed to think, however, that Toby's hopes would be disappointed; and the small stranger being forthwith committed to the charge of my mother, she soon settled the question by pronouncing her to be a remarkably fine healthy little girl, the child of Europeans, and from her dress, and the handsome coral ring and gold chain round her neck, of people of some wealth and quality.

The nurse was carried down into the surgeon's cabin, where Mrs King came instantly to assist him in taking care of her. The poor creature had fainted almost immediately on being brought on deck; when, at length, restoratives being applied, she opened her eyes, she gave a look round expressive of grief and alarm, uttering several words in an unknown tongue.

"It is the child she is asking for, sir," observed Mrs King. "Of course, that would be the first thing in her mind."

That Mrs King was right was proved when the child was brought to her. Several times she pressed it to her bosom, but she had no nourishment to afford it. Then, giving one convulsive gasp, before the surgeon could pour the restorative he had ready into her mouth, she sank back and expired. There was nothing about the woman to show who she was, or whence she had come. Her dress, as I have said, was that of an ayah or native nurse, such as all Europeans employ to take care of their children. Conjecture was rife as to who the little stranger was. What the Captain and officers thought about the matter I do not know. Forward, however, the general opinion ran in favour of her being of exalted birth.

"She is a little lady, no doubt about that," remarked Toby Kiddle, as he scrutinised her delicate features and the fineness of her clothing, and the "Little Lady" she was ever afterwards called.

But to whose charge she should fall was the next question. The Captain had a wife ashore, but he seemed to think that she would not be particularly well-pleased should he present her with an infant to look after. It would be something

CHAPTER THREE.

like reversing the order of things, and it might be difficult to persuade her that he was entirely ignorant of the child's parentage.

"You had better have her, Gunning," he said to the First-Lieutenant of Marines, "you have eight or nine already, have you not? And surely another can make no odds, and your wife will be delighted, I'm sure. Mrs Cobb would not mind standing godmother, I dare say, supposing the little damsel is not christened, and, to make sure, it will be just as well to have that done when we get home. I suppose they can go to heaven without it, but it is a matter I am not very clear about, and it is as well to be on the right side, do you see."

These remarks of the Captain enabled Mr Gunning to think over the matter. He had only joined us a few months, and he had some idea that on his return he should find a further increase to his large family. Though he was a kind-hearted man, and really would have been glad to look after the little stranger, yet he did not consider himself justified in undertaking further responsibilities, in addition to those already upon his shoulders. Still, who could take care of the little girl? The junior lieutenants were all young men, not at all fitted for the office. The surgeon was not exactly the person to whom a female infant could be committed. The master was a good seaman, but a somewhat rough hand, and he and his wife were known to live a cat-and-dog life when he was ashore: whereby the service benefited, as he always took care, for the sake of peace, to keep afloat. Then there was the purser. Her life was not likely to prove a happy one should he assume her guardianship, for as his great and sole pleasure in life seemed to be the laborious occupation of skinning flints, it was not likely that he would afford her a liberal education or a liberal maintenance. He was therefore put out of the question. The only persons, therefore, who appeared at all eligible among the officers were the Captain, the First-Lieutenant, and the Lieutenant of Marines. Mr Schank, when the matter was suggested to him, thought a good deal about it. "Perhaps his old mother would like to look after the little girl, he was sure she would, and so would his sisters, and very fit people they were in many respects, barring the expense she would be to them."

"What say you, Schank? Suppose I help you in that matter. I am in duty bound to do so, and so you will excuse my making the offer," said the Captain, his more generous feelings excited, as he thought of the forlorn condition of the little creature.

Lieutenant Schank thanked him, and promised if his mother would accept the charge not to decline his proposal. In the meantime the Little Lady was consigned to my mother's charge. Next to me and my father, the kind woman soon learned to love her more than anything on earth; in fact, she felt for her as for a daughter. The little creature from the first clung to her, and from the way she looked into her eyes, I really believe thought she was her own mother. At first she would not let Susan King even touch her, and shrieked out with fear. Poor Susan's tender heart was somewhat grieved at this. Her outward appearance and hoarse voice was indeed calculated to frighten a discerning child. However, in time, the Little Lady became reconciled to her, though she still always showed a strong preference to my mother.

CHAPTER FOUR.

I need scarcely say that I now, at all events, had a more powerful rival on board than had existed since Quacko was consigned to a watery grave. As may be supposed, the goat during a long sea voyage, where the food was scarce, gave but a small quantity of milk, only sufficient indeed for the Captain and any guest he might have at breakfast or tea. I do not believe that he would have sacrificed it for the sake of anyone else, but directly the child was brought on board he issued an order that the whole of the milk should be reserved for her use. There was something strange about this, for immediately the goat gave twice the quantity that had for some time appeared on the Captain's table. It was, to be sure, whispered that some of the young gentlemen were fond of milk for their tea, and from that time forward not a drop was ever seen in their berth. Before that time, one or two of them used to boast that they had the art of manufacturing milk out of pipeclay, whereby they accounted for the rare fluid which occasionally appeared on the mess-table.

I remember clearly the funeral of the poor nurse. As the Captain and the First-Lieutenant had considered it important that her clothes should be preserved, in the hopes of assisting in discovering to whom the Little Lady belonged, Mrs King had dressed the body in one of her old petticoats. It was then sewn up in a piece of canvas, with a shot at the feet, and placed on a grating near an open port. The Captain, who had somewhat obfuscated theological views, could not decide whether he was bound to read the funeral service over the poor woman.

"Supposing she is a heathen—and I never heard of these black people being Christians—I shouldn't think it was much in their way, eh, Schank? Would it not be something like sacrilege to bury her in a Christian fashion?" he asked of the First-Lieutenant.

"As to that," observed Mr Schank, "I suspect we are apt to perform the ceremony over a good many who have no more claim to be considered true Christians than she possibly had."

"Well, I suppose it can't do much harm, eh, Schank?" observed the Captain, after a moment's reflection, and the Little Lady's nurse was buried, according to the notion of the crew, in a decent Christian manner; they piously believing that, however she might have lived, she would now at all events have a fair chance of getting a safe passage to heaven. We were during this time standing to the southward, and having rounded the south of Ceylon, we touched at Point de Galle, and afterwards at Colombo, proceeding on to Bombay. Greatly to the disappointment of the ship's company, the "Boreas" was here found to be in such good condi-

CHAPTER FOUR.

tion, that, instead of going home, she was ordered back to the China Seas. Passing through the Straits of Malacca, we returned to Macao.

We were here joined by another frigate, the "Zephyr," of thirty-six guns. Captain Peter Masterman, her commander, presented a great contrast to Captain Cobb. The former was a remarkably fine, handsome man, with dignified manners and calm temper. We received orders soon afterwards to proceed to the Philippine Islands, there to reconnoitre the Spanish force supposed to be collected near their chief town of Manilla, and if possible to cut out from under the batteries which guard the harbour certain richly-laden ships which it was understood had there taken shelter. We were also to attack all their armed dependencies, and to give them as much annoyance as possible as we cruised up the Archipelago.

As soon as we were clear of the land, the crews of the two frigates were employed in making them look as much like French frigates as possible, both as to rigging and hulls. The Philippines, belonging to Spain, consist of a number of islands, the largest of which is Luzon, and is divided into two parts joined by an isthmus about ten miles wide. The capital, Manilla, where the cheroots are made, is situated on a bay of that name. It is a large place, consisting of several suburbs or towns surrounding the city proper, which is built on the banks of the river Pasig. South of Manilla is the fortress of Cavite, situated at the extremity of a tongue of land about two miles long. It protects the entrance to the only harbour in the bay of Manilla. The arsenal is within the fortress, and a number of vessels are built there. It was under the guns of this fortress that we expected to find our prizes, and, in spite of its formidable appearance, to cut them out. As we were running down the coast of Luzon, the large island I have spoken of, we captured a trader of considerable size belonging to the island, but, as she was bound northward, Captain Masterman generously declined detaining her after we had taken out of her all the cash to be found on board, amounting to about six thousand dollars. It was somewhat amusing to see the grateful way in which the Spanish skipper thanked the Englishmen for having so mercifully robbed him, so I have heard my father say. It might have been supposed that they had done him the greatest possible favour, instead of having mulcted him of a pretty considerable sum. He also, to show his gratitude, told us that the squadron in the harbour of Cavite consisted of four sail of the line and four frigates, but that only one ship of each class was at all in a state to put to sea. Our Captain considered that two English frigates were fully able to cope with a Spanish line-of-battle ship and one frigate, hoping to draw them off the land if they could be persuaded to come out of harbour, and to capture them in detail. At all events, the news increased the good spirits of the ship's company, and all on board anticipated some rich prizes.

The next day we came up with several other vessels which were treated in the same liberal manner, although those which were sailing south were allowed to pass unmolested, lest it might have been suspected that we did not belong to the friendly nation which we pretended.

Thus we proceeded on, till soon after sunset we approached the Bay of Manilla, with the French flag flying at our peaks, and to Spanish eyes, looking, I doubt not, like two Frenchmen. We had to pass close to a small island on which a signal-house stands, and it now became doubtful whether we should be detected. However, the Spaniards appeared not to suspect us, and we stood on till we came to an anchor in about fourteen fathoms at the entrance of the bay; both the frigates, however, keeping their topsails at the mast-head, to be ready for a sudden start.

The night was very calm; and sounds from a great distance could reach us across the water. There was no chance therefore of our being surprised, should the enemy have discovered our real character. It became, however, hopeless for us to attempt cutting-out any of the vessels, as we should not have had sufficient wind to carry them off, even when we had taken possession. We, however, kept a very bright look-out, and the men were in good spirits at the thoughts of the work they anticipated the next day.

Before morning dawned, we and our consort got under weigh, and, with French colours flying, slowly worked up the bay, which, being broad and free from dangers, we were enabled to do. Soon after sunrise, three sail were seen to leeward, also apparently bound up the bay. They were soon made out to be gun-boats, and the Captains congratulated themselves on the prospect of quickly capturing them without difficulty. I should have before introduced a personage who, for a time, belonged to the ship—Mr Noalles, our pilot. He was supposed to be a Jersey man, as he spoke French perfectly, and also Spanish, and several other languages. He had been in the China seas for a considerable number of years, though he was still a young man. He had dark, strongly-marked features, somewhat perhaps of a Jewish cast, with large black whiskers, and was powerfully built. He was greatly respected on board, as he was known to be a good seaman and a determined character, but my father used to say there was something about him he could not exactly make out. He messed with the officers, for he was perfectly the gentleman, and possessed of a large amount of information, especially respecting that part of the world. I rather think that it was he who suggested the plan of operations we were now carrying out. Captain Cobb himself, having once spent some time in France as a prisoner, spoke French sufficiently well to deceive a Spaniard at all events, though I suspect a Frenchman would soon have detected him. Several of our men also had been in French prisons, or had lived among Frenchmen, and if they could not speak the language grammatically, they could at all events imitate the sounds of a party of Frenchmen talking together. The uniform of the officers did not differ much from those of the French, while such alterations as were necessary were speedily made. It was a great source of amusement to the men to see the officers who were about to act in the proposed drama going through their parts, Captain Cobb flourishing his hat with the air of a Frenchman, and uttering the expressions with which he proposed to greet his visitors.

"I wonder whether we shall bamboozle the Dons," observed Toby Kiddle, who, holding me in his arms, formed one of a group of seamen collected on the forecastle.

"No fear of that, Toby," observed Pat Brady. "If they once think we are Frenchmen, they are such conceited fellows that they will never find out that they are wrong."

CHAPTER FOUR.

Onward we stood, till soon after breakfast we opened the ships in Cavite Road. The glasses of all the officers were pointed in that direction, when they made out three sail of the line and three frigates—tolerable odds against us, it might be supposed; but they could not do us any harm then, because four of them were without masts and the other two had only their lower masts in, and no yards across. We, therefore, if we could get possession of the gunboats, should be at liberty to commit any mischief we chose along the coast. Three gunboats, at all events, were likely soon to give us an opportunity of having something to say to them. The wind was so light that we made but little way, and thus about two hours afterwards we lay about three miles from Cavite, and the same distance from the city of Manilla. At length, when nearly becalmed, a guard boat was seen coming off to us from Cavite, and as she approached, we made out that she pulled twelve oars, and had several officers and men besides on board.

"Now, Mr Noalles," said Captain Cobb to the pilot, "do your best to induce these gentlemen to come on board. It will not do to let them examine the ship, and then go back and express their suspicions, if they have any."

As the boat came alongside, Mr Noalles, in excellent Spanish, politely invited the officers and men on board. The chief officer introduced himself as the second captain of one of the frigates at anchor in Cavite, and inquired who we were and whence we came. Our pilot in return replied that the "Boreas" and her consort were two frigates belonging to the French squadron in those seas, that we had been cruising for some time along the coast of China, where our crews had naturally become sickly, and that we had come to Manilla for refreshment; as also, should the Spanish Admiral be pleased to accept our services, to form a junction with his squadron; Mr Noalles also said he was desired to express a hope that the Spanish ships would accompany us to sea. Meantime, the seamen who had been stationed near began jabbering French, as they had been directed to do, throwing the Spaniards completely off their guard. The Spanish captain, in reply to what had been said, stated that the Governor had directed him to acquaint the French that their wants should be immediately supplied, "but," he added, "it is with great sorrow that we cannot accompany you to sea, because the truth is, none of our ships can by any possibility be got ready in less than two months, as our crews are sickly; and to confess the truth, we are in want of every species of stores."

The boat meantime was secured alongside, and while the captain and officers accompanying him were invited into the cabin, the seamen were conducted below. Captain Cobb acted his part very well, and probably he was just as well dressed as many of the Republican naval officers of those days, who were in the habit of assuming a somewhat rough exterior and rougher manners. Refreshments were immediately ordered, and our consort having by this time got a considerable way up the bay, Captain Masterman, who had seen the boat come off, arrived on board. Captain Cobb immediately introduced him as the French Commodore, giving the name of an officer who it afterwards turned out was at that time dead. Of this fact, however, the Spanish captain was fortunately not aware, or the ruse would have been discovered.

Captain Masterman was able to speak a little Spanish. Refreshments being ordered, the officers were soon engaged in pleasant and not altogether uninstructive conversation at the table. Our Captain, in return, gave the Spaniards a large amount of information, not likely, it may be supposed, to benefit them very much. A great friend of mine, Charlie Crickmay, one of the Captain's boys waiting at table, afterwards gave me a full account of all that occurred. As the Spaniards were plied with wine by their polite hosts, their hearts opened, and they let out all the information which it was necessary to obtain.

"Now, my excellent friends," said the Spanish Captain, "we will drink success to the united exertions of the Spaniards and French against those rascally British, who come out here and interfere with our trade, and do us so much mischief."

Just then a midshipman came down to say that a large barge and a felucca were coming off from the shore. In reply to the toast, Captain Cobb assured his guests that as far as they were concerned their great wish was that the Spanish and French ships should never fail to fall in with the English, as they had little doubt who would come off victorious.

"Of course, excellent señors, the Spaniards will always conquer their foes, whenever the latter dare stay to encounter their prowess," was the answer.

Our Captains continued to humour the gentlemen for some time till the midshipman, again coming down, informed them that the large boats were nearly alongside. At length, Captain Cobb laying his hand on the Spanish officer's shoulder, looked him in the face.

"My dear sir," he said, "you will pardon us for the little trick we have played you; but the honest truth is, we are not the people you took us for. There is an old proverb which says: 'Deceit is lawful in love and warfare.' In the latter it is at all events. Though we have the flag of France now flying, that of Britain generally floats over our decks, and will, I hope, do so till our ships are paid off at home."

"Señor!" exclaimed the Spaniard, turning pale and gasping for breath, "you surely are joking."

The Captain's answer assured him that he was not. The poor man almost fainted.

"Come, my friend," said Captain Masterman, "we intend you no harm. Here, take a glass of wine, you will find it excellent Madeira, and be assured that many a worse event might have happened to you. All we require is, that you should say nothing to your friends when they come below. You will meet them here presently, whoever they are, and believe us on our honours that we intend no one any harm."

While Captain Cobb entertained his dismayed guest, Captain Masterman went on deck to receive the new comers.

CHAPTER FIVE.

The first boat which came alongside was announced to be the barge of Admiral Don Martin Alaba. She rowed twenty oars, and had on board a rear-admiral and two other officers, one of whom was the Governor's nephew, who came to pay his respects to their supposed friends. The other, a felucca, contained the same number of officers and men, and among them was an aide-de-camp of the Admiral's, who sent his compliments and congratulations to the French, with the information that they would be supplied with all they desired. He also announced, which was less agreeable to us, that several launches with anchors and cables were getting ready to assist the frigates into the harbour.

Unless, therefore, a good excuse could be framed for not going in, our true characters would immediately be discovered. However, as Spaniards are not very quick in their movements, it was hoped that some time would pass before the arrival of the launches, and that an opportunity might occur of taking a few more prizes without bloodshed. The new visitors were ushered down, with every mark of respect, into the cabin, while the crews were handed below as the others had been. The first glance the Admiral caught of the Spanish captain's countenance gave him, probably, some anxiety. This was still further increased when Captain Masterman, with a polite bow, requested his pardon for the trick which had been played off on him and his countrymen.

"What trick!" exclaimed the Admiral. "Surely you do not mean to say that you are not the people we took you for?"

"We must confess that we are not," said Captain Masterman; "we beg to assure you that neither you nor any of your countrymen will suffer the least insult or hurt at our hands. We must, however, request you contentedly to remain on board for a few hours, after which time I have little doubt that we shall be able to set you at liberty."

These remarks reassured the Spaniards, who were further reconciled to their lot when they saw the cloth spread, and a number of covers brought aft by active hands. The table glittered with plate and glass, and numerous well-filled bottles of ruby wine. While, however, the dinner was getting ready, the Spanish officers were invited to take a turn on deck. Their astonishment and vexation had been considerable before; it was now increased when they saw a number of Englishmen come up, dressed in the clothes of the Spaniards, and immediately jump into the Spanish boat. Several of the frigates' boats were also seen at the same time to shove off with their officers and men well armed, and to pull towards the three Spanish gunboats which lay at their anchors just outside the river leading to Manilla. The

Admiral and his officers watched them anxiously. What could they be about? On they went till they were alongside the gunboats. Not a sound of a shot was heard, not a trigger apparently had been pulled. In a short time the gunboats under sail were seen slowly dropping down towards the frigates.

"Dinner is ready," observed our Captain to his guests. "We will inform you of the particulars of what has taken place after you have enjoyed it."

The Spaniards were wise men. They shrugged their shoulders, twirled their moustaches, but said nothing, quickly following their hosts into the cabin. Their eyes could not help brightening up when they saw the good dinner spread before them, for such will, with few exceptions, touch the hearts of mortals of all nations. Toasts were proposed, healths drunk, and the Spaniards began to think that the accounts they had read of British ferocity and British barbarism must have been somewhat exaggerated. Meantime the three gunboats were brought alongside with about one hundred and twenty officers and men as prisoners. Several of their people had managed to escape on shore. The officers acknowledged to their captors that there were a considerable number more gunboats in the harbour, all new and coppered, very fast, and well fitted for service. We, having plenty of provisions on board, our Captain had ordered a good entertainment to be prepared for all the prisoners, who showed no unwillingness to make themselves happy and at home. We had already had a pretty good morning's work, but the Spaniards seemed still willing to present us with another prize, for soon after the gunboats had been brought alongside, a second felucca-rigged boat, pulling eighteen oars, was seen coming off. Several officers were also aboard her. As she came alongside, they were received with the same politeness as the others had been. The principal officer informed us that he was Captain of the port. He requested to know for what reason the boats were detained, saying that if they were not immediately restored the authorities would consider the two frigates as enemies, and not only decline giving them any assistance, but direct the squadron to come out of harbour and drive them off.

"Tell him what we know about the squadron," said Captain Cobb to our pilot.

"Why, my friend," observed Mr Noalles, "you must be aware that you have the larger portion of your squadron without their masts, and that even the others will not be able to follow us for a fortnight at least. We know perfectly well what we are about; in fact, it must be confessed that we are Englishmen!"

The start given by the Captain of the port was even more violent than that of his predecessors. What, had he actually run his head into the lion's den, after so many of his companions had been already caught? However, on being conducted into the cabin, he was received with shouts of laughter from his countrymen, who by this time were feeling the effects of the generous wine they had imbibed. The Spaniards were, however, able to punish us slightly in return by the information they gave, that of the two merchant vessels we had come to cut out, one was aground, and the other had landed her cargo in consequence of the appearance of a suspicious looking ship of war, which we afterwards ascertained was one of our cruisers, whose melancholy fate I shall some day have to relate.

CHAPTER FIVE.

By this time we had fully two hundred prisoners on board, and a happier set of prisoners it would have been difficult to find, for not only had the officers' hearts been made merry, but the seamen had as much grog on board as they could well carry. There could be little doubt that by this time the people on shore must have been fully certain of our real characters. Their suspicions must have been confirmed when they saw a breeze spring up, and that we did not proceed into the roads as they had supposed we should do. Our Captains, who were as generous and liberal as brave, now told the Spanish officers that they should be at liberty to return on shore, offering to present them with the Admiral's barge, the guard boat, and the two feluccas; nor would they even ask for their parole nor impose a restriction of any sort upon them. The Spaniards' astonishment on being captured had been very great, but it was greater still when they received this information. I did not hear what the Admiral said, but I know he made a very long speech, full of grandiloquent words, that he pressed his hands to his heart very often, and in other ways endeavoured to show his sense of British magnanimity. Evening coming on, he and his countrymen took their departure in their respective boats, some of which were rather overcrowded, as, of course, they had to carry the crews of the gunboats which we had detained.

Our ship's company shook hands with all the men as they helped them into their boats, and parted from them with three hearty cheers, as if they had been their dearest friends. As soon as our guests had departed, we once more stood out of the bay with our three prizes, keeping away to the south in the hopes of visiting other places before the information of our true character could reach them. The gunboats were manned, a lieutenant from the "Zephyr" taking charge of one of them, and our junior lieutenant and Mr Oliver having the command of the other two.

They were respectively named by the ship's company the "Bam," the "Boo," and the "Zel". The "Zephyr" took the "Bam" in tow, while we had the "Boo" and the "Zel". It was young Mr Oliver's first command, and with no small pleasure he descended the ship's side to go and take charge of the craft, fully expecting to perform great deeds in her. Many another young man has done the same, and found, after all, his expectations sadly disappointed. I remember perfectly watching the little vessels as they followed in our wake. They were handsome, graceful craft, very well fitted for the work for which they were intended, cruising along shore, and being able to run into harbour again on the appearance of bad weather. Somehow or other Englishmen are apt to think if a vessel can float she is fit to go anywhere, and that there is no considerable difference between smooth water and a heavy cross sea,—a summer breeze and a snorting gale.

Mr Oliver had with him a young midshipman, ten seamen, and a boy—a very much smaller crew than the gunboat had under the Spanish flag. Of course, however, fewer Englishmen are required to man a vessel than Spaniards, not but that Spaniards are very good sailors, but then they have not got the muscle and the activity of Englishmen. As a rule, Spanish vessels are far better found than English craft, and are rather over than under manned. We continued to run down the coast without meeting with any adventure till we sighted the large island of Mindanao.

We were standing off that island one night, when about midnight the ship was struck by a heavy squall. She lay over till her yardarms almost dipped in the ocean. Topsail and topgallant sheets were let fly, and she soon again righted without much apparent damage to herself, but at that instant there was a cry from aft that one of the gunboats had parted.

The night was dark, and those who looked out could nowhere distinguish her. The frigate was, however, immediately brought to. A gun was fired, but there was no report in return. A blue light was next ordered to be lit. No answering signal was to be perceived. The missing boat was the "Zel" under charge of young Harry Oliver. He was a great favourite on board, and many anxious eyes were looking out for him. Another and another gun was fired, and blue lights ever and anon sent their bright glare over the foam-topped waves. While one of these blue lights was burning, one of the men on the look-out whispered to another: "What do you see there, Bill? As I am a living man there is a long low ship under all sail gliding by right in the wind's eye."

"And I see her too! And I, and I!" exclaimed several men in suppressed voices. "Hark? There are sounds. There is music."

"Why, they are singing on board. What can she be? I for one would rather never have looked on her. Can you make out the words?"

"No, I should think not."

"Do you see her now?"

"No, she seemed to shoot right up into that thick cloud to windward."

Such and similar expressions were heard, and the men were still talking about the matter when my father and Pat Brady, who had been below, came on deck. At that moment Mr Schank's voice was heard shouting out "Shorten sail!" and the ship was brought speedily under still closer canvas, barely in time, however, to enable her to bear the effects of the second violent squall which came roaring up from the quarter where the supposed stranger had disappeared. Guns were again fired, and more blue lights burned, and thus we continued waiting anxiously till morning broke. The other gunboat was safe, but it was too certain that the unfortunate "Zel" had foundered, and that her crew and the brave young Harry Oliver and his still more youthful companion had perished. Many hearts on board grieved for their loss. I will not say tears were shed, because, however poets may write about the matter, it is my belief that British seamen are not addicted to express their feelings in that way, unless perhaps occasionally a few do so when they become sentimental with a larger amount of grog on board than usual, but even that is not very common. They are more inclined to become obstreperous and combative on such occasions.

The latter part of our cruise was not likely to prove so successful as the commencement.

Standing to the extreme south of the group, we came off a Spanish settlement, guarded by a couple of forts, and which, as it was of considerable size, our Captains determined to lay under contribution for wood, water, and refreshments. We fortunately captured a felucca a short distance from the coast, and her master was now directed to stand in and make our request for the articles we required known to the authorities of the place. They not understanding our amiable disposition, or supposing that we were the bloodthirsty monsters we had been described, declined acceding to our petitions. There was no help therefore but to attempt to take by force what was denied to our modest request. The wood and water we might have procured elsewhere, but vegetables and fresh meat and other provisions we had no hopes of finding. We accordingly stood in towards the town, hoping that our appearance would overawe the enemy. The Spaniards, however, as soon as we got within range of their guns, opened a hot fire upon us which showed that they fully intended to keep to their resolution of not rendering us assistance. Hungry Englishmen are not well-pleased to be baulked of their provisions. The order was "Out boats and take the fort." Four boats shoved off, under command of Captain Masterman, and made for the shore, in spite of the hot fire with which they were received. One, however, grounded on a sandbank, and several men were hit while they were endeavouring to get her off. The intention was to take the fort. They reached the beach, and on the men dashed, expecting in a few minutes to be engaged in storming the fort. As, however, they were rushing up the hill, a large body of armed men appeared on the top of it, five or six times their number. A braver man than Captain Masterman never stepped; but, unless the enemy were great cowards, they could scarcely hope to drive them off, and to get into the fort at the same time. The walls, too, as they approached them, were seen to be far more difficult to climb than they had expected. Meantime the batteries were keeping up a very heavy fire on the frigates, our guns making but little impression in return. With a heavy heart Captain Masterman gave the order to retreat and the British had to hurry down to their boats, while the Spaniards were rapidly advancing. The latter, however, did not venture to come to close quarters, being well content with their success, but continued firing on the boats as long as they were within reach of their muskets. By this time the frigates had lost several men. The "Zephyr"—her master and three or four men killed, and a midshipman and several men wounded. We lost five or six killed or wounded. Among the latter was Pat Brady, who came on board vowing vengeance against the Spaniards wherever he should meet them. The two frigates, besides, had received considerable damage.

Our wheel was hit, the head of our mizzen-mast wounded, several of our shrouds were cut away, and running rigging and sails much injured. At length a shot cut away two strands of our cable. The gunboats which joined in the fight had escaped with very little damage, although they kept up a pretty hot fire on the fort. There seemed to be not the slightest possibility of our success, and as our chief object was to get wood and water, which certainly could be obtained elsewhere, cutting our cables, we made sail out of the harbour. Altogether we had paid pretty dearly for our morning's amusement.

I give the account, however humbling to our national pride it may be, to show that it is possible for the bravest and most sagacious officers to meet with reverses, and as a warning lesson to others not to think too highly of themselves.

I leave the reader to count up what we did during the cruise, and to judge whether we had much cause for congratulation, I had the account from my father in after years, and, calculating profits and losses, I rather think that the balance was terribly against us.

CHAPTER SIX.

The two gunboats, "Bam" and "Boo," had been a source of anxiety to our Captain, ever since they came into our possession, and fears were entertained, should another gale come on, that they might share the fate of the unfortunate "Zel". Their young commanders were ready to go anywhere in them, but it seemed very unlikely, should they make the attempt, that they would ever reach Canton, to which we were soon about to return. They were condemned therefore to be destroyed. They were beautiful looking craft, but were too likely to prove what the ten-gun brigs of those days often did—coffins for their living crews. Accordingly, all their stores being taken out of them, their crews set them on fire and returned to the frigates. I remember well seeing them blaze away and at length blow up, at which I clapped my hands, having some idea that they were fireworks let off expressly for my amusement. The frigates' damages being now repaired, a course was steered for the north. Being greatly in want of water, we put into another harbour on the coast where it was known that no Spanish settlement existed. The watering parties from our frigates proceeded to the shore, making six boats in all, the men being well armed. They ought properly to have remained for each other, but our boats came off first, leaving the "Zephyr's" to follow. Casks were being hoisted up, when the officers, through their glasses, perceived several men running down to the beach, making signals that an enemy was coming. Instantly all the remaining boats were manned, and away they pulled to the support of those on shore, led by the two Captains. There was no time to be lost, for as they approached the shore they saw our men defending themselves against a vast number of enemies. The natives, as the boats approached, took to flight, but it was evident that the number of our people was greatly diminished. The officer commanding the watering party was alive, though he had with difficulty escaped from the enemy, but two poor fellows lay dead upon the beach, and a third was desperately wounded, and was evidently dying. No less than nine had been carried off as prisoners. Our pilot, Mr Noalles, having accompanied the party, now proceeded with Captain Masterman and a very strong body in search of the natives. These, however, had fled at their approach. At length our party came upon a hut, in which a man was found who appeared by his dress and air to be of some consequence. He was lame from a wound, and had been unable to make his escape. Mr Noalles explained to him that we were in search of our men, and demanded their instant release. He was told that unless they were delivered up, their village would be destroyed, and their corn cut down. He promised to use his influence with his countrymen, and as our people retired to a distance, one or two persons were seen to enter his hut. After waiting, however, a considerable time, no one approached. Again the chief was appealed to, but he declared that he had no power in the place. At length Captain Masterman directed his followers to set the village on fire, while our men rushed into the corn fields, and in a short time made a clean sweep of several acres. Whether or not it was a wise proceeding, I think, is doubtful, for it was too probable that the natives would either kill their prisoners in revenge, or else make them labour as slaves to repay them for the damage they had received. This work being accomplished, the frigates got under weigh, the Captains intending to call off a place farther to the north where the Malay chief of the island resided, for the purpose of making him exert his influence for the recovery of the missing men. We were not very far from the latitude where the unfortunate "Zel" had foundered. Our people very naturally talked of their lost shipmates, and especially of young Mr Oliver, who, as I said, was a great favourite with all of them. My father especially looked on him with much affection, having saved his life once, seemed to regard him almost in the light of a son. We had had a fair wind all the morning, when suddenly it shifted round to the northward, and a sudden squall very nearly took the masts out of the two frigates. As it was impossible to say from what direction the breeze would next come, we continued standing off the land towards the town of Palawan. The wind had moderated, though it still blew strong, and we continued standing to the west, when a small island was sighted on the weather bow. As we drew in with it, Pat Brady, who was one of the look-outs, declared he saw a signal flying from the highest point in sight. I speak of it as an island—it seemed to be little more than a large rock—and the peak of which Brady spoke was forty or fifty feet or so out of the water. The ships' companies had been grumbling considerably at being delayed, as they were anxious to get back to Canton, where, it was hoped, we should receive orders to convoy the homeward-bound merchant fleet. The midshipman of the watch having reported what Pat Brady had seen, after we had run on some distance, the ship was hove to, and the glasses being directed in that direction, a man was made out waving apparently a shirt from the rock. A boat accordingly was instantly lowered and pulled towards it. The man kept his post for some time as the boat approached, making signals to those in her to pull round rather farther to the westward, as the surf beating on that side of the rock would prevent their landing. As the boat's head was once more put off the shore the men caught sight of the person on the rock. Pat Brady, who formed one of the boat's crew, looked up at him with a glance of astonishment.

"I say, Jem," he exclaimed to the man next him, "either that's Mr Oliver or his ghost, as sure as my name is Pat Brady."

"It's his ghost," was the answer, "for there is no doubt the gunboat went down a week ago; and it's not likely he or any other man could have swum out of her."

"By my faith, then," answered Brady, "it must be his ghost; and sure enough he is more like a ghost than anything else."

As they were speaking, the figure disappeared from the summit of the rock.

"I told you so," said Brady, "depend on it, when we land, we may hunt about till doomsday, and we shall never find mortal man on this rock." These remarks were overheard by the other men, who seemed to agree very much with the opin-

CHAPTER SIX. 31

ions of the speakers.

"He is fathoms deep down beneath the water, depend on that," observed another; "we shall never see young Mr Oliver with our mortal eyes again."

At length Mr Martin, the Second-Lieutenant, who had gone in command of the boat, overheard the remarks of the men. He, however, from being somewhat near-sighted, had not observed any likeness in the figure on the rock to his lost shipmate. "Mr Oliver, do you think he is? I only hope so."

"No, sir, we don't think it's Mr Oliver; but we think it is his ghost," blurted out Pat Brady; "and as to finding him, there's little chance we shall have to do that."

"We will have a look for him at all events," answered Mr Martin. "Give way, lads, I see the place he pointed out to us; and if he is a ghost, at all events he has an eye for a good landing-place."

The boat accordingly pulled in, and a small bay was found where the men could land with perfect ease. No one, however, was to be seen, and this confirmed the opinions the seamen had expressed. The island was rather larger than it appeared from the sea, and Mr Martin, leaving a couple of men in charge of the boat, proceeded with the rest inland. They looked about in all directions, and yet no human being could they discover. He at length began almost to fancy that they must have been deceived by some means or other, and yet he was certain that the figure he had observed at the top of the rock was that of a human being. I should have said that when the boat was lowered a bottle of water and a flask of spirits, with a small quantity of food, had also been put into her. This the men carried, it being supposed probable that the person on the rock would be suffering from hunger and thirst.

"It's of no use," observed Pat to one of his companions. "I knew it was a ghost from the beginning, or may be just the devil in a man's shape to try and draw the ship in to get her cast away. We none of us know what tricks he can play."

At length the men began to be positively uneasy, and to wish their officer to return. Mr Martin, however, had determined to examine the island thoroughly, before he gave up the search, being perfectly convinced that he had seen a man on the rock, though why he had afterwards hidden himself was unaccountable.

The distance by water from the rock was, in consequence of the shape of the shore, considerably less than by land, and this might have accounted for their getting there before the person they had seen, but some other reason had now to be found for his not appearing. The more level part of the land had been passed over. No signs of water had been discovered.

"Ah, poor fellow!" exclaimed Mr Martin, "he must, at all events, have suffered greatly for want of that."

They now got near to the foot of the rock, on the top of which the man had been seen. All the sides appeared inaccessible, and it was unaccountable how he could have got up there. This further confirmed the men in the idea that they had beheld a ghost or spirit of some sort. Never, perhaps, before had their officer found greater difficulty in getting them to follow him. They would have done so ten times more willingly against an enemy greatly outnumbering them, with the muzzles of half-a-dozen guns pointed in their faces besides. Mr Martin continued to push on. At length he came to a rock in which was a small recess. Beckoning with his hand to his men, he hurried on, and there he saw, seated on the ground, the person of whom he had been in search, with a boy apparently in the last stage of exhaustion in his arms. He himself was unable to speak, but he pointed to the boy's mouth, and then to his own. Mr Martin understood the signs, and shouted to the men to come on with the provisions. Even then he could scarcely recognise the features of Harry Oliver, or of the young midshipman by his side, so fearfully had famine and exhaustion told on them. The men were soon gathered round the sufferers. Before Mr Oliver would take any of the spirits and water brought to him, he watched to see a few drops poured down the throat of his companion. The effect was almost instantaneous. His eyes, already glazing, it seemed in death, recovered a portion of their brightness, and a slight colour returned to his deadly pale cheeks. A moderate draught of the same mixture greatly restored the young officer, but he was even then unable to speak.

"I told you he was a live man," observed Mr Martin at last to the seamen; "but if you had given way to your fears, you see in a very few minutes more both our young friends would have become what you supposed them already to be."

The men now hurried back to bring some of the boat's oars and a sail on which they might convey the sufferers, for Mr Martin was anxious to get them on board without further delay. After waiting a little time longer, he considered that they were sufficiently recovered to be removed.

Great was the astonishment, and greater still the satisfaction, of all on board when they arrived alongside.

The young midshipman hovered for a considerable time between life and death. Had it not been, I believe, for the watchful care of my mother and the surgeon, he would, after all, have sunk under the hardships he had endured. Not, indeed, till the following day, was Mr Oliver himself able to give an account of his escape. Except the man at the helm, the crew of the gunboat had been forward when the squall came on. He and the midshipman Bramston were standing aft. He recollected, as the vessel sank beneath his feet, catching the lad in his arms, and springing over the taffrail. As to what became of the man at the helm, or the rest of the crew, he could not tell. For a few seconds he was drawn under the water, but returning to the surface again, he found close to him several spars that had been lashed together, but, as it appeared, not secured to the deck of the vessel.

On these he threw himself and his young charge. A current, he supposed, swept them away to the westward. When daylight broke, he could clearly see the frigate; but after he had anxiously watched her, he observed her standing to the southward. He had little hopes of surviving, yet he resolved to persevere to the last. Still the spars afforded but a slight support. He had to dread, too, the attack of sharks. About two hours after daylight, however, he observed floating near him the stock of a large ship's anchor. Leaving young Bramston secured to the spars, towing them, he swam towards it. This afforded him and his companion a far safer resting-place. He was now able to lash several spars to the timber, while another formed a mast, and a second, which he and Bramston cut through with their knives, supplied them with paddles and a yard. On this they spread their shirts, which they split open.

As the sun rose, his beams fell on an island in the far distance. The wind was fair, and towards it they directed their course. The current, too, favoured them. Without this their progress would have been very slow. They soon began to feel the want of water, but Oliver urged Bramston on no account to drink the salt water. The midshipman, on searching in his pockets, happily found a small quantity of biscuit, which he had thoughtlessly put there, he supposed, after supper that very night. This supplied them with food when their hunger became ravenous. Thus they sailed on the whole day. Happily the night was not very dark, and they were thus able to keep the island in sight. It was almost daylight the next morning when at length they found themselves driving in towards the rocks. With great difficulty they kept off, and coasted round to the very bay where Mr Martin had landed. Finding, however, that they could not get in their frail raft, they had after all, having repossessed themselves of their shirts, to swim on shore, Mr Oliver towing young Bramston, who was supported on a spar. They were almost exhausted when they landed, but, finding a shady place under a rock, they fell asleep, and awoke considerably refreshed. A few handfuls of water, in a crevice of a rock, assisted to keep them alive, while they, not without considerable danger, managed to collect some shell-fish from the rocks. Still, they found their strength daily decreasing, till the young midshipman was utterly unable to move. Every day Mr Oliver had climbed to the top of the rock in the hopes of some vessel passing. His joy at seeing his own frigate may be conceived. It was greatly damped, however, on finding that his young companion was, as he supposed, at his last gasp; and had not the Lieutenant and his party arrived at the moment they did, there can be no doubt that the lad would have died. He himself, indeed, was so exhausted, that he could with difficulty find his way down the rock, and after that was unable to move farther.

On our return to the Phillipines, the Sultan, as the chief was called of whom I have spoken, had, we found, recovered our men, who little expected to be rescued from the hands of the savages. We then proceeded to Canton, where we found the homeward-bound merchant fleet ready to sail. We had work enough, I have an idea, in keeping our convoy of old tea-chests, as the merchantmen were called, together. I may say, however, that at length, after no small amount of anxiety to the Captains of the frigates, we arrived safely in the Downs. Our task performed, we were ordered to Portsmouth to be paid off.

CHAPTER SEVEN.

My poor mother was crying bitterly. It was at the thoughts of parting with the Little Lady. In vain my father attempted to console her. Give her up, she said she could not. She loved her almost as her own child. Lieutenant Schank had written home to his mother and sisters, who, in return, had expressed their perfect readiness to receive the Little Lady. But how was she to be conveyed into Lincolnshire? Captain Cobb amply fulfilled his promise by putting a handsome sum into the Lieutenant's hands.

"There, Schank," he said; "it is not you who receive it, remember, it is the little girl, so do not talk of thanking me. I only wish I had been rather more certain of what Mrs Cobb would say, or that I felt considerably more sure than I do that she would be pleased, and I should have liked to have had the Little Lady myself. It would have been a matter of interest to hear about her when one was away from home, and a pleasure to look forward to see her again. She promises to be a sweet little creature. Your womenkind will be well-pleased to see her, depend on that; and I say, Schank, if I can help her on in the world in any way I will do so. Remember, we are old shipmates, so do not stand on ceremony." As Captain Cobb went on talking, and thought of parting from the Little Lady, his heart warmed up; and at that time, I believe, if he had had the will, he would have given her half his property. However, there was one thing to be said of him: in spite of his peculiarities, he was a man who would never depart from his word, and that Mr Schank knew very well. But that in no way detracted from the Lieutenant's generosity, for he had made up his mind to take charge of the Little Lady, whether the Captain assisted him or not. Highly as he esteemed my father and mother, he considered perhaps justly, that they were not in a position to bring up a little girl whose parents were evidently gentlefolks. Be that as it may, it was settled that she was to be sent off as soon as an opportunity should occur, to old Mrs Schank's residence, in the village of Whithyford, Lincolnshire. The difficulty of sending her there was solved by the offer of my mother to convey her herself, with the sanction of my father; indeed, he proposed to go down also, provided the journey could be delayed till the ship was paid off.

"Two children, you see, sir," he said to Mr Schank, "would be rather too much for my good woman to take charge of alone, and I suppose, sir, it would not just do for you to go and help her. People might think what was not the case."

Mr Schank laughed. He had never thought of that, and certainly had not bargained either to take care of one child himself, or to assist my mother in taking care of two.

"By all means, Burton," he said. "I have some business in London which will keep me for a few days, and the Little Lady will give interest and amusement enough to my family till I make my appearance."

The heavy coach took us to London under the escort of Lieutenant Schank, who saw us off for Whithyford in another, far heavier and more lumbering. My father and I went outside; my mother and the Little Lady had an inside place. Behind sat a guard with a couple of blunderbusses slung on either side of him, dressed in an ample red coat, and a brace of pistols sticking out of his pockets. There were a good many highwaymen about at the time, who robbed occasionally on one side of London, and sometimes on the other, and an armed guard, from his formidable appearance, gave the passengers confidence, though he might possibly have proved no very efficient protector if attacked. My father was in high spirits, and pointed out everything he thought worth noticing to me on the road. Each time the coach stopped he was off his seat with me clinging to his back, and looking in at the window to inquire if my mother or the Little Lady wanted anything. Now he would bring out a glass of ale for one, now a cup of milk for the other or for me, or sandwiches, or cakes, or fruit. He had the wisdom never to let me take either ale or grog. "Very good for big people," he used to say, "but very bad for little chaps, Ben."

At length we were put down at the inn at Whithyford. Mrs Schank lived down a lane a little way off the road, and thither, my mother carrying the Little Lady on one arm and holding me by the other, and my father laden with bundles and bandboxes, we proceeded. The cottage was whitewashed, and covered with fresh, thick thatch. In front was the neatest of neat little gardens, surrounded by a well-clipped privet hedge, and the greenest of green gates. Indeed, neatness and order reigned everywhere outside as it did, as I was soon to find, in the interior. The Misses Schank had been expecting us. Three of them appeared at the door. They all seemed much older than Lieutenant Schank. Two of them were very like him, tall and thin, and the other bore a strong resemblance, I thought, to our worthy Captain. Their names I soon learned. There was Miss Martha, and Miss Jemima, and the youngest—a fat one—was Anna Maria. They all shrieked out in different tones as they saw us. Miss Anna Maria seized me in her arms and gave me a kiss, and then, looking at me, exclaimed, "Why, I thought it was to be a little girl! This surely is a boy!" at which her sisters laughed, and bending forward, examined the Little Lady, who was still in my mother's arms, and whom Miss Anna Maria had not observed. Miss Martha at length ventured to take her in the gentlest possible manner and kissed her brow, and said, "Well, she is a sweet little thing; why, Mrs Burton, I wonder you like to part with her," at which observation my mother burst into tears.

"I don't, ma'am, indeed I don't," she answered; when gentle Miss Martha observed, "I did not wish to hurt your feelings, Mrs Burton"; and Miss Anna Maria, who was fond of laughing, said something which made her laugh, and then she laughed herself, so that with between crying and laughing we all entered the cottage and were conducted into the parlour, on one side of which sat old Mrs Schank in a high-back chair, and in a very high cap, and looking very tall and thin and solemn, I thought at first.

My father followed with the bundles and bandboxes, but stood in the passage, not thinking it correct for him to advance into the parlour.

"Who is that?" asked the old lady, looking up and seeing him through the open door.

"Please, ma'am, that is my husband," answered my mother, courtesying.

"What is he?" inquired the old lady.

"A sailor, ma'am."

"Eh, my son is a sailor, my Jack is a sailor, and I love sailors for his sake. Let him come in. Come in, sailor, and put those bundles down; they may tire you. There, sit down and rest yourself. And this is the little girl my son wrote about. Let me see her, Mrs—what is your name?"

"Burton, ma'am," answered my mother.

"Let me see her, Mrs Burton. A very pretty sweet little damsel she is; and whose child is she, do you say?"

"That is what we do not know, ma'am," answered my mother.

"And I am sure I do not," said the old lady, who, I should observe, never was at a loss for a remark.

"Well, that does not much signify; we shall like her for herself. And who is that little boy?"

"That is my son, ma'am," answered my mother.

"Oh! Then he is not the little girl's brother, I suppose?"

"No, ma'am," answered my mother, "though I love the little girl as if she were my own child, and indeed I sorely feel the thoughts of parting with her."

"Very natural, and right, and proper," remarked the old lady. "I am sure I should love such a pretty little damsel, especially if I had nursed her as I suppose you have. However, we will not talk about that just now. You and your husband must stay here for some days, and your little boy too, until this little lady gets accustomed to us. I suppose, sailor, you do not want to go to sea in a hurry? What is his name, my good woman?"

"Richard Burton," answered my mother, "late quarter-master of HM frigate 'Boreas'."

"Well, Richard Burton, you may make yourself at home here, and as happy as you can. My son Jack has written to us about you, only I could not recollect your name."

Although the old lady did not appear at first very wise, she had, however, a fair amount of shrewd good sense, and she was excessively kind, and liberal, and generous as far as she had the means. The ladies had prepared a very nice room for my mother and father, and I had a bed in a corner of it, and they really treated them as if they were guests of consequence.

CHAPTER SEVEN.

While the old lady was speaking, Miss Anna Maria stood laughing and smiling at me, trying to gain my attention and confidence. As I looked at her I thought she must be very good-natured. She was short, and very round and fat, with black twinkling eyes and a somewhat dark complexion, a smile constantly playing on her mouth. Her sisters, as I have remarked, reminded me very strongly of their brother. They all made a great deal of me, and still more of the Little Lady. Having no servants, they did everything themselves, and were busily occupied from morning till night, each having her own department. Miss Anna Maria was cook, and I used to think that perhaps that made her so fat and dark. I took great delight in helping her, and soon learned to peel the potatoes, and wash the cabbages, and stone the raisins for plum puddings. Indeed, knowing well that occupation is useful, not only for small boys but for big ones, she set me to work immediately. Not only did they work indoors but out of doors also, and kept the garden in perfect order, trimming the hedges and mowing and digging. Besides this, they found time to read to their old mother, as well as to themselves; and from the way they talked of books and things, I have no doubt were very well informed, though I was no judge in those days. In the parish in which they had all been born they were looked up to with the greatest affection. They had done much to civilise the people and to keep them from falling back into a state of barbarism, or, I may say, heathenism, for the vicar of the parish was a hunting parson who was seen once a week in the church, where he hurried over the service, and read a sermon which lasted some twelve or fifteen minutes; the shorter the better, however, considering its quality. His horse used to be led up and down by a groom during the time, and as soon as his work was over he remounted and rode off again, not to be seen till the following week unless one of his parishioners died, and he could get no one else to perform the funeral service. He seemed to think that the Misses Schank had a prescriptive right to labour in the parish; but he was excessively indignant when on one or two occasions a dissenting minister came to preach in a barn; and he declared that, should so irregular a proceeding be repeated, he would proceed against him as far as the law would allow. My kind friends' father had had three or four successors. The one I speak of, I think, was the fourth, and, I hope, an exception to the general rule.

"It will not do for us to complain," observed the mild Miss Martha, "but I do wish that our vicar more resembled a shepherd who cares for his sheep, than the wolf he must appear to the poor people of the parish. He takes to the last penny all he can get out of them, and gives them only hard words and stones in return." Miss Martha, however, bless her kind heart, gave the poor people not only gentle words, but many "a cup of cold water," in the name of Christ, and to the utmost of her means assisted her poorer neighbours, as, indeed, did also her sisters. Many a day their meals were dry crusts and tea, when they were giving nourishing food, good beef and mutton, to some of the poor around them, requiring strengthening. I mention these things because it will show that the Little Lady had fallen into good hands. My father and mother did all they could to help them, and certainly their labours were lightened after our arrival. The very first morning my father was up by daylight, with spade in hand, digging in the garden, while my mother helped Miss Anna Maria in the kitchen. Indeed, my father was not a man to eat the bread of idleness either ashore or afloat.

The happiest day we had yet spent was that on which Mr Schank arrived. It was delightful to see the way in which his old mother welcomed him; how she rose from her seat and stretched out her arms, and placed her hands on his shoulders, and gazed into his weather-beaten face; and how his sisters hung about him, and how Miss Anna Maria, who, I ought to say, was generally called the baby, came and put her short fat arms round his neck and kissed him again and again, just as she used to do when she was a little girl. Indeed, just then she evidently had forgotten her own age and his, and probably thought of him just as she did when he came home a young midshipman the first time from sea, proud of his dirk and uniform, and full of the scenes he had witnessed and the wonders of the foreign lands he had visited. He patted me on the head very kindly, and told me he hoped I would some day be as good a seaman as my father. Then he told his sisters that he had been making interest to obtain a warrant for Burton as a boatswain, and that he had little doubt he would get it, for a better seaman never stepped, while it was hard to find a more trustworthy or braver man. "Not that I have any interest myself," he observed, "but I have put young Harry Oliver up to it, and he has plenty of interest, and so he made the application in my name through his friends."

"If it is a good thing, brother Jack, to be a boatswain, I shall be so glad to tell Mrs Burton," said Miss Anna Maria. "She is a very nice good creature, and I should like to make her happy."

"Yes, baby, it is a great rise for a seaman," answered Mr Schank, "and I have no doubt Dick Burton is the man to appreciate it; so if you like, you can go and tell them, for I feel very sure he will obtain it."

I understood very clearly all that was said. Miss Anna Maria, taking me by the hand, hurried off to the kitchen, where my father and mother were sitting. I scarcely know which was the better pleased to hear this good news. I rather think my father was. My mother remarked that it was what her Richard fully deserved; indeed, I rather suspect that if she had been told he had been made a lieutenant or even a commander, she would only have thought that he had received his deserts; but that was all very right and proper. It is a great thing that a woman should have a high opinion of her husband, and it is a very unhappy matter for her when she has not, or at all events when he does not deserve it.

I believe my father had several times proposed leaving Whithyford, and looking out for a ship; but my mother urged him to stay a day or two longer, for she could not bear to part from the Little Lady. At length he said he must go; and though Mr Schank told him that he was welcome to remain, he said that he had been idle long enough, and must now look out for another ship.

"But, Burton, do you intend to take your wife to sea again with you?" asked the Lieutenant.

"I should like to, sir; and yet I am rather doubting about it," he answered, "even if I can obtain permission; but if I do not, she would like to go and pay a visit to her friends in Ireland. It is a long time since she has seen them, and they made her promise to go when she could, and now that I am likely to be a warrant officer, they will look upon her and her boy with more respect than they might have done. Do you see, sir, they are a somewhat upper class of people. Polly loved me, and so we married; but they seemed to think that she was letting herself down greatly in splicing with a seaman, and would not, indeed, for some time have anything to say to her."

Mr Schank reported this to his sisters. They, however, had taken such a liking to my mother, that they had made up their minds to ask her to stay with them instead. They knew that they had a powerful inducement to make her accept their invitation; and Miss Martha, with a good deal of tact, took care to make the offer, holding the Little Lady in her arms, and when she smiled and held out her hands to my mother, very speedily gained the victory. My father was too glad to leave his wife in such safe keeping, and so the matter was soon arranged.

My father was appointed to a sloop of war, which he at once joined, and in which he saw a good deal of hard service.

Several captains applied for Mr Schank, who was looked upon as such an excellent First-Lieutenant, that even his best friends declared that it would be a pity to have him promoted. The Admiralty, however, sent him to look after a young lord in delicate health and indolent disposition, who required a cruise to improve the first, and a man who would do all his work for him, in order that he might indulge in the second.

CHAPTER EIGHT.

The Little Lady grew apace, and flourished under the careful nursing of my mother and the Misses Schank. They gave her the name of Emily, in compliment to an elder sister whom I have not before mentioned—a great invalid, who never left her room. I had, indeed, not seen her, for she was so nervous that it was feared I might agitate her. The Little Lady was, however, once taken in to her, and she was so pleased that she insisted on seeing her every day. She was, I afterwards learned, not only an invalid, but occasionally affected in her mind, from some great grief which had occurred to her in her youth.

Time rolled on. I was somewhat spoiled, I think, by the kind ladies, who treated me completely as if I had been in their own position in life, and took great pains to teach me all I was then capable of learning.

At length my father came back to Whithyford. He could not remain long, for he had been appointed to another ship. He told my mother that he had been so unhappy without her that he had got leave to take her and me with him, as I was now big enough to go to sea. My mother was too sensible a woman not to know that she must some day of necessity part from the Little Lady, and though it was like wrenching her very heartstrings, she, without hesitation, agreed to accompany her husband and take me with her. Our kind friends were, I know, very sorry to part with us. The old lady folded her arms round me, and kissed me on both cheeks, and on my forehead, and blessed me, and told me she hoped I should be as brave and good a man as her son, and also as my father. The frigate was fitting out at Portsmouth for the Mediterranean station. She was the "Grecian," of thirty-eight guns, commanded by Captain Harry Oliver, who, three years before, had been a Master's mate in the "Boreas". He having since then served two years as Lieutenant, and one as Commander, had just been posted to her. Some men in Mr Schank's position would have declined serving as First-Lieutenant under an officer who had before served under him, but Mr Schank had no pride of the sort, and when Captain Oliver applied for him he readily consented to accept the offer.

There was every probability of our having a happy ship. I have mentioned a young midshipman—Leonard Bramston—he was our junior Lieutenant, having lately got his promotion; but the person above all others I was delighted to see was Mrs King, whose husband had joined the frigate. Bill King proposed also himself applying for a warrant as gunner. However, for the present, he had come to sea with his old rating as quarter-master. While the ship was fitting out, my mother and Mrs King lived on shore. One Sunday we went to the Marine Barracks, where we heard that Sergeant Killock and Tom Sawyer were stationed. They were great-

CHAPTER EIGHT. 41

ly pleased to see me. The Sergeant tried to persuade my mother to let me remain on shore and turn into a drummer boy, at which I was very indignant, holding a blue-jacket to be a being of far superior grade, and a blue-jacket I hoped shortly to become. I was rather small just then, but not smaller than some of the midshipmen who had joined our frigate for the first time. Mere mites of boys were frequently then sent to sea, who looked more fit to wear pinafores, and be attended by nurses, as far as size was concerned; and yet, though now and then they got into mischief and did not do very wise things, yet occasionally they performed very gallant actions, such as men twice their age might have been proud of, requiring judgment and discretion as well as courage. At length we went out to Spithead and took our powder on board. Blue Peter was flying, the remainder of the stores for the officers came on board, the ship was cleared, the band struck up, the seamen tramped round with the capstan bars to a merry tune, the topsails were sheeted home, and with a blue sky above us and bright water below, we stood down the Solent towards the Needle passage. It was a gay and beautiful sight. I had been so long on shore that I had almost forgotten all about a ship. The men looked so smart and active, for Mr Schank had taken care to get a picked crew, which some officers in those days could get and some could not; the Captain and Lieutenants and midshipmen in their new uniforms looked so spruce, and the marines so trim and well set up, that I could not help rejoicing that I was once more afloat, though I did not forget my kind friends at Whithyford, nor the dear Little Lady. We passed out at the Needle passage, with Hurst Castle on one side and the tall pointed white rocks off the west end of the island on the other, not ill-called Needles, sighting Weymouth, where the good old King George the Third was accustomed to reside. Bless his memory, say I, for, though he might have had his faults, he was a right-honest true-hearted man—brave as the bravest of his subjects, and firm too; though those who opposed him called his firmness obstinacy. However, I am talking of things of which I knew at that period of my career nothing at all.

I had grown by this time into a stout, hardy-looking lad, tall and proportionably broad, so that I looked much older than I was, and thus I was already rated as a boy on board the ship, though I was the youngest on board, and likely to remain so for a considerable time. When people saw my mother, who looked remarkably young, and pretty as ever, they could scarcely believe that I was her son. Few people retain their health and good looks as she did. Running across the Bay of Biscay we sighted Cape Finisterre, rounding which we stood in for the coast, in hopes of picking up some of the Spanish Guarda Costas or any of the enemy's merchantmen. However, when standing in for Finisterre Bay the wind dropped and we lay perfectly becalmed, rolling gently to the swell which nearly at all times sets in on that coast.

Evening was approaching. Our young Captain walked the deck with impatient strides. Though so gentle and quiet in his manners there was a spirit in him that ever desired activity. Several times his glass was turned towards the distant shore. He then summoned the master and examined the chart. We had fallen in, the day before, with a Portuguese Rasca, from the master of which a good deal of information had been obtained, and as an honest man and a patriot it was supposed that it could be relied on. Captain Oliver and Mr Schank were in consultation for some time. We guessed there was something to be done. Now, I thought to myself, I should like to see some fun. They are planning something, that is certain. I wonder what it can be. In a short time the cutter and barge were ordered away, it being understood that Mr Schank would take the command of the former and would be accompanied by Lieutenant Spry of the Marines, while the Third-Lieutenant, Mr Bramston, took charge of the barge. Including marines and blue-jackets the party mustered rather more than forty in all. They waited till dusk to leave the ship. This just suited my plan of operation. As the arms, provisions, and other articles were being lowered into the boat, I managed to slip down and to stow myself away in the barge forward under a sail. I required but little space for hiding away. Just at dusk the two boats shoved off, and away we went towards the shore; I heard the men say that the object of the expedition was to cut out several luggers lying in a small harbour with a town at the further end of it. We had a long pull, for we were at such, a distance from the coast that the frigate could not have been seen from it. At all events the inhabitants of the town would not have suspected that any boats would come from a vessel whose topgallant sails could only just have been visible. At length, after pulling for some hours, the lights on shore were seen, and in a short time the boats came off the mouth of the harbour; but then it was found that the luggers were some little way up it, and that a strong fort guarded the town and entrance. Mr Schank and the Lieutenant of Marines agreed that the first thing to be done was to take the fort. We could not land close to it on account of the rocks, and therefore had to pull some distance to the south before the party could get on shore.

When they all left the boats I had no fancy to remain behind, and therefore scrambled out after the rest, although one of the boat-keepers attempted to stop me by catching hold of my leg. I escaped him, however, and ran on among the men.

"Hillo, little chap! Where did you come from?" exclaimed several of them as they first discovered me.

I replied that I wanted to go and help them fight the enemy. I was passed to Mr Schank. "Why, Ben," he said, "what business have you to be here? What can you do?"

"Please, sir, I can carry your flask if you will let me, or if anybody is hit I can stay by them and help them."

"I have a great mind to send you back, Master Ben."

I entreated that I might be allowed to go on. Perhaps he thought there might be as much risk for me if I remained in the boat as there would be should I accompany them. He therefore, greatly to my delight, allowed me to go on with the party. On we pushed. Mr Schank, it appeared, had been on shore before at the place and knew the position of the fort. We had a heavy tramp, however, especially for him with his wooden leg, which sank into the soft sand every step he took, and he sometimes had to rest his arm on a man's shoulder to help him get along, but his courage and determination were at all times equal to any emergency. On we went

CHAPTER EIGHT. 43

till we could see the dim outline of the fort across the sand; it was a great thing to approach without being discovered, for, although we had determined to get in at all hazard, if we could take the Spaniards by surprise, the work would be far more easy. There was no cover, but we could only hope that the enemy would not be on the look-out for us, or that if they were, their eyes would be turned towards the harbour, the entrance-gate being on the land side. I own, at last, I felt my legs aching with walking over the soft sand. I began to wish that I had remained on board. The men must have suspected how it was with me, and at last one of them took me up and carried me on his shoulders, and then another and another, for even my additional weight was likely to tire the stoutest had they carried me long. At last the fort rose before us. Mr Schank in a low whisper ordered the men to move forward crouching down to the ground, to step softly, and not to utter a word. On we went, so close together, that had anybody watched us, we might have looked like some huge animal moving on, or the shadow of a cloud passing over the ground. Our leaders hurried on. The drawbridge was down. The marines were ordered to level their bayonets and the blue-jackets their pikes, and charge on. It was the work of an instant. The Spaniards were totally unprepared for our coming at that moment, although, as it turned out, they had been informed of our being in the neighbourhood, and a gun was found pointed for the purpose of sweeping the passage should the fort be attacked. Before, however, it could be fired, the gunners had taken to flight. In a few seconds we were in possession of the fort.

Our men were pretty well knocked up with their long pull and march over the sand, and the country might soon be raised, and overwhelming forces sent against us. The order was, therefore, given to spike the guns, which was very speedily done. The fort was found to contain eight brass guns, twenty-four and twelve-pounders, with a considerable garrison. Part of them, as we entered, laid down their arms to save their lives, while the remainder scrambled over the walls, and made their escape to the town. Our boats had, meantime, made their way into the harbour, which, now that we had possession of the fort, they could do without molestation. As soon as all the damage had been done to the fort which time would allow, we once more embarked in the boats, and made a dash at the luggers, which yielded without striking a blow. Directly we had taken them, however, and had begun to move down the harbour, a battery on the opposite side, which we had not yet seen, opened its fire, and continued sending shot after us, which could not however have been very well aimed, for neither the boat nor the prizes were once struck. It is possible that the powder was bad, and the shot fell short. As we approached the mouth of the harbour we saw that the whole neighbourhood was roused. Beacon fires were blazing, guns firing, and musketry rattling away in all directions. As we were getting through the passage, a pretty sharp fire of musketry was opened on us, but though the shot fell thickly, no one was struck, though the boats and vessels were so frequently. It was my first battle, and a very bloodless one, for I do not believe a Spaniard or Englishman was hurt. Our six prizes were very acceptable, for they were laden with wine, which was pronounced very good of its sort. It was broad daylight by the time we got near the mouth of the harbour, and the land-breeze blowing enabled us to carry out our prizes without difficulty, and with them under convoy we sailed for Lisbon, where a good market could be found for their cargoes.

When I got on board, instead of being received as a hero crowned with victory, my father seized hold of me, and looked me sternly in the face.

"Ben," said he, "have you thought of the misery and anxiety you have been causing your mother? She has been in a fearful taking about you ever since you went away. How could she tell that you had not slipped overboard? I could not say that you had not, myself; but I have heard of boys doing just as you have done, and so I guessed pretty well the state of the case. But I tell you, boy, I never saw her suffer so much. I almost thought it would be the death of her."

"Oh! Flog me, father! Flog me!" I cried out; for I could not bear the thoughts of having made my mother unhappy. "Tell Dick Patch to lay it on thick. The harder he hits the better. I did not think, father, what I was doing; indeed, I did not."

"No, Ben, I will not have you flogged," he answered, "your mother's sufferings have been punishment enough for you. I believe you did it without thought, indeed, I know you did; and just do you go and have a talk with her, and see how pale and ill she looks; and I hope that will be enough to make you never go and do a thing again which will cause her anxiety and grief. The time will come when you will have to run all sorts of risks and dangers, but it is a very different thing to run your head into danger from fool-hardiness, and to go into danger because it is your duty." These remarks of my father made a deep impression on me. I hurried below, and there I saw my poor mother looking more ill and distressed than I had ever seen her:—her eyes red from weeping, and her cheeks pale and sickly; and then when she told me how much she had suffered, I burst into tears, and promised never to play her such a trick again.

We took several other prizes on our way to the South; indeed, Captain Oliver showed, that, young as he was, few officers were likely to prove more active or energetic in their duties. He was well off and did not seem to care for the prize-money. He thought of duty above everything else. It was his duty to injure the trade of the enemy as much as possible, and he did so to the very best of his power.

CHAPTER NINE.

Some time had passed since the "Grecian" had entered the Mediterranean. We had not been idle during the time—now cruising along the coast of Spain and France, now down that of Italy, now away to Malta, sometimes off to the East among the Greek Islands. We had taken a good many prizes; indeed, I may say that all our expeditions had been planned with judgment, and carried out with vigour. I had a very happy time on board, for the men treated me with kindness, and I was so young that even the officers took notice of me. To Mr Bramston, especially, I became much attached. As he had known me in my childhood, he took more notice of me than anyone else. It has been my lot through life to lose many kind friends, but I must acknowledge that they have been as often replaced by others. When Mr Schank heard from home, he never failed to send for me or my mother, to give us an account of the Little Lady; indeed, Mr Bramston and others, as well as our Captain, took a warm interest in her, and always seemed glad to hear that she was going on well. Altogether, we were looked upon as a very happy and fortunate ship. However, a dark reverse was to come.

We were returning from Malta, and had run some way along the coast of Italy, when the look-out from the mast-head discovered a sail on the lee-bow. It was just daybreak. The sun rising over the distant land, which lay like a blue line on our starboard side, shed his beams on the upper sails of the stranger. The frigate was kept away a little, and all sail made in chase. We continued standing on for a couple of hours, when the wind drew more aft, and with studden-sails rigged on both sides we glided rapidly over the smooth water, gaining considerably on the chase. She must have discovered us, for she was now seen to rig out studden-sails, and to make every attempt to escape. She was pronounced to be a large polacca ship; and from the way she kept ahead of us, it was very evident she was very fast. This made us more eager than ever to come up with her. The general opinion was that she was a merchantman, very likely richly-laden, and would undoubtedly become an easy prize. Our people were in high spirits, making sure that they were about to add a good sum to their already fair amount of prize-money. I cannot say that these thoughts added much to my pleasure, considering the very small share which would fall to my lot, but my father would probably be very much the richer. In those days, it was no uncommon thing for a seaman to return from a cruise with a couple of hundred pounds in his pocket; and of course, under those circumstances, the share even of a warrant officer would be very considerable. Mr Schank, I doubt not, was thinking of the many comforts he would be able to afford his family at home; and Mr Bramston, who had another reason for wishing to add to his worldly store, was hoping that he might be able to splice his dear Mary all the sooner, and leave her better provided for when he had to come away again to sea.

Hour after hour passed by. There was the chase still ahead and though we had gained considerably on her, still there were many probabilities of her escaping. The fear was that we might not get up to her before nightfall, and that then in the darkness she might escape. The men were piped to dinner, and of course the conversation at the mess-tables ran on the probabilities of our capturing the chase.

Some time afterwards, just as the watch on deck had been relieved, the main topsail gave a loud flap against the mast. The other sails, which had before been swelling out, now hung down.

"The wind is all up and down the masts," I heard my father remark, with a sigh; and going on deck, such we found indeed to be the case. Scarcely a cat's-paw played over the surface of the water, while our canvas hung down entirely emptied of wind. It was a time when Captain Cobb would have almost cracked his cheeks with blowing for the purpose of regaining it. Captain Oliver, however, did no such thing, but, taking his glass, directed it towards the chase.

"She is in our condition," he observed to Mr Schank.

"She is not likely to get away from us, at all events," remarked the First-Lieutenant, taking a look at her also.

"I think, Schank; we may, however, make sure of her with the boats," observed the Captain. "It will not do to give her a chance of escaping, and she may get the breeze before we do."

"Certainly, sir," answered Mr Schank. "It will be as well to secure her, for fear of that."

"Well, as there is no great glory to be gained, I will let Mr Mason and Bramston go in the boats," said the Captain.

The frigate's boats were accordingly called away. The two lieutenants and my father and a couple of midshipmen went in them, with altogether about seventy men. It was a strong force, but the ship was very likely to have sweeps, and even a merchantman might offer some resistance unless attacked by overpowering numbers. The people cheered as they pulled off, and urged them to make haste with the prize. Never did an expedition start with fairer prospects of success, and we fully hoped, before many hours were over, to have the chase under English colours. She was between four and five miles away at the time; but though the pull was a long one, the men laid their backs to the oars for fear of a breeze springing up before they could get alongside. My mother had shown considerable anxiety on former occasions when my father had gone away on dangerous expeditions, yet, in the present instance, she seemed quite at ease, as there appeared to be no danger or difficulty in the enterprise. Though no man ever loved his wife better than my father did my mother, yet this never prevented him volunteering whenever he felt himself called upon to do so, however hazardous and trying the work in hand. As may be supposed, no one thought of turning in that night. All hands were on the watch, expecting to see the ship towed by the boats, or some of the boats returning with an account of their capture. The Captain and First-Lieutenant

CHAPTER NINE. 47

walked the deck with easy paces, every now and then turning their night glasses in the direction of the ship, hoping to see her, but still she did not appear. At length the men began to wonder why the ship had not come in sight, or why the boats did not return to give notice of what had occurred. Afterwards they grew more and more anxious, and they imparted their anxiety to my mother. Our gunner, Mr Hockey, who was somewhat superstitious, now declared that he had dreamed a dream which foreboded disaster. The substance of it I never could learn, nor did he say a word about the matter till some time had passed and the boats did not appear. He was a man of proverbs, and remarked that "a pitcher which goes often to the well gets broken at last," by which he insinuated that as we had been hitherto successful in our expeditions, a reverse might be expected. All the boats had been sent away. The Captain's gig was under repair, but there was a small dinghy remaining. Mr Hockey went aft, and volunteered to pull in the direction the ship had been seen, in the hopes of ascertaining what had become of the boats. The Captain was as anxious apparently as he was.

"Certainly, Mr Hockey," he answered.

Just then the sound of oars in the distance floated over the calm water.

"Stay, there are the boats," he said.

They approached very slowly. At first it was hoped that they might be towing the ship; but though they were evidently drawing near, no ship could be distinguished. At length they came in sight. The Captain hailed them. The voice of a young midshipman answered: "Sad news, sir! Sad news!"

"What has happened, Mr Hassel? Where is the ship?"

"Beaten back, sir, beaten back!" was the answer, and the speaker's voice was almost choked. The boats, as they got alongside, were seen to be full of people, but they were lying about over the thwarts in confused heaps, those only who were at the oars appearing to move. My mother was at this moment fortunately below. The gunner came down and entreated her to remain there. I, however, had gone up on deck, and was eagerly looking about, expecting to see my father arrive. Mr Hassel was the first to come up the side. He staggered aft to the Captain to make his report. Meantime whips were rove, and, one after one, those who that afternoon had left the frigate in high health and spirits were hoisted up dead and mangled in every variety of way. Nearly thirty bodies were thus brought on deck. Many others were hoisted up and carried immediately below, where the surgeon attended them, and of the whole number only seven were able to walk the deck steadily. I eagerly looked out for my father. He was not among those unhurt. Among the dead I dared not look. I hurried below, hoping to see him under the hands of the surgeon, but neither was he there. My heart sank within me. I hastened to the main-deck. There, with a lantern, I met my poor mother frantically scanning the faces of the slain, who were laid out in a ghastly row. Eagerly she passed along, bending over the pallid features of those who a few hours before had been so full of life and courage, jokes escaping their lips. Now as she looked at one, now at another, a glance told her that the corpse was not that of her husband.

"Oh! Mother! Mother! Where is father?" I cried out at length, as I caught sight of her.

"I know not, my boy, I know not," she answered. "Oh! Burton, Burton! Where are you? Has no one seen my husband? Can anyone tell me of my husband? Where is he? Where is he?" she frantically exclaimed, running from one to the other, when she found that he was not among those brought on board.

"The boatswain!" said some one. "Bless her poor heart, I don't like to utter it, but I saw him knocked overboard as he was climbing up the polacca's side. He would not have let go had it not been for a thrust in his shoulder, and he was hit, I know, while he was still in the boat."

"Who is that you speak of?" asked my mother, hearing the man's voice.

"Bless your heart, Mrs Burton, but I am sorry to say it," answered Bill Houston, one of the few who had escaped unhurt. "I was close to him, but he fell by me before I could stretch out a hand to help him, and I doubt, even if we had got him on board, it would have been much the better for him, he seemed so badly hurt. I did not hear him cry out or utter a sound."

The lantern my mother had been holding dropped from her hand as she heard these words. All hope was gone. "Oh I give me back my husband I give me back my husband!" she shrieked out. "Why did you come away without him?"

"Oh! Mother! Mother! Don't take on so!" I exclaimed, running up to her. She put her hands on my shoulders and gazed in my face.

"For you, Ben, I would wish to live, otherwise I would rather be down in the cold sea along with him." Then again she cried out frantically for my poor father. Her grief increased mine. Seeing the state she was in, Bill King, who had remained near her, hurried down to fetch his wife, who was attending on the wounded. She did her best to soothe my poor mother's grief, and not without difficulty she was led away to my father's cabin; and there, placed on his bed, she found some relief in tears. I did my best to comfort her, but I could do little else than weep too. Perhaps that was the best thing I could do; there is nothing like sympathy.

"Oh! My boy! My boy!" she exclaimed, "you are still left to me; but the day may come when you will be taken away, as your poor father has been, and I shall be all alone—alone! Alone!"

Then she burst forth in an Irish wail such as I had never heard before. It was curious; because, though an Irish woman, her accent, under ordinary circumstances, was but slightly to be detected. Mrs King, having done all she could, returned to her duties among the wounded, of whom there were upwards of thirty, several of them mortally.

From Bill Houston, who had come to inquire for my mother, shortly afterwards, I learned the particulars of what had occurred. The boats approached the ship, all hands being fully persuaded that they had little more to do than to climb up her sides and take possession. As, however, they drew near her, and were just about to dash alongside, a tremendous fire of grape, musketry, and round-shot was opened on them from her ports, which were suddenly unmasked. In spite of this, although numbers were hit, Mr Mason ordered them to board the ship.

CHAPTER NINE.

Scarcely had he uttered the words than a shot laid him low, poor Mr Bramston being wounded at the same time. Still the attempt to board was made, but as they climbed up the sides they found that boarding nettings were triced up the whole length of the ship, while pikes were thrust down on them, and a hot fire of musketry opened in their faces. Again and again they attempted to get on board, and not till nearly all were killed or wounded did they desist from the attempt. Young Mr Hassel, the midshipman, being the only officer left alive, then gave the order to retreat, though it was not without difficulty that they could push off from the ship's sides. The darkness of the night saved them from being utterly destroyed. The enemy, probably, had not been aware of the tremendous effect of their own fire, and expected another attack from our men, or they would undoubtedly have continued firing at the boats after they had shoved off. Some distance had been gained, however, before the ship again commenced firing, and the aim being uncertain, very few of her shot took effect.

The next day was the saddest I had ever known. Our kind young Captain felt the loss more than anyone. Really, it seemed as if his heart would break as he walked along the main-deck, where our dead shipmates were laid out. He paid a visit also to my mother, and endeavoured to comfort her as well as he could.

"I owe your brave husband much, Mrs Burton," he said. "We have been shipmates a good many years altogether, and he more than once saved my life; I cannot repay him, but I can be a friend to your boy, and I will do my utmost to be of assistance to you. I cannot heal your grief, and I cannot tell you not to mourn for your husband, but I will soothe it as far as I can."

Then came the sad funeral. Had the frigate been engaged in a desperate action with a superior force we could scarcely have lost so many men as we had done in this unfortunate expedition. I thought the Captain would break down altogether as he attempted to read the funeral service. Two or three times he had to stop, and by a great effort recover his composure. There were the two lieutenants and a young midshipman, and upwards of twenty men all to be committed to the ocean together. Curiosity brought me up to see what was going forward, and though I looked on quietly for some time I at length burst into bitter tears. I thought there is my poor father—he had to go overboard without any service being read over him.

CHAPTER TEN.

Soon after the funeral was over I was sent for into the Captain's cabin. I found him and Mr Schank seated there.

"Ben," he said, "my boy, we have been talking over what we can do for your poor mother. The best thing, I think, will be for her to return to her home on the first opportunity, and I daresay we shall find a ship homeward-bound at Malta, on board which she can get a passage, while we will do our best to raise funds to place her as much as possible at her ease as to money matters. Now, Ben, I wish to stand your friend; but you are very young still to knock about at sea without a father to look after you, and I propose, therefore, that you should return with your mother. After you have had schooling for a year or two on shore, you shall rejoin this ship or any other I may command, and then your future progress will much depend on your own conduct. You will behave well, I have no doubt you will; but if not, I cannot help you forward as I desire."

I did not quite comprehend what the Captain proposed, but I understood enough to know that I had a friend in him, and I accordingly thanked him for his good intentions. I was still standing hat in hand in the cabin, for the Captain seemed disposed to ask me further questions, when the surgeon entered to make his report of the state of the wounded.

"What, more dead I more dead!" exclaimed the poor Captain, as his eye glanced on the paper.

"Yes, sir," was the answer. "Turner and Green have both slipped their cables. I had very little hopes of either from the first. There are one or two more I am afraid will follow them before many days are over."

The Captain hid his face in his hands, and a groan burst from his bosom. "I would that I had gone myself. It would be better to be among the sufferers than have this happen," burst from his lips.

Mr Schank tried to console him. "No blame, sir," he said, "could be attached to you. It was very unlikely that such a ship should have made so determined a defence, and no forethought could have enabled you to act differently."

"Yes, yes," answered the Captain, "but to lose all these brave fellows in such a way," and again he groaned.

No one spoke for some minutes, till at length the surgeon observed that he hoped Mr Hassel would do well, as his wounds, though severe were not dangerous.

"From what I can learn, sir," he observed, "he behaved with great judgment and courage, and I believe it was through him that the boats got away without further damage."

When the surgeon had gone, the Captain once more addressed me, and made inquiries about my mother's family and the place of their residence. I, of course knew very little, but I gave him all the information I possessed.

"But, perhaps, Mr Schank," I said, "you will let us go and pay your family a visit. Those were happy times we had there. I think my mother would rather go there than anywhere else."

Mr Schank who was not at all offended by the liberty I took, replied that he thought the idea a very good one. When, however, my mother was asked, she said that she would rather go and be among her own people, if they would receive her. The truth was, I think I remarked, that her friends were much above my father's position; and now that she would have a pension, and a good deal of prize-money, she felt that she could return and be on an equality with them, as far as fortune was concerned. These ideas were, however, not on her own account as much as on mine, as her great ambition was that I might rise in the world. It was, I truly believe, her only weakness, if weakness it could be called, for she was proud of me, and I suspect thought a good deal more of me than I deserved. After this misfortune, we shaped a course for Malta, for the purpose of replacing the officers and men we had lost, and from thence the Captain intended to send home my mother and me. Towards evening, three or four days after the occurrences I have described, several sail were perceived inside of us, that is to say, to the east. As we were to windward, we stood down towards them till we made out a line-of-battle ship, two frigates and a brig. As there was no doubt they were enemies' ships, our Captain determined to watch them during the night, to ascertain in what direction they were proceeding. They, however, objected to this, and were soon seen crowding all sail in chase. We had now to run for it; and though the "Grecian" was a fast frigate, we well knew that many of the Frenchmen were faster, and that, short-handed as we were, it was too certain that we should be captured if they came up with us. Fortunately the breeze continued, and we made all sail the frigate could carry. But not only could we distinguish the enemy still in chase, but the opinion was that they were rapidly gaining on us. I remember coming on deck and looking out, seeing on our lee-quarter, far away through the gloom, their dark outlines as they came on in hot chase. I, saw that everybody was anxious, and I heard several of the men talking of Verdun, and the way prisoners were treated there. For the men this was bad enough, but for the officers to be made prisoners was sad work. Unless they could make their escape or get exchanged, all prospect of advancement was lost, as was the case with many; the best part of their years spent in idleness. I understood enough, at all events, to be very anxious about the matter.

I went below, I remember, and told my poor mother; she, however, seemed indifferent as to what might occur. Indeed her grief had stunned her, and she was incapable of either thinking or speaking. As morning approached the wind fell, and when daylight broke the sails hung up and down against the masts. We were in a perfect calm, while not three miles off appeared the French squadron. All hopes of escape seemed over, and the men began putting on additional clothing and stowing away their money in their pockets, as seamen generally do when capture is certain, and often when they expect to be wrecked. The officers walked the deck looking very anxious, but the Captain and Mr Schank kept their eyes about on all sides. At length a few cat's-paws were seen playing over the water. The First-Lieutenant pointed them out to the Captain. His eyes brightened somewhat. They came faster and faster. And now the sails once more felt the power of the wind, and away we went pretty quickly through the water. Ahead of us lay a small island, towards which the frigate steered. As we approached it we saw the ship-of-the-line still following us, while the two frigates and corvette stood away round the west side. Their object was very clear. They hoped thereby to cut us off.

"We may still disappoint them," I heard Mr Schank observe.

"I trust so," said the Captain; but though he kept up his confidence, his countenance was very grave. For some time we kept well ahead till we reached the southernmost end of the island, when once more the wind falling we lay almost becalmed. We could see to the east the two frigates and the corvette, their canvas filled by a strong breeze, but the line-of-battle ship was out of sight, hid by a point of land. The former might have been five or six miles off, but they were coming up at the rate of six knots an hour. There was no sign of the breeze reaching us. Our escape seemed almost impossible. Mr Schank's courage, however, never failed—at least, it never looked as if it did, and he seemed to be saying something to the Captain which gave him encouragement. One of the frigates was considerably ahead of the rest. At all events we were not likely, therefore, to yield without striking a blow, and if we could by any means cripple her before her consorts could come up, we might afterwards be better able to deal with them. Still there was the line-of-battle ship, and she would be down upon us before long. A French prison in very vivid colours stared even the bravest of our men in the face. The officers were looking at their watches. Within little more than half-an-hour, unless we could get a breeze, we should be hotly engaged, and then, unless we could beat our enemy in ten minutes, there would be little prospect of getting away. On she came over the blue ocean. Looking at the land, we could see a line, as it were, drawn between us. On our side the water was smooth as a mirror; on the other, still crisped by the fresh breeze, and glittering in the sunlight. It was very tantalising. On the leading Frenchman came, faster and faster. Still the breeze did not touch our sails. At length we could clearly count her ports, and she appeared in the pure atmosphere even nearer than perhaps she was. Suddenly she yawed. A white puff of smoke was seen, and a shot came whizzing across our bows. Another followed. It struck us, and the yellow splinters were seen flying from our sides. The men stood at their quarters ready to begin the fight.

"Not a gun is to be fired till I give the order," cried the Captain.

"That will not be long, I fancy," I heard one of the men say, as I with other boys brought up the powder from below.

The frigate still held the breeze and was approaching. Yet our Captain let her get nearer and nearer. In vain, however, our people waited for the order to fire.

CHAPTER TEN.

Several more shots came flying over the water, and the Frenchmen seemed now convinced that they had got us well within range. Suddenly luffing up, the enemy fired her whole broadside. The shot came flying about us, but did no great damage.

"Trim sails!" cried the Captain, and we edged away towards the blue line I have mentioned, the wind just then filling out our canvas. Meantime the Frenchman remained involved in a cloud of smoke. Again and again she fired her broadside, only hiding herself more completely from view; while her sails, which had hitherto been full, were now seen to flap against her masts, and away we went with an increasing breeze. We could just see the line-of-battle ship hull down on one side, and the two frigates and corvette becalmed on the other, utterly unable to move, while we were slipping through the water at the rate of seven or eight knots an hour.

"I thought it would be so!" exclaimed Mr Schank, increasing the rapidity of his strides as he paced the deck, and rubbing his hands with glee. On we went. In a short time not a trace of the Frenchmen could be discovered, nor did we sight another enemy till we entered Malta harbour.

Captain Oliver and Mr Schank were as good as their words. They mentioned among the inhabitants the circumstance of my father's death, and that his widow and child were on board, and very soon collected a considerable sum of money, which they presented to my poor mother. Her excessive grief had now subsided, and a settled melancholy seemed to have taken possession of her. An armed store-ship which had discharged her cargo at Malta was returning home, bound for Cork; and on board her our kind friends procured a passage for my mother and me. We had a sad parting with our numerous shipmates. The men exhibited the regard they had for my mother by bestowing on me all sorts of presents; indeed, the carpenter said he must make me a chest in which to stow them away. My mother felt leaving our kind friend, Mrs King, more than anything else. It was curious to see the interesting young woman, as she still was, embracing the tall, gaunt, weather-beaten virago, as Mrs King appeared to be.

"Cheer up, Polly, cheer up," said the latter. "You have lost a kind husband, there is no doubt of that, but you have got your boy to look after, and he will give you plenty to think about—bless his heart! The time will come, Polly, when we will meet again, and you will have grown more contented, I hope; and if not, we shall know each other up aloft there, where I hope there will be room for me, though I cannot say as how I feel I am very fit for such a place." Mrs King went talking on, but my poor mother could make no answer to her remarks, sobs choking her utterance. Her tears did her good, however, so Mrs King observed, and told her not to stop them. I was glad to find that the Captain had appointed Bill King as acting boatswain of the frigate. The midshipman, Mr Hassel, who had been seriously injured in the unfortunate expedition, took a passage home in the store-ship. Who should we see on going on board but my old friends Toby Kiddle and Pat Brady. Pat was overjoyed at seeing us, though he looked very sad when he heard of my father's death.

"Arrah, it's a pity a worse man hadn't been taken in his stead," he observed, "but it can't be helped, Polly. Better luck next time, as Tim Donovan said when he was going to be hung!"

Pat had been to see his friends, he said, in the West of Ireland, and Toby Kiddle had been wrecked on the same coast, and having found his way across to Cork had there, with his old messmate, entered on board the store-ship. She was to return to Cork, which was very convenient to us, as my mother could thus more easily travel to the West of Ireland where her family resided.

The name of the vessel was the "Porpoise," and she was commanded by Captain Tubb. He put me very much in mind of Captain Cobb, except that he was considerably stouter. We sailed with a convoy of some fifty other vessels of all sizes and rigs; the larger portion having generally to lay to for the "Porpoise," which, with her Captain, rolled away over the surface of the Atlantic in the wake of the rest. Captain Tubb declared that his ship was very steady when she had her cargo on board, but certainly she was very much the contrary under the present circumstances, and Toby Kiddle remarked that it was a wonder she did not shake her masts out of her.

My poor mother could very seldom be persuaded to come on deck, but lay in her cabin scarcely eating anything, or speaking to anyone except to me, and even then it seemed a pain to her to utter a few words.

From the account I gave Toby and Pat of Captain Oliver, they were very eager to serve again with him, and they promised that should they ever have the chance of finding him fitting out a ship, they would immediately volunteer on board.

I was very glad to hear this, because I hoped they would do so, and that I again should be with them. We had not a few alarms on our homeward voyage from the appearance of strange sails which it was supposed were enemies' cruisers. We, of course, should have been among the first picked out. However, we escaped all accidents, and at length arrived in the Cove of Cork. As may be supposed, Toby Kiddle made many inquiries about the Little Lady. When my mother got to Cork, her heart somewhat failed her at the thought of going among her own kindred under the present circumstances, and she began to regret that she had not agreed to pay a visit in the first place to Lieutenant Schank's family, where she would have had the consolation of looking after the little girl. However, it was now too late to do that. We therefore prepared for our journey to the West. Pat insisted on escorting us, declaring that he had plenty of money and did not know what else to do with it. Toby, however, remained on board the old "Porpoise," intending to go round in her to Portsmouth, where she was next bound with provisions. It was no easy matter making a journey in the West of Ireland in those days. There were the coaches, but they were liable to upset and to be robbed.

Although, therefore, posting was dear, Pat settled that such was the only becoming way for the widow of the "Grecian's" late boatswain to travel. My mother at length consented to go part of the way in a coach, performing the remainder in a chaise, when no coach was available.

The place for which we were bound was Ballybruree, a town, it called itself,

CHAPTER TEN.

on the west coast of the green island. Her father, Mat Dwyer, Esquire, he signed himself, and her mother, were both alive, and she had a number of brothers and sisters, and a vast number of cousins to boot. But I must reserve an account of our reception at Rincurran Castle, for so my grandfather called his abode, for another chapter.

CHAPTER ELEVEN.

"Ben, my boy, you are approaching the home of your ancestors," exclaimed Pat Brady, who was seated on the box of the old battered yellow post-chaise, on the roof of which I had perched myself, while my poor mother sat in solitude inside. "They are an honoured race, and mighty respected in the country. You will see the top of the ould Castle before long if you keep a bright look-out, and a hearty welcome we'll be after getting when they see us all arrive in this dignified way—just like a great foreign ambassador going to court. It is a fine counthry this of ours, Ben, barring the roads, which put us too much in mind of our run home in the 'Porpoise'. But we have mighty fine hills, Ben. Do you see them there? And lakes and streams full of big trout, and forests. But the bogs, Ben, they beat them all. If it was not for them bogs, where should we all be? Then the roads might be worse, Ben. Hold on there, lad, or you will be sent into the middle of next week. But Ben, my boy, as the song says:—

"'If you'd seen but these roads before they were made,
You would have lift up your hands and blessed General Wade'."

Thus Pat continued running on as he had been doing the whole of our journey. It was certainly hard work holding on at the top of the chaise, as it went pitching and rolling, and tumbling about over the ill-formed path, which scarcely deserved the name of a road. Still every now and then I sprang to my feet to look out for the castle which he talked about. I had seen of late a good many castles on the coast of the Mediterranean, Gibraltar, and Malta besides. I had some idea that Rincurran Castle must be a very fine place.

"Arrah! Ben, and there it is as large as life. Sure it's a grand mansion, barring it's a little out of repair!" shouted Pat, as, turning an angle of the road, we came in sight of a tall, stone, dilapidated building, with a courtyard in front, and two round pillars on either side of the entrance-gate. The pigs had possession of the chief part of the yard, which was well littered for their accommodation, leaving but a narrow way up to the entrance-door.

I quickly scrambled down from the roof to assist Pat Brady in helping my mother out of the chaise. Poor dear, overcome by her feelings, she was leaning back, almost fainting, and scarcely able to move. At length the door opened, and an old gentleman appeared in a scratch wig, with an ominously red nose, and clothed in a costume which, in its condition, greatly resembled his habitation. An old lady followed him, somewhat more neatly dressed, who, on seeing my mother, hastened to the door to receive her.

"What! Is this our daughter Mary?" exclaimed the old gentleman; "and that young spalpeen, can that be her boy?" he added, looking at me in a way which did not seem to argue much affection.

"Of course it is, Mat; and is it you, Mat, the head of the Dwyers, not remembering your childer?" exclaimed the old lady, casting on him a scornful glance. On this my grandfather gave my mother a paternal kiss, a repetition of which I avoided by slipping round on the other side, where Pat caught me, and presented me to the old lady. She then took me in her arms and gave me an affectionate embrace. The tears dropped from her eyes as she looked at my mother's pale countenance and widow's dress.

"I don't ask what has happened, Mary," she said; "but though the one for whom you forsook all is gone, you are welcome back to the old home, child."

"Ay, that you are, Mary!" exclaimed my grandfather, warming up a little. "To be sure, grand as it once was, it has been inclined for many a day to be tumbling about our ears. But it will last my day, and there is small chance of your brothers, Jim, or Pat, or Terence, ever wishing to come and stop here, even if it's living they are when I am put under the green turf."

While Pat was settling with the post-boy, my grandmother conducted my mother and me into the parlour. The more elegant portions of furniture, if they ever existed, had disappeared, and a table, with a number of wooden-bottomed chairs and a huge ill-stuffed sofa, were all that remained. A picture of my grandfather in a hunting-suit, and a few wretched daubs, part of them of sporting scenes and part of saints, adorned the walls. Such was the appearance of the chief room in Rincurran Castle. My aunts were not at home, two of them having ridden to market, and the others being on a visit to some neighbours. At length two of them came riding up on rough, ungroomed ponies, with baskets on their arms. Having taken off the saddles, they sent their animals to find their way by themselves into the open stable, while they entered the house to greet my mother. They were not ill-looking women, with rather large features, and fine eyes, but as unlike my mother as could well be. So also were my other two aunts, who shortly after came in. They all, however, gave their sister Mary a hearty welcome, and, with better tact than might have been expected, made no inquiries about her husband, her dress showing them that he was gone. I found that she had been brought up by a sister of her mother's—a good Protestant woman, residing near Cork, where my father had met her. My grandfather was a Romanist, though my grandmother still remained as she had originally been, a Protestant. The rest of her daughters attended the Romish chapel. My mother had not been at home since she was quite a girl, and I soon found had entirely forgotten her family's way of living, and their general habits and customs. She therefore very soon began to regret that she had not accepted Lieutenant Schank's invitation to visit his family. Pat Brady made himself very agreeable to his cousins, and had such wonderful stories to tell them that he was a great favourite. I had plenty to amuse me; but there seemed very little probability of my getting the education which Captain Oliver had recommended. The castle also was not over well provisioned, potatoes and buttermilk forming the staple of our meals, with an over-abundance of pork whenever a pig was killed; but as it was necessary to sell the better portions of each animal to increase the family income, the supply was only of an intermittent character. My grandfather made up for the deficiency by copious potations of whisky; but as my mother objected to my following his example, I was frequently excessively hungry. I was not surprised therefore that my uncles did not often pay the paternal mansion a visit; they all considering themselves above manual labour, in consequence of being sons of a squireen, were living on their wits in various parts of the world, so I concluded from the bits of information I picked up about them.

I could not help remarking the contrast between Rincurran Castle and Mr Schank's neat little cottage in Lincolnshire—the cleanliness and comfort of one, and the dirt and disorder and discomfort of my grandfather's abode. My mother, who had sufficient means to live comfortably by herself, had had no intention of remaining long with her parents, but had purposed taking a cottage in the neighbourhood. When she discovered the state of things at home she had offered to assist in the household expenses, and having done this her family were doubly anxious to retain her. As however, she found it impossible to mend matters, she resolved to carry out her original intention. The search for a house was an object of interest. In a short time she discovered one at the further end of Ballybruree, which, if not perfection, was sufficient to satisfy her wishes. Here, at the end of a couple of months, she removed, in spite of the disinterested entreaties of her relatives that she should take up her permanent abode with them. Her health soon improved, and I grew fatter than I had been since I landed on the shores of old Ireland.

Our new abode, though very much smaller than Rincurran Castle, was considerably neater, yet not altogether such as would be considered tidy in England. The roof was water-tight, and the chimneys answered their object of carrying up the smoke from the fire beneath. The view from the front window was extensive, ranging down the broad and unpaved street, along which I could watch the boys chasing their pigs to market, seated on the hinder parts of donkeys, urging them forward by the blows of their shillalahs. Now and then we enjoyed the spectacle of a marriage party returning from the chapel, at the further end of the street, or still more boisterous funeral procession; when, of course, as Pat Brady observed, "It 'ud be showing small honour to the decased if all the mourners weren't respectably drunk, barring the praist, and bad luck to him if he could not stand up steady at the end of the grave. Sure he couldn't have a head for his office."

Such, however, as was our new house, my poor mother was glad to get it. We had been located there two or three weeks, and my mother had now time to give me some instruction in the arts of reading and writing. She was thus engaged, leaning over the book placed on her lap by the side of which I stood, when we were startled by a voice which said, "Top of the morning to you, Mistress Burton."

We looked up, and there stood in the doorway a rubicund-nosed gentleman, in a green coat and huge wonderfully gay coloured cravat, leather breeches, and top-boots, with a hunting-whip under his arm, a peony in his buttonhole, and a white hat which he flourished in his right hand, while he kept scraping with his feet, making his spurs jingle.

CHAPTER ELEVEN.

"Your servant, Mistress Burton. It is mighty touching to the heart to see a mother engaged as you are, and faith I would not have missed the sight for a thousand guineas, paid down on the nail. Ah! Mistress Burton, it reminds me of days gone by, but I won't say I have no hopes that they will ever return," and our visitor twisted his eyes about in what I thought a very queer way, trying to look sentimental.

"To what cause do I owe this visit, Mr Gillooly?" asked my mother, perhaps not altogether liking his looks, for I rather think his feelings had been excited by a few sips of potheen. Her natural politeness, however, induced her to rise and offer him a chair, into which, after a few more scrapes and flourishes of the hat, he sank down, placing his beaver and his whip upon it by his side.

"It is mightily you bring to my mind my dear departed Mistress Gillooly," he exclaimed, looking very strangely I thought at my mother. "She was the best of wives, and if she was alive she would be after telling you that I was the best of husbands, but she has gone to glory, and the only little pledge of our affection has gone after her; and so, Mistress Burton, I am left a lone man in this troublesome world. And sure, Mrs Burton, the same is your lot I am after thinking, but there is an old saying, 'Off with the old love and on with the new;' and, oh! Mistress Burton, it would be a happy thing if that could come true between two people I am thinking of."

My mother might have thought this very plain speaking, but she pretended not to understand Mr Gillooly, and made no answer.

"Is it silence gives consent?" he exclaimed at last with one of those queer turns of his eyes, stretching out his hands towards my mother.

"Really, Mr Gillooly, seeing I have been a widow scarcely a year, and have seen but little of you at my father's house, I cannot help thinking this is strange language for you to use. I loved my husband, and I only wish to live for the sake of our boy, and I hope this answer will satisfy you."

"But when you have seen more of me, Mistress Burton, ye'll be after giving a different answer," exclaimed our visitor. "Ye'll be after making a sweet mistress for Ballyswiggan Hall, and it's there I'd like to see ye, in the place of the departed Molly Gillooly. It was the last words she said to me—'Ye'll be after getting another partner when I'm gone, Dominic, won't ye now?' and I vowed by all the holy saints that I would obey her wishes, though to be plain with you, Mistress Burton, I little thought I could do so to my heart's content, as I did when I first set my eyes on your fair countenance."

Much more to the same effect did Mr Gillooly utter, without, however, I have reason to believe, making any impression on my mother's heart. Without rudeness she could not get rid of him; and he, believing that he was making great way in her affection, was in no wise inclined to depart. Mr Gillooly, I may remark, was a friend of my grandfather's, a squireen, with a mansion of similar description to Rincurran Castle, though somewhat less dilapidated. His property enabled him to keep a good horse, drink whisky, wear decent clothes, attend all wakes, marriages, and fairs, and other merrymakings, and otherwise lead a completely idle life. Mr

Gillooly's visit had extended to a somewhat unconscionable length, when a rap was heard at the door, and my mother told me to run and open it; observing as she did so, "It's not all people who so want manners as not to knock before they intrude into a lone woman's house."

This severe remark of my gentle mother showed me that she was by this time considerably annoyed by our visitor's continued presence. The person who now entered wore a brown suit, with a low crowned hat on the top of his curled wig. I recognised him as Mr Timothy Laffan, one of the lawyers of Ballybruree. Though short, he was a broad-shouldered, determined-looking man, with a nose which could scarcely be more flattened than it was, and twinkling grey eyes which looked out knowingly from under his shaggy eyebrows. He cast an inquisitive glance round, and then, paying his respects to my mother, took the seat which I had brought him.

"A good boy, Ben," he said, patting my head. "I came to see how you were getting on in your new house, Mrs Burton, as is my duty as a neighbour. Your servant, Mr Gillooly. I was after thinking that the next time you came into Ballybruree ye would be giving me a call to settle about that little affair. There's nothing like the present time, and may be you will stop at my office as you go by, and arrange the matter offhand."

The lawyer's eyes twinkled as he spoke. Mr Gillooly began to fidget in his chair, and his countenance grew redder and redder. He cast a glance at his whip and hat. Suddenly seizing them, he paid a hurried adieu to my mother, and turning to the lawyer, added, "Your servant, Tim Laffan. I will be after remembering what you say"; and away he bolted out of the door.

I almost expected to hear the lawyer utter a crow of victory, for his comical look of triumph clearly showed his feelings. I had reason to believe that he also was a suitor for the hand of my mother, but I do not think he gained much by his stratagem. Her feelings were aroused and irritated, and at length he also took his departure, after expressing a tender interest in her welfare.

CHAPTER TWELVE.

My mother's good looks, amiable disposition, and reputed fortune raised up a host of admirers, greatly to her annoyance, for she had, or fully thought she had, made up her mind to live a widow; or at all events, as she told my Aunt Ellen, if she married anyone it should be a sailor, in respect to my father's memory. I liked Ellen more than any of my other relations. She was more like my mother than the rest of her sisters. She had much of my mother's beauty, though with more animal spirits, and was altogether on a larger scale, as I think I have said. She was engaged to marry a certain Mr Pat Kilcullin, who I heard was a gentleman of property some distance further west; and that he had a real castle and a good estate, somewhat encumbered to be sure, as became his old family and position. How many hundreds or thousands a year it might once have produced I do not know; but as he and his father before him, and his grandfather, and other remote ancestors had generally taken care to spend double their income, it could not but be supposed that he and they were occasionally in difficulties. As, however, his father had lived, so my intended uncle purposed living also. I will not describe the wedding further than to say that my grandfather was nearly out and out ruined by it. He and his guests all got gloriously drunk. Mr Gillooly and Tim Laffan fell out about my mother, and came to blows in her presence. They were separated by two of the other guests—a certain Dan Hogan, a good-looking exciseman, who was also a suitor for her hand, and Captain Michael Tracy, the master of a merchantman, who had lately come home after a few successful trading voyages to the West Indies. As he, however, was the most sober of the party, he came worst off in the fray, and had not my mother come to his rescue with the aid of her sisters, he would, I have an idea, have been severely handled. Whether or not he was touched by this exhibition of her courage I do not know; but he certainly from that day forward became her warm admirer, and certainly if she showed a preference to anyone it was to him. I did not suppose I had so many relations in the world as turned up at that feast, of high and low degree: the greater number, however, it must be confessed, were of the latter rank. The bride looked beautiful, and the bridegroom in the height of his feelings invited all the guests to pay him a visit that day fortnight at Ballyswiggan Castle. The bridegroom was taken at his word, and though I rather think my Aunt Ellen might have been somewhat annoyed, there was no means of escaping. My mother was, however, unwilling to be present at so uproarious a scene as she knew pretty well was likely to take place; but my grandfather and her sisters insisted upon her accompanying them, and of course I went with her. Some of the guests, however, were not likely to make their appearance, and for the best of reasons Mr Laffan and Dan Hogan could not be present, as it was well-known that no lawyer nor exciseman had ever ventured to set foot in the district in which Ballyswiggan Castle was situated. Most of the guests went on horseback, as the approach was scarcely suited to wheeled carriages. My grandmother was too infirm to move, but my grandfather mounted a rawboned back which had carried him in his younger days, and my aunts and mother rode on their rough ponies. Pat Brady, who, finding himself so happy on shore, had put off going to sea, and I rode together on a beast which we had borrowed for the occasion.

Ballyswiggan Castle was situated amidst fine wild scenery within sound of the roar of the mighty Atlantic. The building itself was in a somewhat dilapidated condition, but exhibited signs of having been once a place of importance. Some out-houses had likewise been strewn with fresh straw to afford sleeping accommodation to a portion of the guests who could not find room within, while sheds and barns had been cleared out for the reception of their steeds.

"Ye are welcome to Ballyswiggan, by my faith ye are!" exclaimed Uncle Pat, as our party arrived, a sentiment which was uttered by Aunt Ellen without any pretension to mock modesty, while she laughed heartily at the complimentary remarks which were passed on her good looks and high spirits.

"Small blame to Rincurran Castle if I am not after getting somewhat stouter here than I did under my paternal roof," she answered, intending to allude simply to the meagre fare of her ancestral mansion, though from the giggles of some of the ladies, I rather suspect they put a different interpretation upon the remark. To say the truth, Ballyswiggan Castle had been stored with all sorts of provisions, and no end of casks of whisky, so that there appeared little chance of the guests starving or having to suffer from dry throats. We, with other visitors from a distance, arrived the day before the dinner and ball were to take place. On that morning, Peter Crean, steward and factotum to my uncle, awoke him with the news that a ship of war was beating into the Bay, "And sure," he observed, "it would be a fine opportunity, Mr Kilcullin, to show your loyalty and love to His Majesty's government, to invite the officers. They will make a fine show in the ball-room too, with their gold lace coats, and white breeches, and may be may make some of the gentlemen jealous, and just bring matters to a close, which have been kept off and on for some months past. The mothers will be pleased, and the girls will be thanking you from the bottom of their hearts."

This sage advice was instantly followed by my uncle, who, habiting himself in his wedding suit, ordered his horse that he might ride down to the Bay, and be early on board to give the proposed invitation. There were no fears about it being accepted, and, as may be supposed, it formed the subject of conversation at the breakfast-table when it was announced where my uncle had gone. His return was accordingly looked for with no little anxiety, especially by the young ladies of the party, including my three spinster aunts. Mr Kilcullin was not very long absent.

"They will all come!" he exclaimed, throwing up his hat, "and faith, they're a fine set of gentlemen. She is a frigate, they tell me, but her name has escaped me, and it is my belief they will toe and heel it with the best of you, gentlemen, and may do something towards breaking the hearts of some of you young ladies. How-

CHAPTER TWELVE. 63

ever, we will do our best to make them welcome, for the honour of ould Ireland."

As the hour of dinner approached, the guests began to arrive in considerable numbers; and carts, and cars, and waggons came bumping and thumping over the uneven path, though the greater part made their appearance on horseback. I was looking out of a window which commanded the approach to the castle, when I saw coming along the road a large party of naval officers, whose well-known uniform I at once recognised as they drew nearer, and I fancied I knew two of those who led the way. On they came; I could not be mistaken. There were Captain Oliver and Lieutenant Schank, and several other officers and midshipmen whom I remembered on board the "Grecian". I ran to my poor mother with delight to tell her this. She turned pale, recollecting the sorrow she had gone through when last she saw them.

"I cannot face them," she said; "but you go, Ben; they will be glad to see you; I should feel out of place in their company, and though my family may be as good as that of many among them, they knew me under such different circumstances, that I should not like to be sitting at table with them."

On hearing my mother make these remarks, I too was seized with a bashful fit, but she insisted on my going down to meet them; and at length mustering courage, I ran downstairs. Captain Oliver did not at first know me, but Mr Schank recognised me at once.

"What, Ben, my boy, what brings you here?" he exclaimed.

I soon explained that Mr Kilcullin had married my aunt, and that my mother and I were among the guests.

"Ah! I always thought she was above her position on board," he observed to Captain Oliver, who, when he found out who I was, shook me warmly by the hand.

"Well, Ben, recollect I shall keep to my promise, and when your mother can spare you, I will take you with me."

"I hope we shall see her, Ben," observed Mr Schank, kindly; "I should like to shake hands with her." I told him how she felt on the subject.

"Oh!" he said, "that cannot signify. Tell her we shall not half enjoy the evening unless she comes down." The officers now arrived in the entrance hall, where my uncle and aunt were standing to welcome their guests. Of course they received them with all due honour.

"We're in a wild part of the country, Captain Oliver and gentlemen, but we will show you, at all events, that we have hospitable intentions, however roughly we may carry them out," said my uncle.

The great dining-hall was very soon filled, and several adjoining rooms, the guests of inferior quality, of whom there were a good many, making themselves happy in separate parties wherever they could find room to sit down. Among those most active in attending to the wants of the guests, and directing the other serving-men, were Peter Crean and Pat Brady, who was a host in himself, for though second cousin to the bride, he did not at all object to acting the part of a servant. As room was scarce, I was among the picnickers outside. The feast was progressing, when I saw Pat Brady come up to Peter Crean, pulling, for him, a wonderfully long face.

"Faith Peter!" I heard him say, "I do not at all like his looks. There's a hang-dog expression about him, and to my mind he's a bailiff in disguise!"

"A what?" exclaimed Peter. "Has one of them vipers ventured into the neighbourhood of Ballyswiggan? Faith, then, it would have been better for him had he never seen this part of the country, for it will never do to let him go boasting that he set his foot in it without being discovered. Where is he?"

"He is just now outside the gate," answered Pat; "but I told two or three of the boys to keep him talking, and on no account to let him come beyond it. I think they have just got an idea that he will not be altogether a welcome guest."

"I have no doubt who he is, then," observed Peter Crean. "I have been expecting him. And, sure, he must not see the master, or he would be spoiling the fun of to-day, and for many a long day afterwards. Here, Pat, you go and talk to him, and I will just make arrangements to receive him."

Peter Crean was a man of action. A small room was cleared of visitors, a table prepared with viands and various liquors. This done, Peter hurried out to receive the guest. His suspicions were thoroughly confirmed on his inspection of the man.

"Your name, sir," he said, "that I may make you welcome to Ballyswiggan Castle. My master is just now particularly engaged with a few guests, but he will be happy to see you when the wine is on the table; and, in the meantime, you will just come in and satisfy your appetite. You have had a long ride since you took anything to eat, barring maybe the whisky, which is not quite so rare on the road."

"My name is Jonas Quelch, at your service," answered the stranger, "and I come from England, though I have been living for some time in Dublin. It's a fine city, that Dublin."

"Faith it is, Mr Quelch," observed Crean; "and fine people in it, and rogues in it, and the rogues sometimes come out of it, and when they do they are pretty glad to get back again, for we don't like rogues in these parts, Mr Quelch. But I will not keep you sitting on your horse; that will be taken to the stable, and you will just come in, as I said, and partake of the scanty fare this poor part of the country can afford."

He spoke in a satirical tone. Mr Quelch, holding his riding-whip in his hand, as if for defence, followed him into the house. Peter. Crean was, however, all courtesy and attention. He entreated his visitor to make himself at home, and helped him abundantly to the good things in the dishes placed before him, nor did he omit to ply him with whisky. Glass upon glass he induced him to pour down his throat, till I began to wonder how he could swallow so much without inconvenience. He was evidently a hardened vessel. Crean, however, had not yet done with him. He now placed before him a flagon of claret.

"Faith, this is the stuff for a gentleman," he observed. "You may just empty the bottle, and feel none the worse, but rather much the better than when you began."

The stranger, nothing loath, followed the advice of the steward. By degrees, however, Mr Quelch's speech became thick, and his conversation more and more incoherent. Crean watched him with a wicked look in his eyes, continuing to press the liquor more and more warmly upon him.

"Come, now, Mr Quelch, just let's begin another bottle. I have always found, where one bottle confuses a man's head, a second one puts him all to rights again. Now, I should not be surprised but that you are beginning to feel a little fuddled."

"You are right, friend," answered Mr Quelch, though the words were jerked out in a manner indicative of his state.

"Just so; and, now, follow my advice. Take the other bottle to cure you. We never like a stranger to come to this part of old Ireland without showing him due hospitality."

Mr Quelch, unaccustomed to claret, drank it as he would beer, and before he had finished the second bottle, on the top of almost an equal quantity of whisky, his head began to nod, and finally it dropped down on the table, where he let it remain, completely overcome.

CHAPTER THIRTEEN.

I was describing, at the end of my last chapter, my uncle's uninvited guest—Jonas Quelch—dead drunk, with his head on the table. I sat at the further end of the room watching proceedings. Peter Crean gave a well-satisfied nod, and then left the room. In a short time he returned with Pat Brady, and a bundle of papers in his hand. Without much ado, they commenced an examination of the pockets of the stranger, and produced from them several documents. One of them, as Peter ran his eyes over it, seemed to excite his excessive indignation. However, producing one from among his own papers, of a similar size and appearance, he sat down and wrote off several paragraphs, which seemed to afford him and Pat infinite amusement. This, with some other papers, which he had taken from the stranger's pockets, he then returned to them. This done, he and Pat—having removed the provisions and jugs—left the stranger still sleeping, with his head resting on his arms, as before, I soon got tired of watching, and made my way into the banqueting hall, from which shouts of boisterous merriment were proceeding. His guests were, indeed, doing ample justice to my new uncle's good cheer, and speeches and songs were succeeding each other in rapid succession. Sometimes, indeed, two or three of the guests seemed disposed to sing or speak at the same time, one exciting the other, and adding not a little to the Babel of tongues. At this state of affairs the ladies took their departure, though not without several gentlemen rushing after them to bring them back. "Are ye after leaving us without a sun in the firmament!" exclaimed one. "The stars are going out, and we shall be in darkness presently," cried another. "A garden without roses is a sorry garden, by my faith!" exclaimed a third. "What shall we do without those beautiful eyes beaming out on us?" shouted a fourth. However, in spite of the flatteries and efforts of Mr Tim Gillooly and his companions—for he was among the most demonstrative of the party—the ladies made their escape to an upper room. Curiosity at length prompted me to go back and see what had become of the stranger. As I entered the room, he lifted up his head and looked about him, evidently wondering where he was. At length he rose to his feet, and with unsteady steps began to pace backwards and forwards.

"This won't do," he said to himself. "I am not in a fit condition, I have a notion, to execute this writ. However, it must be done. That liquor was not bad, or I should not feel as comfortable as I do. If now I can get a basin of water, and pour some of the cold liquid down my throat, I shall be soon all to rights again. I wonder when that foolish old steward will come back. He seemed to fancy that I had some favour to bestow on his master by the way he treated me. However, these Irish have very poor wits, and it is no hard matter to impose on them."

While he was speaking, Peter opened the door. The stranger made his request,

CHAPTER THIRTEEN.   67

with which he promised to comply. In a short time, Pat appeared with a basin and a jug of water. "I am your man now," exclaimed Mr Quelch, having dipped his head several times in the cold water, "and shall be happy to pay my respects to your master."

"To be sure, sir, to be sure," answered Pat. "He is with his friends in the great hall, and you will be welcome as all gentlemen from England are sure to be. You have only to go in and make your bow and give your message, and depend upon it you will get a civil answer, whatever else you get, and be requested to sit down and make yourself happy with the rest."

Peter, on this, led the way, followed by Mr Quelch. He did not observe that a number of women and others who had been feasting outside brought up the rear. A large party followed him into the hall, where he enquired for Mr Kilcullin, as he said, that he might make no mistake. "There he is to be sure, at the end of his table, where a gentleman, with a beautiful wife always should be," answered Peter, pointing to the lord of the mansion, who, with his guests, appeared to be enjoying himself amazingly without any consciousness of the approach of a bailiff.

"Your servant, sir," said Mr Quelch, advancing towards him, and drawing from his pocket a long document.

"The same to you, I beg your pardon, what is your name?" said Mr Kilcullin, with a complacent smile. "You are welcome to Ballyswiggan, as all honest men are, and if they are not honest, by the powers they had better keep away! And what is that paper with which you are about to favour me?"

"Perhaps, sir, you will read it," said Mr Quelch, with a somewhat doubtful expression in his countenance.

"Certainly!" exclaimed my new uncle, "with the greatest pleasure in the world. Now listen, friends and gentlemen all. This is to give notice to all present that the bearer—Jonas Quelch—has come across the Channel to the west side of ould Ireland, on a fool's errand. There are many more like him, may be, but he must understand that he will have to go back the way he came, or else consent to be deported forthwith to the coast of Africa, to live henceforth among the black sons of the soil, for whom alone he is a fit associate."

The astonishment of Mr Quelch on hearing this knew no bounds. Scarcely recovered from the effects of his ample potations, the little sense he possessed entirely forsook him. He began to storm and swear, and declared that he had been vilely tricked. Loud peak of laughter from the guests present were the only answer he received.

"Come, come, Mr Quelch!" exclaimed Peter Crean, touching him on the shoulder. "You have your choice, my boy, but, by my faith, if you go on abusing Irish gentlemen in this fashion, you will be sent off sooner than a Kilkenny cow can leap over the moon to the country where the niggers come from, and it will be no easy matter for you to find your way back again, I'm after thinking." This answer only increased the anger of the unhappy bailiff. The consequence was that he found himself seized by several of the men around, and amid the varied cries of the guests quickly hurried out of the hall. Derisive shouts of laughter followed the unhappy man as he was carried away. Most of the guests had, in their time, taken part in a similar drama to that which was about to be enacted, and knew full well how the man was to be treated. The carouse continued till it was time to clear the room for the ball. Several of the guests had to be borne off, and their heads bathed in cold water to make them fit companions for the ladies in the dance. Meantime, Jonas Quelch was carried back to the room he had left, where Crean plied him with a further supply of whisky under the excuse of keeping up his spirits.

"Faith, my friend, we bear you no ill-will," observed the steward, "but you should have known that in this part of ould Ireland it's against the law to execute writs. Such a thing never has been done, and it would be contrary to our consciences ever to allow it to be done, and, therefore, though it's your masters are to blame, it's *you* who will have to bear the consequences."

Mr Quelch, however, by the time these remarks were made, was scarcely in a condition to understand their full meaning; and he was shortly again reduced very much to the condition in which he had been before he had gone into the hall. At this juncture a party of men entered the room, one of them telling him that they had come to conduct him on board the ship which was to convey him to the coast of Africa. In vain he urged that he had no wish to go there, and that he would do anything, even to going back to the country from which he had come, if that would satisfy them. No excuses, however, were available. Away he was carried, in spite of all his struggles, down to the sea-shore, where a boat was waiting, as he was told, for him. As I preferred remaining to see the dancing, I can only give the story as I afterwards heard it. In spite of his struggles he was placed in the boat, which immediately pulled off into the bay, where he quickly found himself transferred on board a vessel which lay there at anchor. He was carried down below, and placed in a small cabin by himself.

"We will treat you decently," said one of the men, who appeared to be the leader of the party. "There are just two things you will have to do, you must understand, or have a chance of being knocked on the head. You must not attempt to get out, and you must ask no questions. It is to the coast of Africa we are going to carry you, and to the coast of Africa you must go. The voyage will not be a long one if we have a fair breeze, and they are dacent sort of people where we are going to land you; may be they will make you a prince of their country, and let you marry a princess, but you will understand that if you love your life, on the shores of ould Ireland again you will never venture to set foot."

The unfortunate Mr Quelch could make no resistance. All his expostulations were in vain. He heard, as he fancied, the anchor being got up and sail made, and was fully under the impression that he had begun the voyage which was to carry him away for ever from his native land. The man who had first spoken to him again came below.

"We wish to treat you as a jintleman, though may be it's more than you deserve," he said, "so we will not stint you in liquor. You shall have as much as you can pour down your throat, for I have a notion you will not get an over abundant

CHAPTER THIRTEEN. 69

supply when you reach Africa. It's a fine country, I am told, though a little more sandy than ould Ireland."

As may have been discovered, one of Quelch's failings was his fondness for liquor, and he soon imbibed enough to bring him into a state of unconsciousness. He thus had very little idea how the time passed. As soon as he awoke he found another bottle placed by his side. Thus he could not tell whether he had been days or weeks on board the ship. All that he knew was, that he had been fearfully tossed about, and often horribly uncomfortable. It had not occurred to him to feel his beard, in so confused a state was his mind. At length he heard the Captain's voice calling him.

LOOKING UP HE SAW, TO HIS HORROR AND DISMAY, SEVERAL BLACK MEN DANCING AND SHRIEKING.

"Come up, if you please, Mr Quelch, we are off the coast of Africa, and it is time for you to be on shore. We will just see you comfortably landed, and then wish you farewell."

The shades of evening were just settling down over the land, when Mr Quelch made his appearance on the deck. He could not distinguish objects distinctly, but he saw before him high hills and a sandy beach. On looking over the side he discovered a boat with six black men in her.

"Good-bye, Mr Quelch," cried the friendly Captain, as he took Mr Quelch's arm. "Good luck go with you. May be the niggers will look after you when they have put you on shore, but don't trust them too much, for it's small love they have for white men."

Poor Quelch did not feel very comfortable on hearing this, but though inclined to resist, the butt end of a pistol which was sticking out of the Captain's belt, and which that gentleman significantly began to handle, reminded him that resistance was useless. With a trembling heart he stepped into the boat. He was soon conveyed on shore. From the suppressed laughter of the crew, and from the broad grin which, as far as he could distinguish, appeared on their countenances, he had an idea that they were inclined to be amused at his expense.

"Dare, massa," said one of them, "step on shore. Welcome to Africa. Make yourself at home. De king of de country come and see you by-and-by. He very fond of eating men, but no eat you, me hope."

Poor Jonas was compelled to obey, and being placed on shore, the boat again pulled away. Soon after she had disappeared round a rocky point he heard loud shouts coming from inland, and looking up he saw, to his horror and dismay, several black men dancing and shrieking, and showing by their gestures their intention of coming down, and of making him the chief article of their supper. He was now utterly overcome with terror, and dared not leave the shore lest he should fall into the hands of his enemies. Yet, as he had not been supplied with food or water, he was under the dread of dying from hunger or thirst. He sat himself down disconsolately on a rock. The shouts continued round and above him, which made him shrink within himself for fear.

"Oh, if ever I get back home to England it is the last time that I will undertake to serve a writ in the West of Ireland, at all events," he said, over and over again to himself. Still the savages did not descend, though he every instant expected to see them rushing towards him. At length the sounds ceased, and he sat himself down on the rock, where he remained all the night long, afraid of moving lest he should find himself attacked by them.

The morning broke. He saw a large ship in the offing, and after some time a boat left her side and came towards the spot where he was sitting. "Oh!" he thought to himself, "if I could get on board that ship how happy I should be." No sooner did the boat's bow touch the sand than he ran towards her. "Oh! Take me on board! Take me on board out of this savage land!" he exclaimed. "I will do anything to serve you! I will make myself generally useful on board! There is nothing I will not do. Oh! Take me away out of the power of these blackamoors!"

CHAPTER THIRTEEN.

"You may enter as a seaman, perhaps," answered the midshipman, in command of the boat. "If you will promise to do that, we will take you on board, but we have no idlers, and if you do not know your duty you must learn it as quickly as you can."

Without further ado Quelch was lifted into the boat, which soon returned to the frigate. He found that she was the "Grecian" frigate, and that she was standing on and off the land, waiting to take the Captain and some of the officers on board. He, however, was at once regularly entered, and found himself speedily transferred into a man-of-war's-man. Scarcely had he signed the papers, than loud peals of laughter broke from the seamen round him. None, however, would explain the cause of their merriment. At length once more the frigate put about and stood towards the land. As he gazed at the shore, he could not help fancying that its appearance was very much like that of the neighbourhood of Ballyswiggan. At length he put the question to one of the people standing near him.

"Why, my boy," was the answer of an old quarter-master, "you have been nicely bamboozled. This comes of attempting to serve a writ in this part of the world. As to the coast of Africa, you have never been nearer it than you are at this present moment, nor much further from the place from which you started. However, take my advice; many a better man than you has found himself on board a man-of-war, and has had no cause to regret having done his duty."

Jonas Quelch had the sense to see the wisdom of this counsel, and fortunately, being an unmarried man, made the best of his case, and, I can answer for it, became a very fair sailor in a short time, though his besetting sin occasionally interfered with his happiness and liberty, and brought him more than once into difficulties.

CHAPTER FOURTEEN.

I interrupted my narrative with an account of Mr Jonas Quelch's adventures, with which I shortly afterwards became acquainted. I wish I could describe the ball which followed the dinner I have already mentioned; how perseveringly the ladies danced country dances and jigs, and how furiously the gentlemen flung about, sprang here and there, rushed up and down the room, and performed antics of every possible description, such as might have astonished the more sober professors of the art across the channel. My mother stole into a corner of the room, where she could see without being observed, and nothing would induce her to go further. Although Captain. Oliver found her out, and entreated her to join in what was going forward, she refused to dance even with him.

"I could not resist joining in the fun as you do, Mrs Burton," said Mr Schank, "but I am afraid the ladies would object to my hopping up and down the room, lest I should come down upon their tender feet with my timber-toe, so I am obliged to abandon the sport I delighted in in my younger days." Mr Gillooly, also, at length discovered her, and was far more persevering in his efforts to induce her to take part in the dance, though with no more success.

"Sure, Mistress Burton, you would not be after breaking a jintleman's heart, which is as soft as butther whenever he is thinking of you!" he exclaimed, pressing his hand on his bosom and looking up with an expression which he intended to be extremely captivating.

"Indeed, Mr Gillooly, but it is more likely that any heart you have got would be after melting rather than breaking," remarked my mother, observing the fiery countenance and the violent perspiration into which her swain had thrown himself. "My dancing days are over, and had I not supposed that the gentlemen here would have had the good taste not to press me to do what I dislike, I should not have ventured into the room."

Nothing abashed, however, by this answer, Mr Gillooly continued to pour out his compliments into my mother's ear, and she had to be still more explicit before he would receive a refusal. At length he left her, and was soon afterwards seen rushing about, as before, with one of my aunts, or with some other young lady of equal powers of endurance. Captain Oliver, after this, sat himself down by my mother's side.

"Your boy has grown into a fine big lad," he observed, "and though he is somewhat young, still I think he is strong enough to hold his own in a midshipman's berth, and if you are disposed to let him go, I am ready to take him."

CHAPTER FOURTEEN.

"A midshipman's berth!" exclaimed my mother, and a choking feeling came into her throat. "Surely you cannot intend such advancement to my boy—the boatswain's son. I never wished him to be above his station, and if he were to rise to be a boatswain like his dear father, I should be well contented."

"Do not say that, Mrs Burton. His father was a fine seaman, and would have been an honour to the quarter-deck himself. I promised to befriend your boy, and I can do so far more if he is in the rank of a midshipman than if he is simply one of the ship's boys. From what I see of your relations and friends, indeed, though to be sure some of their doings are a little eccentric compared with our English notions, yet their position is such that their young relative should be placed in the rank of a gentleman. Say no more about it, I will assist him, and so I am sure will Mr Schank, in procuring his necessary outfit. That matter, therefore, need not trouble you, and I hope in a short time that he will pick up so much, prize-money that he will be able to support himself till he attains the rank of Lieutenant."

Of course my mother could offer no objection to this very generous proposal. All she pleaded was, that I might remain a short time longer with her on shore. Lieutenant Schank then came in with a proposal which he had to make. It was that she should return to his mother's house, where I might employ my time to advantage in obtaining the instruction which I could not get at Ballybruree. This offer she gladly accepted. Indeed, she told me that she had herself thought of returning to Whithyford, in order to avoid the persevering addresses of Mr Gillooly and her other admirers. The frigate was to remain on the coast for a week or ten days, after which time she had been ordered to go round to Portsmouth to refit. Captain Oliver, therefore, kindly offered my mother and me a passage, should she in the meantime be able to make arrangements for her departure. For this proposal she was very grateful. A journey across the whole width of Ireland and England was both difficult, hazardous, and very expensive, if performed in a comfortable manner. I was delighted with the thoughts of meeting again the Little Lady with the kind Misses Schank; for I must confess that the habits and customs of my relatives did not suit my taste much more than they did that of my mother. As to the ball, I need not further describe it. The ladies who came from a distance occupied all the upper rooms in the house, while the gentlemen were stowed away in the lower rooms and out-houses, many of them, however, little knowing how they got to bed or where they were.

Great was the lamentation her friends expressed when my mother's determination of going to England was made known; indeed, some considered that a decided insult was offered to her native country. Mr Gillooly, indeed, made some remarks as to her motives, which certainly did not further his cause.

We set off the next day for Ballybruree with the rest of our party, my uncle and aunt inviting us to return to Ballyswiggan, there to remain till the frigate was ready to take us on board. Mr Tim Laffan, who showed much good feeling, undertook to dispose of my mother's few possessions, and in the course of a few days placed in her hands a sum which she considered even more than their value.

"Well, Mrs Burton, I had hoped other things," he said, as he shook her warmly by the hand, as she was mounting her pony to proceed to Ballyswiggan, "but I know enough about ladies' hearts to be aware that they are more difficult to manage than the toughest lawsuit."

Dan Hogan was away on duty, and we were off before he returned, but Captain Michael Tracy insisted on walking by my mother's side all the way to Ballyswiggan; indeed I could not help thinking that if anyone was to win her heart, he was likely to be the happy man. We had a somewhat moving scene when bidding farewell to my grandfather and grandmother.

The old gentleman, indeed, wept bitterly as he was apt to do, especially after his tenth tumbler of whisky and water, provided it was of the full strength. I need not say anything more about him at present. We reached Ballyswiggan Castle in safety, the small amount of property my mother wished to retain following us in a cart. Mr Kilcullin was very kind, and my aunt promised to write occasionally, and let us know how the rest of the family got on. She was, indeed, the only one of her sisters who was much practised in the art of penmanship, the others having spent most of their time in gaining a knowledge of horseflesh, in riding up and down the country, and in practising certain very useful domestic duties. I certainly did feel very proud, and so I think did my mother, when the boat from the frigate came to fetch us on board, and we were seated in the stern sheets with our boxes in the bows, a young midshipman in a fresh bright uniform steering. A short, somewhat stout man pulled the stroke oar. He looked at my mother very hard. At length a beaming smile came over his broad countenance, and he could no longer help giving her a look of recognition. I thought I knew him. He was no other than my old friend Toby Kiddle. Still, as the midshipman treated us with so much respect, he evidently thought it did not become him to address us. Our friends on shore, I should have said, saluted us with loud shouts as we pushed off. "Long life to Ben Burton!" cried a voice. "May he live to be an admiral, and an honour to old Ireland, and may he never forget the land of his ancestors." My mother waved an adieu. Her heart was too full with a variety of emotions to speak.

"Is Ben Burton your name?" said the midshipman, looking at me. "I understand you are going to join us. You are a lucky chap, for our ship is a happy one, and we are likely to see a good deal of service."

When we got on board, one of the first people I set eyes on was Pat Brady.

"I could not help it, Ben," he said. "Some of the boys got round me and talked of old times, and faith, though I was living on shore like a gintleman, after all I could not resist the look of the trim frigate, and the thoughts of the fighting and the fun on board. But, Ben, I hear you are to be one of the young gintlemen, and I know my place too well and your interests ever to be claiming relationship with you. You will understand that, Ben. If ever you can do me a good turn I am sure you will, and I need not tell you that when we are boarding an enemy's ship, and you are in the thickest of the fun, Pat Brady won't be far off your side. Just tell your mother that, for may be I may not have an opportunity of speaking to her as I would wish."

"He is a good honest fellow, that cousin of ours," said my mother when I told

CHAPTER FOURTEEN. 75

her. "It is just like him, and I am very thankful to think that you have so true a friend among the men. If you behave wisely and kindly to them, depend upon it you will always be able to get work done, when others much older than yourself will fail, and that more than anything else will gain you the approval of your superior officers."

The Third-Lieutenant of the frigate had gone home on sick leave, and his cabin was given up to my mother. She told me she felt very strange occupying a berth aft when she had been so long accustomed to one in the fore-part of the ship. It was satisfactory to see as much attention paid her as if she had always occupied the position of a lady. Indeed I may say with satisfaction that she was well deserving of all the attention paid her, while in her manner and conversation she was thoroughly the lady. I was said to take after her, and, at the risk of being considered vain and egotistical, it is satisfactory to believe I did. "It would be a shame not to place that boy on the quarter-deck," I heard the Captain observe to Mr Schank one day, when he was not aware how near I was. "He looks, and is, thoroughly the gentleman, and will make a smart young officer, depend on that."

I was delighted to find myself on board ship again, and if the choice had been given me I suspect that I should have remained rather than have accompanied my mother back to Whithyford. After we had doubled Cape Clear a sail hove in sight, to which we gave chase. She was a large brig, and soon showed us that she had a fast pair of heels, by keeping well ahead. All sail was pressed on the frigate, and yet, after chasing several hours, we appeared to be no nearer to her. Still Captain Oliver was not a man to strike to an enemy, or to give up a chance of making a prize as long as the slightest possibility of doing so remained. All night long we kept in her wake; she probably expecting a fog, or a change of wind, or some other circumstance to enable her to alter her course without being perceived by us. The night, however, was very clear, and when morning broke there she was still ahead. It was evident, also, that we had gained on her considerably.

"I say, Ben, our skipper and First-Lieutenant are licking their lips at the thoughts of the prize we shall pick up before the day is many hours older," observed my friend Tom Twigg, the midshipman who steered the boat which brought us on board; he had ever since then marked me as an object of his especial favour. He was a merry little fellow, with the funniest round face, and round eyes, and round nose possible. He often got into scrapes; but he declared that, like a hedgehog or slater, or woodlouse, he always managed to roll himself out of them. "I rather think the skipper has entered you on the books that you may have a share in the prize we are going to make," he observed. "It will not be very great, but it is something, and no man on board will grudge it you." About noon we got the brig under our guns, when she hauled down her colours, and proved to be a richly-laden Letter of Marque. It was very pleasant returning into port with her, and this circumstance put everybody on board in good humour, the Captain and Lieutenant Schank especially, who of course had large shares.

"I wish I could accompany you, Mrs Burton," said Mr Schank, when we reached Portsmouth; "but that is impossible. You must let me frank you up, however, to my mother's. I dare say by this time you pretty well know how to manage on the road. Pay the postboys well, and take care that youngster does not tumble off the roof and break his neck." Of course my mother thanked the Captain and all the officers for the kindness she had received on board. They insisted on her saying nothing about the matter; indeed, they declared they had not done enough, and would not let her go till they had made her accept a purse of gold, which they declared would have been my father's share of the prize just taken had he been alive. Lieutenant Schank had written on before to announce our coming. The old lady, therefore, and the three Misses Schank were on the look-out for us as our post-chaise drove up to the cottage, while I saw poor Mrs Lindars looking out at an upper window from the room she occupied, and there in the midst of the ladies downstairs was the Little Lady, a perfect little fairy she looked among the three mature Misses Schank. Miss Anna Maria held her up in her arms, and the little girl cried out, "Oh! Mamma, mamma, I know you are my mamma, though I have got four other mammas here." She had grown very much, and instead of going off in beauty, had become one of the most perfect little creatures I ever set eyes on. Nothing could be more hearty than the welcome we received, and the dear old lady told my mother that she must look upon herself as one of the family, and only help the other ladies just as much as she felt inclined. Mrs Lindars, soon after we arrived, begged we would come up, and the Little Lady, taking me by the hand, led the way. There was something very striking in the affectionate and tender way the Little Lady addressed Mrs Lindars; indeed it for the moment struck me that they were something alike, though one was somewhat advanced in life, and the features of the other were scarcely yet formed. Mrs Lindars welcomed my mother very kindly. "And Ben has indeed grown into a fine lad," she observed. "And Emily, too, you see her greatly improved, Mrs Burton. Ben, you must be her champion if she requires one. Alas! I fear she will. I trust her fate may be happier than mine."

"Yes, ma'am, I will fight for her, that I will," I answered, looking at Emily; "not that I think anyone would ever be so wicked as to try and harm her." The poor lady smiled sadly and shook her head.

"Beauty is rather a snare than a protection," she observed.

Of course I did not exactly understand her meaning; I heard afterwards, though I think I have already alluded to the fact, that the poor lady had, at a very early age, married a foreigner, calling himself Lindars, and that she had one child, a girl. Her husband, after frequently absenting himself, returned to Whithyford, when one day he and the child disappeared. The poor mother was left in an agony of doubt as to what had become of her infant, persuading herself that it had been murdered. A letter, however, at length reached her from her husband, saying that he was on the point of leaving England, and that he purposed carrying the child with him. From that day she had never received the slightest intelligence of her husband or daughter. Her brother Jack had been absent from home at the time of her marriage, and five years passed away before he again returned, so that he had been unable to assist her in her inquiries. I was placed for instruction under the care of an old gentleman residing in the village, who had formerly been a schoolmaster. He was well able to impart to me the knowledge I most required, and as I was very anxious to learn, I made considerable progress. My spare time

CHAPTER FOURTEEN.

was spent almost entirely in the company of little Emily. I was never tired of attending on her. As was then the custom, she wore a little red mantle as a walking dress. One day we were out in the fields, when she ran off in chase of a butterfly. At the further end of the field a bull was grazing, having been turned out to indulge his sulky humour by himself. The sight of the red cloak fluttering over the green meadow suddenly excited his rage, and with a loud roar he came rushing up towards it. I saw the little girl's danger, and quick as lightning darted towards her. The cloak was fortunately secured by a very slight string. I tore it off and told her to run on; while, seizing the cloak, which I at once guessed was the cause of the bull's rage, I darted off in a different direction. The animal followed, as I had expected. On he came, however, at a speed which was likely soon to bring him up to me. It was some distance to the nearest hedge. Towards that, however, I made my way, as the best means of escape. The bull was not five yards from me. The hedge was thick and high. Into it or over it I must go, or run the certainty of a toss. I sprang towards the hedge. Just at the spot I reached was the stem of a small tree; one branch alone had escaped the pruner's hatchet. Throwing the cloak against the hedge, I seized the bough and sprang to the top—not a pleasant position, considering the brambles of which it was composed. The bull, with a loud roar, dashed into the hedge below me, into which he fixed his head, tearing up the ground, and making the bushes shake all round. I looked out and saw that Emily had reached the gate in safety; but how to descend was now the difficulty, for if I jumped back into the field out of which I came the bull would probably again attack me, whereas, on the other side, I could not descend without the risk of tearing my clothes and scratching myself with the brambles.

"Thou be a brave lad; I seed it all!" exclaimed a voice near me, and looking down I saw a person who appeared to be a farmer, standing on the further side of the hedge.

"Jump into my arms, I'll catch thee, lad," he added, seeing the predicament in which I was placed. I willingly did as he bid me, and, caught by his arms, reached the ground in safety. "We must have the little maiden's cloak, though," he said, laughing. "I will bring up some of my men, and we will soon handle the old bull." He was as good as his word. Five or six farm servants soon made their appearance with a stout rope, which they threw over the bull's neck and led him quietly off, while, accompanied by the farmer, I passed through a gate a little way on, and, securing the cloak, crossed the field to where Emily, still in a great fright, was waiting for me. The farmer insisted on accompanying us home. He was well-known, I found, to the ladies, and with great glee he recounted to them my exploit, bestowing more praise on me, I thought, than I deserved. Emily, however, declared that he was right, and that if it had not been for me, she was sure the bull would have tossed her up into the moon, or at all events as high as the moon.

My mother was now busily employed in preparing my outfit, and many a tear did she shed over her work when she thought that I was soon to be separated from her. A letter came at length from Captain Oliver, saying that the frigate was ready for sea, and that I must come at once down to Portsmouth. Fortunately my friend Farmer Cocks was going up to London, and undertook to escort me thus far, and from thence he was to see me off in the coach for Portsmouth. I will not describe my parting. There was a good deal more crying than I like to think of, and the dear Little Lady wept till her heart seemed about to break. However, her tears probably soon dried up, but my poor mother's sorrow was likely to be far more enduring.

"Thou art a brave, honest lad, Ben Burton," said the good farmer, pressing a five-pound note into my hand as I was about to mount on the top of the Portsmouth coach. "Thou wilt have plenty of use for this in getting thy new clothes for sea; but if not, spend it as thou thinkest best. I have no fear that thou wilt squander it as some do, and mark thee, shouldst thou ever want a home to come to, thou wilt always find a warm welcome at Springfield, from my good dame and me." I pocketed his gift with a sincere "Thank you," and he wrung my hand warmly, again and again, until I got fairly out of his reach on to the top of the coach.

CHAPTER FIFTEEN.

Captain Oliver had directed me to meet him at the "George," and I found him standing on the steps of that aristocratic hotel to which very few midshipmen of those days ever thought of going. My mother, being well acquainted with the internal economy of a man-of-war, had provided me with a chest of very moderate dimensions, at which no First-Lieutenant, however strict, could cavil. It and I were deposited at the hotel, and the waiter, seeing the kind way in which the Captain treated me, must have taken me for a young lord at least, and ordered the porter to carry it forthwith inside.

"That will do," said the Captain, as he eyed it. "And now you must come and get measured for your uniforms, and procure other necessaries, as I hope we may be off in two or three days at furthest."

I found that Captain Oliver had paid off the "Grecian," and commissioned a new frigate, the "Orion," to which most of his officers and men had been turned over, and that she was about to proceed to the Indian station. "There was no use telling your poor mother this," he observed. "The thoughts that you would be so long separated from her would only have added to her grief at parting from you, and as far as you are concerned, my boy, the time will soon pass by, and you will come back nearly ready for a swab on your shoulder."

The tailor, under the Captain's inspection, having examined the contents of my chest, made a note of the things I required besides. My outfit was soon complete.

"And now, my lad, my coxswain will take charge of you and your chest," said the Captain, "and see you safely on board."

Greatly to my delight, Toby Kiddle soon afterwards made his appearance. "Why, Mr Burton," he said, and I thought his eyes twinkled as he addressed me with that title. "Why, you see, the Captain's last coxswain slipped his cable a few months ago, and as I was one of the Captain's oldest shipmates, and he knew he could trust me, he has appointed me, and I never wish to serve under a better captain." Having purchased a few other articles with Farmer Cocks' five-pound note, which Toby Kiddle suggested I should find useful, we chartered a wherry to go to the frigate.

Among other things I got two or three pounds of tobacco. "You see, Mr Burton, if you deal it out now and then to the men, it will show them that you have not forgotten them; and though you are on the quarter-deck, that you are not proud, as some youngsters show themselves, but still have a kindly feeling towards them."

I gladly followed his advice. As we approached the "Orion," and I observed her handsome hull, her well-squared yards, and her trim and gallant appearance, I felt proud of belonging to so fine a frigate. The boatswain's whistle was piping shrilly as we went up the side, and as my eye fell on the person who was sounding it, I had an idea that I recollected him. I asked Toby who he was. "Your old friend, Bill King," he said. "I wanted to see whether you would remember him; I am glad you do. It is a good sign when old friends are not forgotten."

While Kiddle got my chest up, and paid the boatman, I went and reported myself to Mr Schank as come on board; and very proud I felt as I stepped on the quarter-deck in my bran-new midshipman's uniform. The First-Lieutenant, who was stumping on his wooden leg here and there with active movements, watching the proceedings of the various gangs of men at work in different ways, stopped when he saw me and smiled kindly. He had grown thinner, if not taller, since I last saw him, and looked somewhat like the scathed trunk of a once lofty poplar, battered and torn by a hundred tempests.

"You know the ways of a ship, Ben, pretty well, but as you are still somewhat small, I have asked Mr Oldershaw—one of the mates—to stand your friend, and he will give you a help also in navigation. And, Ben, mind, do not you be ashamed of asking him anything you want to know. You may live a long time on board ship, and still learn nothing about seamanship, if you do not keep your eyes open, and try to get others to explain what you do not understand." As Mr Schank spoke, he beckoned to a grey-headed old mate who just then came on deck. "This is the youngster I spoke to you about, Mr Oldershaw," he said. "You will have an eye on him, and I hope you will be able to give a good report of his behaviour." I naturally looked up at my protector's countenance, and was well-satisfied with the expression I saw on it. He soon afterwards took me down below, and on my way told me that I was to be in his watch, and that if I did not become a good seaman before the cruise was up, it should not be his fault.

"You see, Ben, I feel an interest in you on many accounts. I entered before the mast, and was placed on the quarter-deck, much as you may be said to have been, and was also left an orphan at an early age. I have not been very fortunate as to promotion; indeed, though my family were very respectable in life, I had no interest. I suppose some day I shall be made a lieutenant, and then I do not expect to rise much higher; but a lieutenant is a gentleman by rank, and though the half-pay is not overwhelming, yet, as I have saved a little prize-money, I shall have enough to keep me till I am placed under the green sward. When I visit some quiet churchyard, I often think how sweet a resting-place it would be after having been knocked about all one's life on the stormy ocean, and after having met with so many disappointments and sorrows."

I do not know what induced Oldershaw to speak to me in that way, for in truth he was one of the happiest and most contented people on board, so it seemed to me. While others grumbled and growled he never uttered a word of complaint in public, but took everything as it came, in the most good-humoured manner. He was a true friend to me from that time forward, and gave me many a lesson in wisdom as well as in other matters, which was of value to me through life.

CHAPTER FIFTEEN. 81

Tom Twigg who was the only midshipman I knew, received me cordially. There was another young gentleman, who, though he might have been older, was considerably smaller than I was. There was a roguish, mischievous look about the countenance of Dicky Esse, which showed me at once that I must be prepared for tricks of all sorts from him. Another mate was seated in the berth, to whom Oldershaw introduced me. His name, I found, was Pember. He was a broad-shouldered, rough-looking man, with a suspiciously red countenance and nose, his features marked and scored with small-pox and his eyelids so swelled, that only a portion of the inflamed balls could be seen. He uttered a low growl as I entered.

"We have kids enough on board already," he observed. "They will be sending the nurses with them next."

"Never fear, Pember, he will soon grow out of his kidhood," observed Oldershaw. "We want young blood to supply the place of us oldsters when we slip off the stage."

"You mean to be placed over our heads, and to trample us down," said Pember. "Why there is our skipper. I was a passed midshipman when he came to sea, and now he is a post-captain, and I am where I was, and shall be probably to the end of the chapter."

As soon as I could leave the berth I hurried to the boatswain's cabin, to which Bill King had just then descended. "You do not remember me, Mr King," said I, shaking him by the hand, "but I recollect you, and that you were one of my father's oldest shipmates, and my mother's kindest friend."

"Bless my heart, Ben, is it you?" he exclaimed, for he really had not at first known me. "Well, I did not think it. I am glad, that I am, boy, to see you, whom I have dandled in my hands many a time, come to sea on the quarter-deck. You must be an admiral, Ben, some day, that you must. Those who have sent you to sea must give you a shove upwards while you have still youth and strength and health in your favour. To many, promotion comes too late to do them any real good. When hope is knocked out of a man he is fit for very little in this world, or rather, I should say, nothing!"

"And Mrs King?" I asked; "how is she?"

"I could not bring her on board again, Ben, but she is very well, and as strong and active as ever. She has set up a coffee-shop in Gosport, which gives her something to do, and will help her to keep the pot boiling till I get back."

We had a fine run down Channel, and a fair wind carried us along, till we were in the latitude of the Azores. Our orders were, not to go out of our way, but to do as much damage and harm to the enemy as we conveniently could on our voyage to the South. We consequently kept a bright look-out, in the hopes of falling in with a ship worth capturing. Several times we had chased vessels, but they either managed to escape us during the night, or proved to be neutrals. At length, however, when about twenty leagues to the north of Teneriffe, we saw a sail standing apparently towards that island. That she was a Spaniard seemed probable, and there were great hopes that she might prove a merchant vessel. We made all sail, hoping to overhaul her before the sun went down, but she was a fast craft, and kept well ahead of us. Hour after hour passed by. All the glasses on board were constantly turned towards her. Great doubts at length began to be entertained of our capturing her after all. In our berth, especially, some of the young gentlemen were ready to sell their expected share of the prize-money, while others of more sanguine temperament were not unwilling to buy. Dicky Esse, especially, wanted to purchase my share.

"What will you give, Esse?" I asked, not, however, making up my mind that the transaction was a very wise one.

"Ten shillings would be handsome, but I have no objections to give you thirty. She is very likely to be in ballast, and we are more likely still not to catch her, so that you at all events will be the gainer of thirty shillings."

"I should not object to the thirty shillings, but if we take her I may possibly get thirty pounds, and more than that if she is a richly-laden craft."

"Don't have anything to do with the business, Ben," exclaimed Oldershaw. "I do not bet, and do not intend to begin, but I say there are five chances to one that we shall take her, so keep your prospects in your pocket, my boy, and I hope they will prove good ones." Although the hammocks were piped down at the usual hour, very few officers or men turned in. It was well-known that Captain Oliver would not let the chase escape as long as there was a prospect of getting hold of her. There was a bright moon, and by the master's calculation we should sight Teneriffe before dawn. A sailor's eye alone could have made out the shadowy form of the chase ahead of us, but not for a moment was she lost sight of. The wind fell as the night drew on, and the sea became calm, rippled over only by little wavelets, upon which the moonbeams played brightly. It was a lovely night. Bright as was the moon, many of the stars were to be seen also, vying with her in splendour. Yet here were we, with thousands of stars looking down upon us, about to commit an act of rapine and slaughter, for such, lawful as it might be thought, was the deed we were about to do. It was Oldershaw's watch, and I was walking the deck with him. I made some remark of that sort. He responded to it.

"Yes, Ben," he said, "I wonder what the bright seraphic beings up there—for surely there must be such in that pure heaven above us—are thinking of the proceedings of us mortals down here below. We have to fight, and it is right to defend our country, but I tell you, Ben, I have seen a good deal of it, and, putting what people call glory aside, it is very fearful, disgusting, dirty work. It makes a man feel like a devil for a time, and it is devilish, there is no doubt about that. I am in for it, and I expect to have plenty more of the same sort of work to do, but I am very sure that for men to kill each other is hateful to the God who made us. There is only one thing worse, and that is when they lie, and cheat, and deceive each other, and it seems often to me that more than one-half of the world is employed in doing one or the other."

"Have we gained much on the chase, Mr Schank?" asked the Captain, who just then appeared on deck.

"The best part of a mile, sir, I should think, in the course of the last hour. If the

CHAPTER FIFTEEN. 83

wind does not fall still more, we shall come up with her soon after daylight. She is heavily laden, and requires a breeze to send her along."

Oldershaw at length persuaded me to go below and turn in, promising to have me called should anything occur. When I came on deck in the morning, as the hammocks were piped up, the chase was still some distance off, running in for the land, which appeared on our starboard-bow. We followed her pertinaciously, however, though, as the wind frequently shifted, we did not gain upon her as at first. At length, however, we saw her run in for a bay with a fort on one side of it. "We have her safe now," observed Captain Oliver to Mr Schank. "Before this time to-morrow I hope she will be ours."

Having reconnoitred the bay, and found that the fort was rather too strong to attack in the day, Captain Oliver stood off the land once more. It soon became known that a cutting-out expedition was in contemplation, and the men were busily employed in sharpening their cutlasses, and looking to the locks of their pistols. From the appearance of the chase, there was no doubt that she was a merchant vessel, and it was hoped would offer no great resistance. Every precaution which prudence could dictate was taken. Four boats were ordered to be got ready, and towards evening we again stood in for the land. A bright look-out had been kept all day, so that there was no risk of the expected prize having made her escape. I greatly longed to be in one of the boats, but Oldershaw told me there was no use asking, as he was sure the Captain would not let me go. He, too, was disappointed, finding that he was not to be one of the party. The Second and Third Lieutenants, with Pember and the master, commanded the two boats, and, all things being ready, away they pulled. They had got to some distance when it was discovered that they had gone without signal-rockets or port-fires. Oldershaw, on this, volunteered to carry them in the dinghy, and I begged that I might accompany him.

"Well, look after the boy, and take care he gets into no mischief, Mr Oldershaw," said the Captain, "and he may then go."

I was delighted. Toby Kiddle and Pat Brady offered to pull the boat, for, of course, she had no regular crew. Two other men also volunteered, and away we went. The other boats, however, had got a long way ahead. We could only just distinguish the dim outline of the bay. We pulled rapidly on, when, just as we were at the entrance of the harbour, suddenly, from the deck of the ship, there burst forth loud shouts and cries, the flashing of pistols and musketry, and the clashing of steel, the sounds coming over to us across the calm water. Our men were hotly engaged, of that there was no doubt, but, from the frequent flashes of pistols, and the shouts of Spaniards as well as Englishmen, it was doubtful which was gaining the day. The contest was evidently a fierce one. Oldershaw's blood, in spite of his principles, was quickly up, and he evidently thought very little about me or anything else, except getting on deck as fast as he could, and joining in the fray. Our crew strained every nerve to get alongside. As we pulled by, the shouts and cries increased. The whole deck seemed one blaze of fire from the rapid discharge of pistols and muskets, while every now and then fearful shrieks burst from the bosoms of those who had been cut down. The ship was a high one, and there was some difficulty in climbing up out of our small boat.

"Here's a lower port open!" exclaimed Pat Brady, springing up and hauling himself into it. We all followed, and found ourselves the sole possessors of the lower-deck. Whether our people had the fore or after part of the deck we could not ascertain. We were about, however, to make our way up, when we caught sight of several figures descending. They were Spaniards, going apparently to the magazine for more ammunition. Before they were aware of our presence, our men had sprung upon them and cut them down. Scarcely had they ceased to breathe when three other persons came down, apparently for the same object. Led by Oldershaw, Kiddle and Brady with the others were upon them, and they too were cut down. It being supposed, probably, that they were skulking, a still larger number of people came down to look them up in the same incautious manner, and before they had time to cry out they also were slaughtered. An officer and several more men, swearing fearfully at the cowardice of their companions, now jumped below, and were in like manner cut down. I scarcely like to say how many people were killed in this fearful way. Our men now made a dash aft with such fury that the Spaniards on deck thought only of defending their lives. Two dead bodies came tumbling down the hatchway, as well as another poor fellow, only half killed, with a desperate wound on his shoulder. I should say from the way he groaned, and an exclamation he uttered, I felt sure he was an Englishman. I ran up to him, "Who are you?" I asked. It was one of our men.

"Is that you, Mr Burton?" he answered, in a faint voice. "It is going hard with us, for the ship was full of people and they are fighting well." Oldershaw, who just then came up, heard the words. "We will turn the tide then!" he exclaimed. "Come on, lads!"

We on this made our way forward, and reached the fore hatchway. Pat Brady sprang up first, shouting, "The ship is ours! The ship is ours!"

Oldershaw then taking the lead, we rushed aft, where our men were fighting with a number of Spanish soldiers and seamen. With loud shouts we dashed at our enemies, who, not seeing our numbers and supposing that a fresh set of boarders had gained the deck, began to give way.

We pressed on them, those who refused to yield or escape over the taffrail being speedily cut down. The ship was ours, but we had still a good deal to do. We had lost several people, killed and wounded, and we had a large number of prisoners to keep in order. As yet the garrison in the fort, not knowing who had gained the day, had not commenced firing at us. We had time, therefore, to secure our prisoners. Sail was then made on the ship, and her cable being cut, the boats towed her head round. The topsails were sheeted home, and with a light land-breeze we stood out of the bay. Having to pass pretty near the fort, Mr Tilhard, the Second-Lieutenant, ordered the greater number of the people to go below, he and Kiddle taking the helm; while the few who remained on deck were directed to keep close under the bulwarks. It was fortunate that these arrangements were made, for, as we drew near, the Spaniards began to pepper us pretty sharply with round-shot and musketry, the bullets flying thickly about us, while several shots struck the hull. Had they been better gunners they might have done more damage. Happily no one was hurt, though the sails were riddled and the white planks laid

CHAPTER FIFTEEN.

bare in several places.

As soon as the fight was over I thought of the poor fellow who had been tumbled below. I went to look for him with a lantern. For some time I could not discover where he was, for several Spaniards who had been killed had fallen down at the same spot. Pat, who accompanied me, at length discovered him. "He will not want any more human aid," he observed, holding the lantern to his face. "The Spaniards have already done for him." Whether, if instant aid had been afforded him, the man might have escaped, I do not know, but his wound was a desperate one, and he had apparently bled to death. We were received with loud cheers from the frigate's decks, as in the grey dawn of morning we passed close under her stern.

CHAPTER SIXTEEN.

Our prize—a ship of six hundred tons, and mounting fourteen guns—called the "Santiago," proved to be of considerable value. A prize crew being put on board, we steered for Saint Helena, where it was possible we might find a purchaser, and if not, Captain Oliver resolved to take her to the Cape. Fortunately, at Saint Helena we found the officers and crew of an Indiaman, which had been burnt at sea; and the Company's agent there was very glad to purchase our prize, and send her on, most of the goods being suitable to the Indian market. On concluding the bargain, the agent presented the Captain with a couple of young tigers. They were somewhat inconvenient pets, though they would have been valuable had we been going home. However, as we had no others on board, he accepted them, thinking they might serve to amuse the ship's company, and having an idea, I believe, that they might be perfectly tamed. We in the midshipmen's berth welcomed them with glee, and at once began to teach them to perform all sorts of tricks. They would let us ride on their backs, and they learned to leap through hoops and over ropes, and they would rush round and round the deck at a rapid rate, and soon they became the most playful, engaging creatures possible. Oldershaw was the only person who expressed doubts about their amiability.

"If I were the Captain, I would clip their claws and draw their teeth before I would let them play with you youngsters," he observed. "Their tricks may be playful now, but they will serve you a scurvy one before long, or their nature is more changed than I believe it to be."

Of course we laughed at his prognostications, and continued to amuse ourselves with our pets as usual. The Cape was reached. We took on board a supply of live and dead stock, having now a long run before us across the Indian Ocean, into that part of the world where I had first seen the light—the China Seas. We had several sheep and a supply of hay to feed them on. Some of the men had an idea that our tamed pets would gladly feed on the hay, but their carnivorous teeth refused to munch it. They, however, turned suspiciously hungry glances towards the newcomers. Oldershaw observed it, "They have probably never eaten sheep or midshipmen," he observed, "but the nature to do so is in them, and depend upon it their nature will have sway if we give them the opportunity." However, as the animals were tolerably well-fed, and were carefully caged, they gave no exhibition when anyone was watching them of their evil propensities, if they possessed them. When our stock of fresh meat was exhausted, first one sheep and then another was killed to supply the Captain and officers' tables, a portion falling to the lot of some of the men's messes. Their skins, which were peculiarly fine, were cleansed and prepared by the armourer, who happened also to understand the trade of a currier. Two of them were hung up to dry, when it came into the brains of Tom Twig and Dicky Esse to clothe themselves in the skins, and in high glee they came prancing about the deck, baa-ing away, imitating two frolicsome lambs, with a tolerable amount of accuracy. They afforded much amusement to us, their messmates, and not a little to the men who happened to be on deck. Not content with amusing us, off they went, into the neighbourhood of the tigers' cage. It ought to have been shut, and generally was shut. So exact was their imitation of nature that the beasts, after watching them with great eagerness for some moments, could no longer resist their natural propensities. With fierce leaps they rushed against the door of their cage. It gave way, and out they sprang. One bound carried them on to the backs of their expected prey. In another instant Tom and Dicky Esse would have been torn to pieces, had they not, in a way midshipmen alone could have done, slipped out of their skins, and rolled pale with terror across the deck. The animals, finding only the dry skins, were about to make another spring, when the man who had charge of them and had witnessed the scene, came rushing up with his stick of office, and several other men coming to his assistance with ropes, the savage creatures were forthwith secured. Both the midshipmen were rather more frightened than hurt, and in consideration of their terror they escaped any further consequences of their conduct which was looked upon by the First-Lieutenant as somewhat derogatory to the dignity which they were in duty bound to maintain.

After leaving the Cape, we were constantly becalmed, and then, getting further east, fell in with a hurricane, from the effects of which nothing but first-rate seamanship, under God's Providence, could have preserved the frigate. We were now getting much in want of water, and Captain Oliver, unwilling to go out of his way to any of the settlements to obtain it, resolved to search for a supply at the first island we should fall in with. At length we came in sight of a large island, with yellow sands, and green palm trees waving in the breeze. Nothing could be more attractive, but it appeared that nobody on board had been there before. The master knew the existence of the island on the chart, but whether it was inhabited or not, or by whom, he could not say. As no anchorage was found, the ship was hove to, and three boats, with casks, under the command of the Second-Lieutenant, and my friend Oldershaw, and Pember, were directed to go on shore. I went with Oldershaw, and Twigg and Esse went in the other boats. We pulled into the bay abreast of the ship, where, between two projecting rocks, we found an excellent landing-place, and not far from it a stream of water, clear and limpid. As no natives appeared, the opinion was that that part of the island, at all events, was uninhabited, and this made us somewhat careless. All the casks being filled, the boats were sent back for a fresh supply, as we could not hope to find a better place for filling up with that important necessary. Pember, directing Tom Twigg to take charge of his boat, invited Dicky Esse and me to accompany him meantime on a stroll to see the island farther inland. He directed Toby Kiddle and Pat Brady to follow with a couple of muskets.

"Not that they will be wanted," he observed; "but if we do fall in with any natives, it will make them treat us with respect."

"If I were you, Pember, I would not go far from the bay," observed Oldershaw, as he shoved off.

IN ANOTHER INSTANT TOM AND DICKY ESSE WOULD HAVE BEEN TORN TO PIECES.

"You are always uttering warnings, old Careful," muttered Pember; and, leading the way, he turned his back on the sea and proceeded inland.

The country was very beautiful. We soon came to a grove of cocoa-nuts, when Pember proposed that we should procure a supply. This, however, was more easily thought of than done. Pat Brady, who was the most active of the party, declared that he could manage it after the native fashion. He and Kiddle having placed the muskets against a tree, were considering the best way of mounting. We went first to one tree and then to another, to find one which seemed most easy to climb, with a satisfactory reward at the top of it for our trouble. Having made a band of sufficient strength with our handkerchiefs, Pat commenced his ascent. He had got some way up, Kiddle having helped him as far as he could reach, when suddenly a dozen dark-skinned savages sprang out from among the trees, and before we could draw our pistols they had brought us all to the ground. Forthwith they proceeded to bind our arms behind us. Pat, seeing there was no use going higher, came gliding down the tree, and was secured in the same manner. We endeavoured to make them understand that we had desired to do them no harm, and that if the cocoa-nuts were theirs, we should be happy to pay for them. Whether they understood us or not I cannot say, but without more ado, three of them attaching themselves to Pember, and a like number to each of the other men—one black fellow, however, only taking charge of Dicky and another of me—they dragged us off into the interior. In vain Pember struggled and expostulated. The fierce gleam of their dark eyes, and the keen blades of their glittering creeses which they flourished before us, showed that it would be dangerous to dispute the point with them. All we could do, therefore, was to move forward as they insisted, hoping that, when our absence was discovered, a strong party might be sent in pursuit of us, and that we might be recovered. We had not gone far when they were joined by another band of a similar number, and we could not help suspecting that they had been watching us all the time, but seeing so many armed men round the boats had not ventured to attack us. This made us still more regret our folly in having ventured alone into the country. On, on we went. We had great reason to fear that they had no intention of restoring us. At length they stopped at a village of bamboo huts, covered with cocoa-nut leaves, from which a number of women and children came forth to gaze at us. The children went shrieking away when they saw our white skins, while the women advanced cautiously and touched us, apparently to ascertain whether the red and white would come off.

"Faith, they take us for white niggers!" said Pat Brady, observing the look of astonishment, not unmixed with disgust, with which the women regarded us. "It's to be hoped they won't set us to work as we do the blacks, though, to be sure, it would be better than eating us, and I don't like the looks of those fellows at all, at all."

"Depend upon it, if they don't eat us they will make us work, or why should they otherwise carry us off?" observed Kiddle. "These Malay fellows make slaves of all the people they can lay hands on. If it was not for that they would cut our throats."

These remarks made Dicky Esse and me feel very uncomfortable, till Pember observed that perhaps they had carried us off in the hopes of obtaining a ransom. This idea kept up our spirits a little; but as they continued to drag us on further and further into the country, our hope on that score greatly decreased. At length we reached another village, in which was a large hut. Under the shade of a wide-spreading verandah in front of it an old chief was seated on cushions; a dozen half-naked savages with drawn swords standing behind him. He was dressed in a dark-coloured turban, with a shawl over his shoulders, a belt, in which were three or four formidable looking daggers with jewelled hilts, and a curved sword by his side. His dark countenance was unpleasantly savage and morose, and we felt that our lives would be of little value if they depended upon the amiability of his disposition. Our captors arranged us before him, and then appeared to be explaining how they had got possession of us. He smiled grimly at the narration. As Pember, Dicky Esse, and I were placed in advance, it was evident that our captors looked upon us as of more value than the men. This made us hope that they were entertaining some thoughts of allowing us to be ransomed, for in every other way the men were likely to prove more useful to them than we should.

After our captors had said all they had to say, the old chief made a few remarks in return. Before he had ceased speaking, several of his guards advanced towards us with their sharp-looking swords glittering in the sunbeams. It was a moment of intense anxiety. It seemed evident they intended to kill us. We could, however, neither fly nor defend ourselves.

"I say, Ben, have you said your prayers?" whispered Dicky to me. "If not, it is time to begin."

Pember prepared to meet his fate with dogged resolution, his dark red countenance turning almost to an ashy hue. Kiddle and Brady, as I cast my eye on them, were evidently preparing to show fight.

"Knock the fellow next you down, Pat," said Toby, "and get hold of his cutlash. I will treat mine the same, and if we cannot get away we will die game."

Suddenly our expected executioners stopped, and stood waving their weapons at a short distance from our necks. The chief continued haranguing for some time, and when he ceased others stepped forth from the crowd and addressed him. Whether or not the chief had intended to kill us, we could not ascertain, but having kept us in most disagreeable suspense for half-an-hour or more, though it seemed several hours, the men with the swords faced about, and marched back to their former position. Our guards then carried us off to a hut at a little distance, into which we were all thrust, several men standing outside as a guard over us. After some time they brought us a mess of grain of some sort, well seasoned with pepper.

"I suppose they don't intend to kill us, or they would not give us this," observed Pat, taking a handful from the bowl, as, of course, we were left to feed ourselves, with our fingers. "Faith, it's not so bad, after all."

His example was followed by Dicky and me, and after a time Pember and Kiddle, unable any longer to restrain their appetites, also commenced eating. A supply of dry leaves and long grass, with several carpets, were brought in, and we were given to understand that they were to serve us as beds. This sort of treatment again raised our hopes that our captors might give us our liberty on receiving a ransom. Our difficulty would be to communicate with the ship.

"They cannot expect any very large sum for us," observed Pember, who, deprived of any stimulant, was getting sadly out of spirits. "The Captain would not consent to pay much for me, I am afraid, and you two youngsters are worth little enough."

"Speak for yourself," answered Esse. "I rather think the Captain sets a higher estimation on me than you do."

"Whether or not, for the honour of the flag they will not desert us," I observed.

Pember on this gave a faint sickly laugh.

"Few inquiries would be made at the Admiralty as to what had become of an old mate and two youngsters. Expended on a watering party—killed by savages. Such would be our epitaph, and the matter would be settled to the satisfaction of all parties."

No wonder, considering the circumstances, that our conversation did not take a more lively tone. Pat Brady, to be sure, did his best now and then to get up a laugh, but with very poor success.

"Keep silence, man!" exclaimed Pember, at last, in a surly tone. "You will be singing out in a different way to-morrow morning when they get the ovens ready."

"Faith, I suppose they would be after making me into an Irish stew, or a dish of bubble and squeak!" exclaimed Pat, whose spirits were not to be quelled even with the anticipation of being turned into a feast for cannibals. I had an idea, however, that the people into whose hands we had fallen were not addicted to such practices, and was, therefore, not much influenced by the remarks which Pember occasionally made as to our probable fate. We were allowed to pass the night in quietness, and next morning another bowl of food was brought to us, with a basket of fruit of various sorts, very acceptable in that hot climate. We waited anxiously, expecting the arrival of a party from the frigate, either to rescue us by force, or to offer a ransom for our liberty; but no one appeared, nor did any of the natives, except the man who brought the food, come to the hut. Once, during an interval of silence, Esse declared he heard firing, but though we listened with all our might, the sounds reached no other ears. After a time, indeed, we all fancied we heard the boom of great guns, but even of that we could not be quite certain. Night again came round, and no one had come to look for us.

CHAPTER SEVENTEEN.

Several days passed by; we were still prisoners, and all hope of being rescued by our friends vanished. We came to the conclusion that they supposed we were killed, especially as Kiddle told us he had known of several boats' crews having been cut off by the natives in those seas. What was to be our fate we could not tell; it was not likely to be a pleasant one, at all events. One day the whole village appeared to be in commotion; loud shouts were heard, and presently the door of our hull was thrown open, and several men entered, who dragged us out into the midst of a large crowd collected in the open space in front of it. Among them was the old chief whom we had seen on the day of our capture; a number of the men had hoes and other implements of agriculture. After a good deal of palaver, a hoe was put into Pember's hands, and signs were made to him that he was to go to work with it. Toby and Pat had hoes given to them also. Esse fancied that we should be allowed to escape.

"They think us too little to work, I hope," he observed; but scarcely were the words out of his mouth than we both of us had implements put into our hands, and a pretty heavy whip being exhibited, signs were made to us that we should join our companions. We were forthwith marched off to a field where several natives were already at work. Apparently it belonged to the old chief, for he sat on a raised spot at the further end, under an awning, watching the proceedings with a complacent air which especially excited Pember's wrath. When, also, at times the old mate relaxed in his labours, a dark-skinned fellow with a turban on his head, who seemed to act the part of an overseer, made him quickly resume them by an unmistakable threatening gesture. Thus we were kept at work till late in the evening, when we were all allowed to knock off and go back to our hut, where a larger amount of food than usual was awarded us. Next day we were called up at early dawn, and the hoes again were put into our hands. Sometimes the overseer, and sometimes one of the other men, came and showed us how to use them. All day long we were kept at work with the exception of a short time, when we were allowed to rest and take some food which was brought to us in the fields. We could no longer enjoy any hopes of regaining our liberty. It seemed as if we were destined to be turned into slaves, and to be worked as hard as any negroes in the West India plantations. At first Pember was very miserable, but abstinence from his usual liquor at length, I think, did him good, and he grew fatter and stronger than he had been since I first knew him. Still he persisted that he was dying, and should never again see the shores of England. The rest of us did our best to keep up our spirits, Esse and I told stories to each other, and formed plans for escaping. Some of them were very ingenious, and more or less hazardous; most, in reali-

CHAPTER SEVENTEEN.

ty, utterly impracticable, because, not knowing where we were, and having no means of getting away from the coast, even had we made our way to the shore, we should very soon have been brought back again. I might spin a long yarn about our captivity, but I do not think it would be interesting. Our days were monotonous enough, considering we were kept at the same work from sunrise to sunset. What a glorious feeling is hope! Hope kept us alive, for in spite of every difficulty we hoped, some time or other, to escape. At length one day as we were working, the old chief as usual looking on, a stranger arrived, and, going up to where he was seated, made a salaam before him. After a palaver of some minutes, which I could not help thinking had reference to us, the old chief called the overseer, and sent him down to where we were working. He went up to Pember, and made signs to him to go to the chief.

"Sure that's a message for us!" exclaimed Pat Brady. "Arrah, Ben, my boy, you will be after seeing your dear mother again; and the thought that she has been mourning for you has been throubling my heart more than the hard work and the dishonour of labouring for these blackamoors. Hurrah! Erin-go-bragh! I am right sure it's news that's coming to us."

By this time the overseer had spoken to Kiddle, and finally we were all conducted up to the chief. What was our astonishment to see the stranger produce a letter and hand it to Pember. It was written by the captain of a frigate, stating that having heard that some British seamen were detained by a petty chief, he had gone to the Rajah of the country, who had agreed that they should be liberated. The letter was addressed to any officer, or the principal person who was among them, advising them to follow the messenger, who could be trusted. The old chief seemed very indignant, but the envoy was evidently determined to carry out his instructions.

"Sure he need not grumble," observed Pat Brady, "the big thief has been getting a good many months' work out of us, and sure that's more than he had any right to. Still we will part friends with him, and show him that we bear him no ill-will." On this, Pat, not waiting for the rest, went up and insisted on shaking the old chief cordially by the hand; the rest of us, with the exception of Pember, did the same. I need scarcely say that it was with no little amount of satisfaction that we began our march under the guidance of the Rajah's envoy. I doubt if any of our friends would have known us, so changed had we become during our captivity. Rice and other grain diet may suit the natives of those regions, but it certainly does not agree with an Englishman's constitution. We were all pale and thin, our hair long and shaggy, our clothes worn and tattered. We had darned them and mended them up as best we could with bits of native cloth, but in spite of our efforts we officers had a very unofficerlike appearance; while the two men might have served for street beggars, representing shipwrecked sailors, but were very unlike British men-of-war's men. Eager as we were to get on, we made little progress across the rough country, and not till nearly the close of the second day did we obtain a glimpse of the bright blue sea. Our hearts bounded with joy when we saw it. Still more delightful was it to gaze down from a height which we reached on the well-squared yards and the white deck of a British frigate which lay at anchor in the harbour below us. Pat threw up his hat and shouted for joy. He was the only one of us who retained anything like a hat; only an Irishman, indeed, would have thought of preserving so battered a head-covering.

"Sure it serves to keep my brains from broiling," he observed, "and what after all is the use of a hat but for that, and just to toss up in the air when one's heart's in the mood to leap after it?" So near did the frigate appear that we felt inclined to hail her to send a boat on shore, though our voices would in reality have been lost in mid-air, long before the sound could reach her decks. We should have hurried down to the shore, had not our guide insisted on our proceeding first to the Rajah's abode, where he might report our arrival in safety and claim a reward for himself, as well as the better to enable the Rajah to put in his own claims for a recompense. We were still standing in the presence of the great man, when a lieutenant and a couple of midshipmen with about twenty armed seamen made their appearance in the courtyard. Dicky Esse and I no sooner caught sight of them than, unable to restrain our eagerness, we rushed forward intending to shake hands with them.

"Hillo, what are these curious little imps about?" exclaimed one of the midshipmen, as we were running towards them.

"Imp?" exclaimed Dicky. "You would look like an imp if you had been made to hoe in the fields all day long with the sun right overhead for the best part of half-a-year. I am an officer like yourself, and will not stand an insult, that I can tell you!" This reply was received with a burst of laughter from the two midshipmen; but the lieutenant, guessing who we were, received us both in a very kind way, and Pember with Kiddle and Pat coming up, he seemed highly pleased to find that we were the prisoners he had been sent to liberate. The frigate, he told us, was the "Resolution," Captain Pemberton, who, having heard through some of the natives that some English seamen were in captivity, had taken steps to obtain our release.

"We told the Rajah that if any of you were injured, or if his people refused to restore you, we would blow his town about his ears—a far more effectual way of dealing with these gentry than mild expostulations or gentle threats. And now," he added, "if there are no more of you we will return on board." In a short time we were standing on the deck of the frigate. Her captain received us very kindly, and soon afterwards we made sail. The frigate being rather short of officers, we were ordered to do duty till we could fall in with our own ship. Pember grumbled somewhat, declaring that he ought to be allowed to rest after the hardships he had gone through. People seldom know what is best for them, nor did he, as will be shown in the sequel. Both Dicky Esse and I were placed in the same watch, as were our two followers. The "Resolution" had not fallen in with our frigate, and therefore we could gain no tidings of any of our friends, and as she, it was supposed, had sailed for Canton, we might not fall in with her for some time. We cruised round and about the shores of the numberless islands of those seas, sometimes taking a prize, and occasionally attacking a fort or injuring and destroying the property of our enemies whenever we could meet with it. One night, while I was on watch, I found Kiddle near me. Though he did not hesitate to speak to me as of yore, yet he never seemed to forget that I was now on the quarter-deck.

CHAPTER SEVENTEEN.

"Do you know, Mr Burton," he observed, "that I have found an old acquaintance on board? He was pilot in the 'Boreas,' and he is doing the same sort of work here. I never quite liked the man, though he is a fair spoken enough sort of gentleman."

"What! Is that Mr Noalles?" I asked.

"The same!" and Toby then gave me the account which I have before noted of that person.

"That is strange!" I said. "I really fancied I had seen him before. Directly I came on board it struck me that I knew the man, and yet of course I cannot recollect him after so many years." He was a dark, large-whiskered man, with a far from pleasant expression of countenance. The ship had been on the station some time, and rather worse for wear and tear. We had not been on board long, when one night as I was in my hammock I felt it jerk in a peculiar manner, and was almost sent out of it. I was quickly roused by a combination of all conceivable sounds:—the howling of the wind, the roar of the seas, which seemed to be dashing over us. The rattling of ropes and blocks, the creaking of bulkheads, the voices of the men shouting to each other and asking what had happened, were almost deafening, even to ears accustomed to such noises.

"We are all going to be drowned!" I heard Dicky Esse, whose hammock slung next to mine, sing out. "Never mind, Dicky," I answered, "we will have a struggle for life at all events, and may be, as the savages did not eat us, the sea will not swallow us up."

Finding everybody was turning out, I huddled on my clothes as best I could, and with the rest found my way on deck, though I quickly wished myself below again, as it was no easy matter to keep my footing when I was there, and preserve myself from slipping into the sea, which was dashing wildly over our bulwarks. The ship was on her beam-ends. By the light of the vivid flashes of lightning which continued incessantly darting here and there round us, I saw the Captain half-dressed, with his garments under one of his arms, shouting out his orders, which the lieutenants, much in the same state as to costume, were endeavouring to get executed, their voices, however, being drowned in the tempest. For some minutes, indeed, even the best seamen could scarcely do anything but hold on for their lives. One thing appeared certain: either the masts must be cut away, or the guns hove overboard. It seemed impossible, if this could not be done, that the ship would continue above water. Suddenly with a violent jerk up she rose again on an even keel with her topmasts carried away, and the rigging beating with fearful force about our heads.

"Clear away the wreck!" shouted the Captain. Such was now the no easy task to be performed. The officers, however, with axes in their hands, leading the way, sprang aloft, followed by the topmen. Blocks and spars came rattling down on deck to the no small risk of those below. At length the shattered spars having been cleared away, head sail was got on the ship, and off she ran before the hurricane, the master having ascertained that we had a clear sea before us. When morning dawned, the frigate, which had looked so trim at sunset, presented a sadly battered appearance, her topmasts gone, the deck lumbered with the wreck, two of the boats carried away, a part of the lee-bulwarks stove in. The carpenter too, after going below with his mates, returned on deck and reported that the ship was making water very fast. "We must ease her, sir," I heard him say, "or I cannot answer for her weathering the gale." The Captain took a turn or two along the quarter-deck, his countenance showing the anxiety he felt.

"It must be done," I heard him say. "Send Mr Block aft." He was the gunner. "We must heave some of our upper-deck guns overboard, Mr Block." The gunner seemed inclined to plead for them.

"It must be done," said the Captain. And now the crew, who would have sprung joyfully to the guns to man them against an enemy, began with unwilling hands to cast the tackles loose in order to launch them into the ocean. Watching the roll of the ship, first one gun was sent through the port into the deep—another and another followed.

"By my faith it's like pulling out the old girl's teeth, and giving her no chance of biting," observed Pat Brady, who was standing near me.

"We will keep a few of her grinders in though, Pat," observed Kiddle: "we must handle them the smarter if we come alongside an enemy, to make amends for those we have lost."

The heavy weight on her upper-deck being thus got rid of, the frigate laboured less, and the pumps being kept going, the water no longer continued to gain upon us. However, it was necessary to work the chain pumps night and day to keep the water under. At length we arrived at Amboyna, where we remained some time repairing damages and refitting the frigate as far as we were able.

"I wish we were aboard our own ship again," said Kiddle to me one day, "for I don't know how it is, but the crew of this ship declare that she is doomed to be unlucky. I don't know how many men they have not lost. They have scarcely taken a prize, and they are always getting into misfortune. It's not the fault of the Captain, for he is as good a seaman as ever stepped, and the officers are all very well in their way, and so there's no doubt it's the ship's fault. Some of the people, to be sure, don't like Mr Noalles, the pilot. They don't know who he is or where he came from, though that to my mind has nothing to do with it, for it's not likely he would be aboard here if he was not known to be a right sort of person."

At length we once more sailed for a place called Booroo, where we got a supply of wood and water, as well as refreshments and stock, and then sailed for the Straits of Banca. As we were standing along the coast, when daylight broke one morning, we saw towards the land a number of vessels, which were pronounced to be pirate prows. In their midst was a large brig, which they had apparently captured. We were standing towards them when the land-breeze died away, and we lay becalmed, unable to get nearer. On this the boats were ordered out, and two of the lieutenants, the master, and a couple of mates took the command. Dicky Esse and I accompanied the Second-Lieutenant. Our orders were to board the prows, and if they offered any resistance, to destroy them. The water was smooth and beautifully blue, while the rising sun tipped the topmost heights of the lofty hills,

CHAPTER SEVENTEEN.

which rose, as it were, out of the ocean, feathered almost from their summits to the water's edge with graceful trees. There lay the brig, while the prows were clustered like so many beasts of prey around their quarry. The pirates seemed in no way alarmed at our approach. Our leader, however, had made up his mind, in spite of their numbers to board the brig, and then, should the prows interfere, to attack them. As soon as this resolution was come to, we dashed forward to get on board her without delay. The pirates seemed scarcely aware of our intention, and before any of the prows had lifted an anchor we were on board. Some forty or fifty dark-skinned, villainous-looking fellows had possession of the brig, but they were probably unable to use the big guns, and though they made some little resistance, we soon drove them forward, a considerable number being cut down, the rest jumping overboard, and attempting to swim towards the prows, which, instantly getting out their sweeps, began to approach us.

CHAPTER EIGHTEEN.

The brig was ours, but we were not to be allowed to carry her off without a struggle. There were certainly not less than twenty prows, each of them carrying from fifty to a hundred men; and though the frigate's guns would have dispersed them like chaff before the wind, she was too far off to render us any assistance. We had therefore to depend upon the guns of the brig for our defence. They had all been discharged probably by her former crew, who had struggled desperately in her defence. Several of them lay about the deck, cut down when the pirates boarded. They appeared to be Dutchmen, with two or three natives. One of the mates and I, with a couple of men, were ordered down immediately we got on board to bring up shot and powder from the magazine. On our way I looked into the cabin. There, a sight met my eyes which made me shudder. Close to the entrance lay on his back a tall, fine looking old gentleman with silvery locks, while further in, two young women, their skin somewhat dark, but very handsome, they seemed to me, and well dressed, lay clasped in each other's arms, perfectly dead. It seemed as if the same bullet had killed them both. We had no time, however, to make further observations, but hurrying down we found that the magazine was open. We immediately sent up a supply of powder, as well as round-shot, which were stowed not far off. We were hurrying on deck again, when I thought I saw something glittering under the ladder. It was a man's eye. Repressing the impulse to cry out, I told Esse what I had seen. At the same moment we sprang down and seized the man, Esse receiving a severe cut as we did so. At the same instant a pistol bullet whistled by my ear. It was shot at the magazine, but happily it was at too great a distance to allow the flash to ignite the powder. Fortunately my right hand was free, and drawing my dirk, I pinned our antagonist through the throat to the deck. He still struggled, but another blow from my companion silenced him for ever. I felt a sensation come over me I had never before experienced, but it was not a time to give way to my feelings. Had I not discovered the man, we should probably in a few minutes have all been blown into the air. The prows were coming rapidly on.

"If we had a breeze we should do well," observed our commanding officer, "but if not we shall have tough work to keep these fellows off." Our guns were loaded and run out. "We must not throw a shot away," observed the Lieutenant. He kept looking out in hopes of a breeze. The topsails had been loosened, and all was ready for making sail. "Cut the cable," he shouted at length.

"Sheet home the topsails! Man the starboard braces! Up with the helm!" Our sails filled and the vessel's head slowly turned away from the shore, just as the nearest prow was a dozen fathoms from us. A couple of shot threw her crew into confusion, and before they could grapple us we glided by them, every instant gathering way. "Give the next the stem," shouted the Lieutenant. We did so, but we had scarcely way enough to do the vessel much injury. The other prows were now gathering thickly round us, and it was time for us to open on them with our guns. The enemy had no great guns, but the instant we began firing, they returned the compliment with matchlocks and javelins, which came flying thickly on board. As we had to fight both sides at once, we had but little time to use our own small-arms. However, while the men were working the guns, Esse and I and another midshipman loaded the muskets with which the men fired while the guns were being sponged and loaded, we youngsters doing our part by firing the muskets which were not used. So rapidly did we work our guns, that many of the prows at a distance hesitated to approach us, while those which got near were quickly half knocked to pieces. "Hurrah! There goes one of them down!" sung out Kiddle, who was hauling in his gun. "And there's another! And another!" shouted others of the crew. The breeze was increasing. Again the prows came on on both sides, but our guns were all loaded, and we gave them such a dose, few of our guns missing, that once more they dropped astern in confusion. The wind had now reached the frigate, which under all sail was standing towards us. When the pirates saw this they well knew that their chance of victory was gone, and the crews of the headmost ones, again firing their matchlocks and darting a few more spears at us, pulled round, and made off with all speed towards the shore. Luffing up, we brought our broadside to bear upon them, and gave them a few parting shots, our crew giving a hearty cheer in token of victory. We were soon up to the frigate, when Captain Pemberton ordered us by signal to run back, and keep as close in shore as we could, in order to watch the proceedings of the pirates. However, before long it again fell a calm, and both the frigate and brig had to come to an anchor. Soon after, the Captain and several officers came on board the brig to examine her, and to ascertain more particularly what she was, and who were the murdered persons on board. Among others was Mr Noalles the pilot. No sooner did he enter the cabin than he started back with a cry of horror.

"What is the matter? Who are those?" asked the Captain, seeing the glance he cast at the dead man and the two ladies.

"Little did I expect to see them thus," he answered. "They were my friends, from whom I have often when at Batavia received great attention. That old man was one of the principal merchants in the place, and those poor girls were his daughters," and again I observed the look of grief and horror with which Mr Noalles regarded them. There had apparently been two or three other passengers on board, but what had become of them, or the remainder of the crew, we could find nothing on board to tell us. The sight of those poor girls, cruelly murdered in their youth and beauty, was enough certainly to make the hardest heart on board bleed, and yet how much worse might have been their fate. A prize crew was put on board the brig, but of course the cabin was held sacred till the murdered people were committed to their ocean grave. At first it was proposed to bury them on shore, but a strong force would have been required had we landed, and as their remains might afterwards have been disturbed, it was determined to commit them to the deep. For this purpose the next morning the Captain came on board the brig with most of the officers, the sailmaker having in the meantime closely fastened up each form in several folds of stout canvas, with a heavy shot at the feet. As Mr Noalles informed the Captain the deceased were Protestants, he used the burial service from the Church of England prayer book. The words, indeed, sounded peculiarly solemn to our ears. All present probably had heard it over and over again when a shipmate had died from wounds in battle or sickness brought on in the service, but their deaths were all in the ordinary way. These people had been cut off in a very different manner. I remember particularly those words, "In the midst of life we are in death." They made an impression on me at the time, and more so from what afterwards occurred. As they were uttered the old man's corpse was allowed to glide off slowly into the calm ocean, into the depths of which it shot down rapidly. The bodies of the poor girls were launched one by one in the same manner, and I could not help jumping into the rigging to watch them, as the two shrouded figures went down and down in the clear water, till gradually they were lost to view. Most of us then returned on board the frigate. Such stores as the brig required were sent to her, as well as a prize crew, and she was then despatched to Amboyna to bring the frigate certain stores which it appeared she required. As our ship was supposed to be cruising in another direction, we remained on board, in the hopes of falling in with her. A light breeze towards evening enabled the brig to get under weigh three or four days after the circumstances I have just related. Esse, who drew very well, made a sketch of her as she stood along the land, the rays of the setting sun shedding a pink glow on her canvas, while the whole ocean was lighted up with the same rosy hue. One side of the picture was bounded by the horizon, the other by the yellow shores and the lofty broken tree-covered heights of the island. We remained at anchor, intending to sail in the morning, should there be sufficient wind to enable us to move. As the sun was sinking into the ocean, the sky and water for a few seconds were lighted up with a glow of brightest orange, which faded away as the shades of night came stealing across the water from the east. In a short time the stars overhead burst forth, and shone down upon us, their light reflected in the mirror-like expanse on which we floated. The heat was very great. Esse and Pember had the middle watch under the Third-Lieutenant of the ship (the second had gone away in the prize). The heat making me unwilling to turn into my hammock, I continued to walk the deck with Esse. Sometimes we stopped and leaned against a gun-carriage, talking, as midshipmen are apt to talk, of home, or future prospects, or of late occurrences.

"That foreign-looking pilot aboard here is a strange fellow," observed Esse to me. "The people think him not quite right in his mind. They say he talks in his sleep, and did you observe his look when he caught sight of the murdered people aboard the brig?" I did not, however, agree with Dicky's notions.

"The man had been employed on board ships of war for many years, I am told," I answered. "And if he was not a respectable character it is not likely that they would take him."

"As to that I have my doubts," answered Esse. "All they look to is to get a good pilot who knows the ugly navigation of these seas, and that, I suppose, at all events, he does. But see, who is that on the other side of the deck?" As he spoke he

CHAPTER EIGHTEEN.

pointed to a person who was standing, apparently looking out at some object far away across the sea.

"Yes, that is he," I whispered. "I hope he did not hear us."

"If he did it does not signify," said Esse. While we were looking at him, the man walked directly aft, and remained gazing, as he had done before, into the distance over the taffrail. The watch at length came to an end. "I shall caulk it out on deck," said I. Esse agreed to do the same. Indeed several of the crew were sleeping on deck—Kiddle and Brady among them. There also was Pember. Indeed it seemed surprising that anybody could manage to exist in the oven-like heat which prevailed in the lower part of the ship. "Sound slumber to you, Burton," said Esse, and he and I before a minute passed were fast asleep. How long we had slept I do not know, but I was awoke with the most terrific roar I had ever heard. I felt myself lifted right up into the air, and then, as it were, shoved off with tremendous violence from the deck on which I was lying, and plunged into the water. Down! Down! I sank. My ears seemed cracking with the continued roar. My breath was going. The horror of deep waters was upon me. Then suddenly I appeared to be bounding up again. I thought it was all a dream; I expected to find myself in my hammock, or in my bed at Whithyford, and certainly not struggling amidst the foaming waters in the Indian Seas.

CHAPTER NINETEEN.

When I came to the surface, I found myself amidst a mass of wreck, and several human beings struggling desperately for dear life. Some were crying out for help, others clutching at fragments of timber which floated near, and others striking out and keeping themselves afloat by their own exertions. I had become a pretty good swimmer, and seeing a part of the wreck above water not far from me, I made towards it. On my way I saw a person clinging to a spar a couple of fathoms off. "Who is that?" said a voice. It was that of Dicky Esse. "Burton," I answered. "Oh! Do help me!" he cried out. "I cannot swim, and I cannot hold on much longer, and if I do not reach the wreck I shall drop off and be drowned!"

"Hold on," I shouted, "and perhaps I may be able to tow the spar up to the wreck. I will try at all events; but do not let go, Dicky! Do not on any account!"

I swam to the spar, and, partly resting on it, shoved it before me towards the wreck, but still I made but slow progress. I was afraid that I should be obliged, after all, to give it up, as I felt my strength going, when a man swimming powerfully reached us. "Help! Help! Do help me!" I cried out. He said nothing, but just touching the spar with one hand, so as not to sink it deeper in the water, he shoved it on till we reached the wreck. The hammock nettings were just above water, and afforded us a better resting-place than we could have expected. "Thank you! Thank you!" I said, as the man hauled Dicky and me into this place of refuge. "What shall we next do?"

"Wait till morning, and if we are then alive, we must get on shore as best we can," he answered. I knew by the voice and accent of the speaker that he was Mr Noalles. The bright stars shining down from the sky gave us sufficient light to distinguish objects at a considerable distance. As we looked out we saw several other persons still alive, some swimming, others holding on to bits of timber. We shouted out to them, lest they should not be aware that they could obtain a place to rest on, at all events, until morning. A voice not far off answered us. "Who is that?" I cried out, for I thought I recognised it. "Toby Kiddle, sir," was the answer. He was swimming up towards us. "I have just passed Mr Pember clinging to a piece of the wreck. I will go back and try to bring him here."

"I will go with you," I said.

"No, no, youngster, stay where you are," observed Mr Noalles; "you will be drowned if you make the attempt; I will go!" The next instant he was striking out in the direction in which Toby was now swimming.

Esse and I watched them anxiously as they disappeared in the gloom. I was

CHAPTER NINETEEN. 103

very thankful to think that Toby Kiddle was alive, but I could not help wishing that Pat Brady had escaped also, as I knew that he had been on deck and close to Kiddle. While we were looking out for the return of our shipmates, another man, one of the seamen, reached the wreck. He said he was greatly scorched, and it seemed surprising that he should have been able to swim so far. There were yet a number of people floating about alive, and when we shouted several voices answered us. Among them I thought I recognised Pat's. "Brady, is that you?" I cried out. "By the powers it's myself, I belave," answered Pat, "but where I have been to, or what I have been about, or where this is happening bothers me particularly. And how I am ever to get to you is more than I can tell."

"I must go to help him," said I to Esse, "for he will be drifted away, even if he manages to cling to whatever he has got hold of."

"But surely he is drifting towards us," observed Esse. "He has got nearer since he began to speak." Such indeed was the case, and even before Kiddle and Mr Noalles returned with Pember, not only Pat, but two or three other men had been drifted up to us. Pat had helped himself along by striking out with his feet, though he was but a poor swimmer; indeed, I have scarcely ever met an Irish seaman who could swim. We could make out other people still floating at some distance. Now and then a cry was heard. We shouted in return, but there was no reply. It was the last despairing utterance of one of our shipmates, before he sank below the surface. Those on the wreck were already so exhausted that no one could go to their assistance. There were rather more than a dozen altogether, I believe, clinging to the wreck. Several of them, from the exclamations they uttered, I found were suffering from scorching, or the blows they had received from falling pieces of the wreck.

Morning at length dawned upon us poor human beings—the sole survivors of the ship's company, who but a few hours before were I enjoying life and strength. Just then the words which I had heard at the funeral came across my mind—"In the midst of life we are in death." How true it had proved to them. It might prove true to us also, for our prospects of escape were small indeed. Pieces of the wreck were floating about around us, and I thought I made out two or three people still holding on to the fragments, but I could not be certain. In the far distance were the shores of the island. It seemed so far off, that we could scarcely hope to reach it; yet reach it we must, if our lives were to be saved. The sea was smooth, and the warmth of the water prevented our being benumbed from being so long in it. Still, as the sun rose, all hands began to complain of thirst. Something must be done, however. I asked Pember what he would advise, as he, being the highest in rank among us, would have to take the command; but his drinking habits had unnerved him, and he answered, incoherently, "We must swim, I suppose, if we cannot get the wreck under way." Esse and I then turned to Mr Noalles. He had occasionally uttered a deep groan, as if in pain. I found that he was severely hurt, partly from the fire, and also from the blows he had received. At first, apparently, he had not been aware how seriously he had been injured. "We must build a raft, lads," he answered at length. "See! Here is the main-yard alongside of us, with the main-sail and plenty of rope hanging on to it. We shall have no lack of materials, but there are not many of us, I am afraid, fit for the work." He spoke too truly. Esse and I had escaped the best. Kiddle, also, was only slightly injured, and two of the ship's company had escaped, while all the rest were more or less hurt, two or three of them very badly. It seemed a wonder they could have got on to the wreck, while Pember, either from external injury or the shock his nerves had received, was likely to be of little use.

While we were looking out for the spars and pieces of timber to form our raft, a round object appeared at a little distance. "It's a pumpkin!" cried one of the men. I darted into the water and struck out for it. Thankful, indeed, was I to get such a prize. I soon brought it back. It was meat and drink to us, and though, divided into so many, there was little for each, yet it might assist in saving our lives. A double share was awarded me, but I declined taking more than the rest. It revived us greatly, and with our strength somewhat restored, we began the building of our raft. Those who could swim every now and then struck off to get hold of pieces of wood to serve our purpose. Among other things the jolly-boat's mast was found, and it was agreed that it would serve us well for a mast for the raft. It was hard work getting up the canvas which hung down in the water, but at length with our knives we cut off a sufficient quantity for a sail. The rope served as for lashing the spars which we had collected together. At length we managed to get a framework formed. Across this we lashed other spars and planks, but it was a very slow business, for some of the men could only use one hand. Others had their legs so injured that they could not move from where they sat; while so greatly diminished was the strength of everyone of us, that we were unable to secure the lashings as thoroughly as was necessary.

"It is to be hoped no sea will be after getting up, or all our fine work will be tumbling to pieces entirely," observed Pat, as he surveyed what we had done.

"This will never do as it is," observed Mr Noalles. "We must build a platform on the top of it, to keep us out of the water."

There was no lack of materials to do as he proposed, and we, therefore, immediately set about building the platform. Its weight brought the lower part of the raft deeper into the water, but that could not be helped. Some hours passed by while we were thus engaged, and again thirst attacked us. We had only eaten half the pumpkin. Some of the men entreated that they might have the remainder. "Give it them—give it them," sang out Pember, "and give me a piece. It is the last morsel we shall probably put into our mouths." The fruit was cut up into twelve small slices, and distributed evenly. Even now I recollect the delight with which my teeth crunched the cool fruit. Every particle, rind and all, was consumed, as may be supposed. We now stepped our mast, and got a sail ready for hoisting. As the raft was small for supporting so many people, great care was necessary in balancing ourselves on it. Mr Noalles, who was evidently suffering greatly, and three of the men who were most injured, were placed on the platform in the centre. The rest of us ranged ourselves round them, Kiddle steering with a spar, which we had rigged as a rudder. There was very little wind; what there was, was blowing in the direction of the low land of Sumatra, which we calculated to be about four leagues off. Mr Noalles told us that some fifteen or twenty leagues to the north of it was

CHAPTER NINETEEN. 105

a Dutch settlement. If we could reach it, we might there obtain assistance. By this time Pember had roused up a little, and was able to assume the command of our frail craft, for when he had his proper wits about him he was a very good seaman. Noalles, meantime, was getting worse and worse. It was nearly two hours after noon before our task was accomplished. We had picked up everything we could find floating about the wreck, but not a particle of food appeared, nor did a cask of water pass near us. What would we not have given for that. All this time the sun, in burning splendour, had been beating down upon our unprotected heads, for most of us had lost our hats. I secured a handkerchief round my head, and Esse did the same.

"Are you all ready, lads?" asked Pember. "Ay! Ay! Sir," was the answer. "Then shove off, and I pray we may reach yonder coast before dark." We glided slowly on. For some time we appeared to be approaching the land. Then, from the way we moved, we discovered that a current was running, and was carrying us to the southward, rather away from than nearer the point we hoped to reach. Mr Noalles, who was just able to sit up, saw what was happening.

"I thought so," he muttered. "With so great a wretch as I am on board, there is little chance of the raft reaching the shore. If the people were wise they would heave me overboard; but, oh! I am not fit to die. I dare not face death and that which is to come after it!"

These words were said in so low a tone that I alone, who was sitting close to him, could understand him.

"Die! Did I say? And yet how often have I faced death, without a moment's thought of the future, or a grain of fear!"

"What makes you then think so much about it now, sir?" I asked. "I hope we shall get on shore, and that you will recover." I was anxious to calm the feelings of the poor man, though I was scarcely surprised to hear him speak as he did.

"Is that you, Burton?" he said, hearing my voice. "They tell me that we have been shipmates before, and that I was on board the ship when you were born; but I don't remember the circumstance."

"I have been told so," I said, "and the man steering, Toby Kiddle, remembers you."

"Ah! Yes, I think I have an idea of your mother—a pretty woman. Where is she now?" And I told him that she was living with Mrs and the Misses Schank, and I added, "There is another sister—a Mrs Lindars, whose husband deserted her."

"Mrs Lindars?" he said slowly, "and is she still alive?"

"Yes," I answered, rather astonished at the question.

"I have been saved another crime!" he muttered between his teeth. He was silent for some minutes. Then he abruptly addressed me. "Burton, I believe I am dying. I should like to make a clear bosom before I go out of the world. A viler wretch than I am has never been borne shrieking through the air by demons to the place of torment. You speak of Mrs Lindars. She is my wife, for that is my real name. I have borne many since then. I was young then, and so was she—very young and very beautiful, I thought. I wished to run away with her, but she would not consent, and we married. At first I thought I could settle down in the country, and support myself by my literary and musical talents. I soon found that this would not bring me a sufficient income to supply my wants, for I had somewhat luxurious tastes. My wife gave birth to a child—a daughter. She was a sweet little creature. I loved her in a way I never loved anything before. Each year she increased in beauty. At length I had an opportunity of obtaining a large sum by committing a crime. A fearful crime it was, and yet I did not hesitate. It was necessary to fly the country. I could not bear the thoughts of leaving my child behind me. It was a cruel act to desert my wife, and still more cruel to carry away the child, for I knew that her mother loved her as much as I did. My wife was ill, and I pretended to take the child to see a relation, from whom I told her I had expectations. I knew she could not follow me. Changing my name, I crossed to France where I had relations. I never cared for gambling, or I should probably quickly have got through my ill-acquired wealth. I had followed the sea during the early part of my life, and soon again I got tired of remaining on shore. I was eager to start on a new expedition, but what to do with my daughter in the meanwhile I could not decide. I ought in common humanity to have sent her back to her poor mother; but had I done so, I was afraid I should not be able again to see her. She was so young when I took her away that she did not know her real name. I therefore carried her to Jersey, to which island my family belonged, and there left her, pretending that her mother was French, and had died soon after her birth. The arrangement having been made, I came out to the Indian Seas and China, and, engaging in the opium trade, made a considerable sum of money. I lost, however, the larger portion, and then once more, seized with a desire to see my child, I returned to Jersey. I found her grown into a beautiful girl. A new undertaking had presented itself to me. I would go out to India, and make my fortune by serving under one of the native princes. I had several times visited that country during my wanderings. My daughter, I knew, would materially aid me in my undertaking. As I placed before her the advantages to be gained in the most glowing colours, and hid what I knew would be objectionable, she willingly consented to accompany me. Her beauty, I felt sure, would enable me to secure a wealthy marriage for her, but, as that might not assist my views, I secretly resolved to throw her in the way of some native prince, and she, once becoming his favourite wife, I felt very sure that I should rise to the highest offices in his court. The degradation to which I was dooming my child did not deter me; indeed, I persuaded myself that I was about to procure a splendid position for her, which she might well be satisfied to gain."

CHAPTER TWENTY.

Mr Noalles, as I will still call him, spoke with difficulty, but some secret impulse, it seemed, made him anxious to disburden his mind. "I make these confessions to you, Burton," he said, "because I want you to convey to my poor wife, should you ever return to England, the expression of my sorrow for the way I treated her; and if you can by any means discover my daughter, that you may tell her, her miserable father died blessing her; though, alas! I feel that blessings proceeding from such lips as mine may turn to curses. But I did not tell you that mercifully she escaped the dreadful fate to which I devoted her. Among the passengers on board the ship in which we went out to India was a young writer. He was pleasing in his manners, but far more retiring and silent than his companions, and I did not for a moment suppose that he was likely to win the affections of my daughter. He had already been in India some years, and was returning after a short absence. He therefore knew the country, and immediately on landing proceeded to his station. I flattered myself that I had got rid of him, for latterly I had observed that my daughter was more pleased with his society than with that of anybody else on board. We remained some time at Calcutta, where, as I expected, my daughter was greatly admired. I, meantime, was perfecting myself in Hindostanee, and gaining information to guide my further proceedings. At length we got off up the country, but on the way I was taken seriously ill. It happened to be at the very station where Mr Bramston was residing. He heard of my being there and instantly called, and very naturally pressed his suit with my daughter. Believing that I was dying, I consented to his becoming her lawful protector, for otherwise I dreaded lest she should be left in the country alone and destitute. Scarcely, however, had the marriage taken place than I recovered, and all the plans I had designed were brought to nothing. I found that my character was suspected, and hastening back to Calcutta, I took a passage on board a ship bound for Canton, again changing my name to that by which you know me. From that time forward I have knocked about in these seas in various capacities, just able to support myself, but ever failing to gain the wealth for which I had been ready at one time to sell my soul. Of the child I had loved so dearly I had never heard. If she wrote to me, her letters must have miscarried, and from that day to this I have received no tidings of her. Often and often I have thought of returning to India, but the dread of being recognised has deterred me, and I felt that my appearance would more likely produce shame and annoyance than afford her any satisfaction or pleasure. Thus all my plans and schemings have come to an end, and such fruits as they have produced have been bitter indeed; I cannot talk more, Burton. Promise me that you will try to find out my daughter and her husband. Bramston, remember,

Charles Bramston of the Civil Service—the Bengal Presidency, and his wife bore the name of Emily Herbert. Herbert was the name I then assumed. She often asked me questions about her childhood, but I invariably led her off the subject, so that of that she knew nothing. Tell her that you saw her father die, and that his last thoughts were of her."

I entreated the unfortunate man to keep up his spirits. I pointed out that we were approaching the shore, and that before many hours had passed we should probably land on it; when, although the Dutch were our enemies, our forlorn condition would assuredly excite their compassion, and induce them to afford us all the relief we could require. "Do not trust too much to them," he answered slowly. "Besides, the natives on this coast are savage fellows, who would scruple very little to put us all to death, and as to getting on shore at all, you will not be there for many hours, depend on that!"

He ceased; appearing very much exhausted from having spoken so long. His sufferings, indeed, also, had become very intense, for the salt water and the heat of the sun had greatly inflamed his legs, which had been severely burnt. His voice, in a short time, almost failed, but his lips continued to move, and I heard him murmuring, "Water! Water! Oh! Give me but one drop to cool my tongue! Where am I? Is this hell begun already? Water! Water! Will no one have compassion on a burning wretch?"

Still, so strong was his constitution, that in spite of his sufferings he lingered on. Another poor man, apparently not more hurt than he was, in a short time sank under the injuries he had received. The man had been sitting up trying to catch a breath of air, when suddenly he uttered a low groan, and fell back on the platform.

"The poor fellow is dead, I am afraid," said Esse, taking up his hand, which fell helpless to the position from which it had been raised. "Can we do anything to restore him?"

"There is no use," said Pember, putting his hand on the man's mouth, "he will never speak again. The sooner we heave him overboard the better."

He was the first of our number we had to launch into the deep. The body floated astern for some time, and we could scarcely help casting uneasy glances at it. "Oh! Look! Look! He was alive after all!" exclaimed Esse. We turned round. The body seemed to rise half out of the water, the arms waving wildly. Then down it sank and disappeared from view. We also expected to hear a shriek proceed from it. "Oh, Pember!" I exclaimed, "why did you let us throw him overboard? What a dreadful thing!"

"Save your sympathy for those who want it, youngster," answered the old mate. "He was as dead as a door nail. Don't fear that. Jack Shark had got hold of his heels, and that made the body rise suddenly out of the water, as you saw him. Well! It will be the lot of more of us before long. I do not like the look of the weather. I wonder what Mr Noalles thinks of it." Noalles, however, was unable to speak. The wind was increasing, and the sea had already got up considerably, making the raft work in a very unsatisfactory manner. We had the greatest difficulty in holding on, while the smaller pieces of timber, which had been less securely lashed to

CHAPTER TWENTY.

the frame-work, began to part. Still we ran towards the island, our sail helping us considerably. As the sea increased, steering became more difficult, while the lower part of the raft was so completely immersed in the water, that we had the greatest difficulty in preventing ourselves being washed off, when the foaming seas came rolling over it. We held on as best we could, by the beckets, which had been secured to the raft for this purpose. We had all now reason to dread that we should lose our own lives; for though the raft appeared to be still approaching the shore, yet so furiously was it tumbled about by the fast rising seas, that we could with difficulty cling on to it, while we could scarcely hope that it would hold together. Noalles, as I have said, had been with Pember and two other men on the platform. A foam-covered sea came roaring towards us. We all held on to the main part of the raft. The sea struck it, and before we could make any effort to secure it, away it was carried, to a considerable distance from us, with our three shipmates still resting on it. It seemed surprising that they should not have been washed off. The same sea carried off one of our number, thus leaving six of us only clinging to the main part of the raft. At the same moment our mast and sail were carried away, and we were left at the mercy of the seas. In vain we endeavoured with the paddles, which we had saved, to get up to the other raft. It appeared to be receding further and further from us, when another sea, similar in size to that which had torn it from the main part, struck it with full force, and hid it from our view. We looked again. The few fragments of the wreck could alone be seen; but our late companions had sunk beneath the surface of the troubled waters, which now leaped, and foamed, and raged above their heads. We had little time to mourn their fate, for we were compelled to look after our own safety. Night was coming on. A dreary prospect was before us. Still Pat Brady kept up his spirits wonderfully. "Sure, Mr Burton, old Mother Macrone of Ballynahinch was after prophesying you would become an admiral one of these days, and sure if we was drownded, we should not live to see it, nor you neither for that matter; and so sure as Mistress Macrone is an honest woman, and spoke the truth, we need not be after throubling ourselves about not getting to land. It will be some time before we can manage to reach it, however." I cannot say that Paddy's remarks had much effect on us, although I fully believe he spoke what he thought to be the truth. We were still a long way from the land, when darkness settled down upon us, and the shattered raft continued tossing up and down on the foaming seas. Every instant we thought would be our last, for we knew that the spars to which we were clinging might be torn from the frame-work, and we might be deprived of our last remaining support. Still, life was sweet to all of us. We who had escaped were the least injured of the party. Twelve had left the wreck, six now alone remained alive, two only of the crew of the ill-fated frigate—Smith, an Englishman, and Sandy McPherson, from the North of the Tweed. They were both brave, determined fellows, but Sandy's spirit was troubled, not so much, apparently, by the fearful position in which we were placed, as by what he called Pat Brady's recklessness and frivolity. Even when thus clinging to our frail raft, now tossed high up on a foaming sea, now sent gliding down into the bottom of the trough with darkness around us, almost starved, and our throats parched by thirst, Brady's love of a joke would still break forth. "Arrah, but it's illegant dancing we're learning out here!" he exclaimed, "though, faith, I would rather it were on the green turf than footing it on the top of the green waves, but we will be safe on shore before many hours are over."

"Ay, laddie, but it's ill dancing o'er the graves of your friends," observed Sandy. "Just think where they are, and where we may be not ten minutes hence. You will not keep the breath in your body half that time under the salt water, and we may, one and all of us, be fathoms deep before five minutes have passed away."

Sandy spoke what we all knew to be the truth, but still we would rather have shut our eyes to the unpleasant fact. It is extraordinary that men should be able to disregard the future, even when on the very brink of the grave. Is it apathy, or stolid indifference, or disbelief in a future existence that enables them to do so? I speak of those without the Christian's hope—men who lead profligate lives; men stained with a thousand crimes; men who have never feared God, who seemed scarcely to have a knowledge of God. I have thought the matter over, and have come to the conclusion that some men have the power of shutting out thought. They dare not let thought intrude for a moment. They struggle desperately against thought. Sometimes thought conquers, and then fearful is their condition. Then the terrors of hell rise up, and they would give ten thousand worlds to escape the doom they know well they have merited. Even now I do not like to think of that night. Slowly the hours dragged on. We fancied as we rose to the top of the sea, that the wind was blowing with even greater force than before, and our frail raft was dashed here and there, with even greater violence than it had yet endured. We felt it breaking up. With a desperate grip we held on to the larger portions of the timber which composed it. At length it parted, and Kiddle and I were left clinging to one part, while our four companions held on to the other. We could scarcely hope finally to escape. The two portions, however, continued floating within hailing distance of each other. We shouted to our friends to hold on. Pat Brady answered with a cheerful "Ay! Ay!" It cheered our spirits somewhat, though not very greatly, it must be owned. From that moment the sea appeared to be going down, and gradually daylight, which we thought had been much further off, stole over the world of waters. Fortunately there were some thin boards still secured to the portion of the raft which supported Kiddle and me. We agreed to tear them up, and with them to paddle towards our friends.

After a considerable amount of labour we reached them, and immediately set to work, as the sea had again become almost smooth, to repair our raft. So thirsty had we become by this time, that it was with difficulty we could avoid drinking the salt water. We counselled each other, however, not to do so, well knowing the ill effects which would be produced. We felt now the loss of our sail, for the wind was setting directly on shore. Still, slight as was the breeze, it assisted us along, when we stood up, which we did by turns, while the rest laboured with the paddles we had constructed. We gazed anxiously at the land, but the current still appeared to be sweeping towards the south. Suddenly it changed, and we advanced with far more rapidity than we had hitherto done. We could now distinguish objects on the shore. We looked out eagerly. No houses or huts were to be seen, nor any vessels at anchor. A heavy surf, however, was setting on the beach, and Kiddle urged us on no account to attempt to land there. This was tantalising, but the danger of having

CHAPTER TWENTY.

our raft upset and being carried out to sea was too great to be encountered. With might and main, therefore, we continued to paddle along the shore, hoping to find some place into which we might stand with less danger. We had to continue for some distance, till at length we got round a point by which the land on the other side was completely sheltered. We could scarcely hope to find a better place. And now, exerting ourselves to the utmost, we made towards the beach. With thankfulness did we hear the timbers grate against the sand. Esse and Brady, who were nearest the shore, attempted to spring on to the beach, but so weak were they, as we all were, that in doing so they fell flat on their faces. Had we not kept the raft off with our paddles, the next sea which came up would have thrown it over them. By great exertions they worked themselves up, however, out of the reach of the water, and the rest of us crawled on shore with more caution. We looked round. No one was to be seen. Our first impulse was to throw ourselves down on the sand and rest, but scarcely had we done so when the sensation of thirst came over us, and weak as we were we set out at once to search for water. The trees came down very nearly to the shore, here and there rocks appearing among them. We soon separated, each one going in the direction in which he hoped he should find the longed-for fluid. I went forward almost as in a dream. My eye at length caught sight of a rock at a little distance. I had a feeling that water would be found not far off. A sound struck my ear—a low, soft, trickling. Yes! It was water, I was sure of it—I almost fell in my eagerness to hurry on. I cannot easily forget the delight with which my eye rested on a natural fountain—a rocky basin, into which a bright stream flowed from a crevice in the rock. I rushed on shouting out "Water! Water!" Eagerly I put my mouth to the pure fountain-head. Oh! How deliciously sweet I found it! I let it run over my face, parched and cracked by the hot sun and salt water. Brady, who was nearest to me, heard me shout. "Hurrah, lads! Hurrah, lads! Here's water!" he cried out, making a few attempts at leaps, as he rushed forward. The others took up the cry, till the whole six of us were putting our mouths to the fountain, for scarcely had I withdrawn mine than I returned again for a fresh draught, the others doing the same thing. It is surprising that we did ourselves no harm by the quantity we swallowed. Brady declared that he heard it fizzing away as it went down his throat, from the heat of his inside.

CHAPTER TWENTY ONE.

Having quenched our burning thirst, our next impulse was to seek for rest. Since we had been sleeping on the deck of the ill-fated frigate, not one of us had closed his eyes. Collecting, therefore, a quantity of dried leaves and boughs, we made a bed, on which we threw ourselves, the boughs forming a shade overhead. In an instant almost I was asleep, and so, I believe, were most of my companions. We had escaped the dangers of the sea, but we had a good many more to encounter. The thoughts of them, however, could not drive away sleep. I was awakened by feeling a gnawing sensation of hunger. It was not so painful, perhaps, as thirst, but it was very trying. I could have eaten a raw lizard had I found it crawling over my face. My companions soon awoke from the same cause, but nothing eatable, animal or vegetable, could we find. We hurried down to the beach, and searched about for shell-fish. Not one could we see.

"It will not do, lads, to stop here to starve," observed Kiddle. "What do you say, Mr Burton? Had not we better push on along the shore, while we have a little strength left, and try and find some natives who may give us food?"

Esse and I agreed at once to Toby's suggestion, and returning once more to our fountain for another draught, we set out along the coast. Esse and I had on shoes, but, after being so long in the salt water, they became shrunk and shrivelled when they dried, and were rather an inconvenience than any assistance in walking. The rest of the party had no shoes, and the hot sands burned and blistered their feet. We dragged ourselves on for about a mile, or it might have been more, when, turning a point, we saw before us in the deep bay a prow at anchor. She was so close in shore, that should we continue in that direction we could scarcely hope to escape the observation of those on board. Should she prove to be one of the fleet with which we had had the scratch a few days before, her people might not be inclined to treat us very civilly. Still, hunger made us desperate. We pushed on, therefore; when, surmounting a rocky height and looking over the ridge, we saw down below us a party of dark-skinned natives, collected at a short distance from the shore, while three or four other prows were at anchor a little further on. Some of the people were squatting round a fire cooking, others were repairing a boat, and others lying on the ground. An old man with silvery beard, whom we took to be a chief, was seated on a carpet, under the shade of a tree, smoking his long pipe, while two or three men squatted at a little distance, apparently ready to obey his commands. We discovered that they had each of them some ugly-looking weapons in their hands, and it suddenly occurred to us that should we make our appearance together, they might, without asking questions, use them upon our heads. I, therefore, undertook to go forward by myself, advising my companions,

CHAPTER TWENTY ONE. 113

if they saw me killed, to make the best of their way off in an opposite direction.

"By the powers, though, but that will never do!" exclaimed Brady. "If anybody's to be killed, I'm the boy, and so just let me go forward, if you plase."

"No, no," I said, "I am young, and much less likely to excite their anger than you would be."

Pat still demurred. At length I had to exert my authority, and directed him to stay quiet while I went forward. I shall not forget the poor fellow's look of anxiety as he saw me creep away down the hill, for I was anxious that the Malays should not discover from what direction I came. I confess that I did not feel quite comfortable about the matter, but I thought to myself, it is just as well to be killed outright as to die by inches from starvation. The Malays were not a little astonished at seeing an English midshipman in their midst, although I certainly had very little of the smart look which belongs to the genus. The guards in front of the old Rajah, as soon as they cast eyes on me, started to their feet with uplifted weapons, at which I halted, and made a profound salaam to the old gentleman beyond them. It had its due effect, for directly afterwards they lowered their swords, and their looks became much less threatening. I thought, therefore, that I might venture to approach, and advancing slowly, I made another salaam. As I could not speak a word of Malay, I had to explain by signs the intelligence I wished to convey. I therefore pointed to the sea, and then put my hands together, rocking them up and down, in imitation of a vessel, and then making the sound of an explosion, I endeavoured to explain that my ship was blown up. Next, I pointed to myself, holding up one finger, adding five others, and then, moving the palm of my hand from the sea toward the shore, indicated that we had just landed. I judged from the expression of the spectators' countenances that they understood me, and, making another salaam, I asked permission of the Rajah to go and fetch my companions. He nodded, and I hurried off. I could not, however, resist the temptation of passing near the fire where the men were cooking. On it was boiling a large pot of rice. I held out my hands, and entreated that the cooks would put some of their food into them. They understood me, and I presently had my hands filled with hot rice, so hot, indeed, that I nearly let it fall. In spite, however, of the heat, my mouth was soon embedded in it. Before I had gone far, I had eaten the whole of it. I made signs that I should like to take some to my companions, but the Malays in return signified that they must come and fetch it themselves. Pat Brady's delight on seeing me knew no bounds. Followed by the party, I quickly returned. We were none of us objects to excite fear. Malay pirates are not much addicted to feelings of pity. Such we believed to be the occupation of the gentry before us. Smith, I found, could speak a little Malay, and, putting him forward as interpreter, we explained more clearly to the Rajah what had happened, and begged him to help us to reach some European settlement, whence we could find our way back to our ship. This request made him cast a suspicious look at us.

"Are you Dutch?" he asked us suddenly.

Smith assured him that we were British.

"He says, sir, it is fortunate we are so," observed Smith to me, interpreting the

Rajah's reply. "They vow vengeance against the Dutch, whom they say tyrannise over them, and declare that if we had been Dutch they would have cut the throat of every mother's son of us."

"If they have any doubt about the matter," exclaimed Brady, "tell them that I will dance an Irish jig, and, by the powers, that's more than any Dutchman could ever do. But I say, Bill, before I favour them with a specimen of my talents, just hint that a little provender will be acceptable down our throats."

Smith explained that we had a great dancing-man among us, an art in which the chief in his sagacity must be aware the Dutch did not excel, and he hinted that not only to the dancing-man but to the rest of us some food would be very acceptable. The Rajah in reply told him, if we would sit down, our wants should soon be supplied. By this time the messes over the fire were cooked, and, with more liberality than I had expected, the Malays placed before us a couple of bowls full of fish and rice. Without ceremony, we plunged our hands into the food, which disappeared with wonderful rapidity down our throats.

"Take care the bones don't stick in your gullets, boys," cried Pat, every now and then turning round to the Rajah and making him a bow. "I say, Smith, just tell his Majesty, or whatever he calls himself, that as soon as I have stowed away as much as I can carry, I will give him a specimen of the jintalist Ballyswiggan jig that he ever saw in his life before."

Paddy was as good as his word, and no sooner was our meal finished than, jumping up, forgetting all his fatigue, he began dancing a real Irish jig with wonderful agility, making the music with his own voice, crying out to us, every now and then, to strike up an accompaniment. The effect was at all events very advantageous to us, for the old Rajah looked on with astonishment and approval as Paddy continued his performance. When he ceased, the chief called Smith up to him, and spoke a few words.

"He asks where you learnt the art of dancing," said Smith.

"Oh! Jist tell his honour, or his riverence, if that title plaises him the better, that it comes natural to an Irishman with his mother's milk. I have danced ever since I put foot to the ground. Just as natural, tell him, as it comes to him and his friends to go out robbing and murdering, and such like little divartisements."

I rather fancy Smith did not give an exact interpretation of Brady's answer; at all events the performance put the old pirate into a very good humour. Seeing the condition of our clothes, which were the worse for having been soaked in salt water so long, he sent a boat aboard his prow, which returned with a supply of Eastern garments. How they were come by we did not inquire. They had never been worn, and were most probably part of the cargo of some captured trader. We very thankfully put them on, and the chief then told Smith that if we liked to lie down and sleep, we should have another meal when we woke up again, provided our dancing-man would undertake to give more of his performances, as he would then have a few other friends as spectators.

"Tell his honour I will do it with all the pleasure in the world," answered

CHAPTER TWENTY ONE.

Brady, making a salaam at the same time towards the Rajah, who seemed highly pleased with his good manners. The chief then pointed to a shady spot, on which his attendants spread some carpets. Here we thankfully lay down, and I do not think I ever slept more soundly in my life, forgetting all the hardships I had gone through. When we awoke the sun was well-nigh dipping into the ocean, and the Malays had finished the repair of their boat. The old chief was, however, still seated on his carpet, with four or five other individuals, habited much in the same way, and all gravely smoking. As soon as we sat up, another bowl of rice and fresh meat was brought us. After we had partaken of it, the Rajah called to Smith, who told Paddy that he was expected to begin his performance.

"With the greatest pleasure in life!" he exclaimed, springing up, "but you must all come and support me, and sing and clap your hands, and toe and heel it, too, every now and then. It will make my dancing go off better, and show the old boy that we wish to do our best to please him."

Paddy's strength having been completely recruited by his sleep and ample meals, he far outdid his morning's performance, and elicited the warmest signs of approval from the spectators of which Orientals are capable. When it was over, all hands got into the boats, the Rajah taking us with him on board his vessel. We had from the first suspected, as was the case, that the prows did not belong to this part of the country. It being evident that the pirates did not intend us any harm, we went to sleep again soon after we got on board, in spite of our afternoon snooze. At daybreak the fleet of prows made sail for the spot where the frigate had blown up. No part of her was, however, now above water. A few seamen's chests were seen floating about, and pieces of the wreck; and the saddest sight of all, here and there, the corpses of some of our late companions. From the way we were treated, we concluded that our friends did not form part of the fleet with which the boats of the "Resolution" had been engaged a few days before, and of course Smith wisely forbore to mention the subject. Finding that nothing more was to be picked up from the wreck, the pirate fleet continued their cruise along the coast, looking out for trading craft, from China, Java, and other parts. At night, when the weather was fine, we kept under way, like a pack of wolves, hoping to come suddenly upon a quarry. In the day-time the fleet would lie hid behind some point of land, so that they might dart out on any unwary passer-by. I learnt a lesson from their mode of proceeding, from which I hoped some day to benefit, should I, in the course of service, be ever sent to look after such gentry. What were their intentions regarding us all this time we could not tell. The old chief, though ready enough to ask questions of us, was not very communicative in return, and Smith could learn nothing from him.

"Perhaps he intends to demand a ransom for us," I observed.

"He may, sir, but I rather think that he will keep us until some day he is hard pressed by any of our men-of-war, and then he will threaten to cut our throats if our friends do not let him get off, and it is my belief he would do it, sir. These sort of people are very civil as long as you please them, but just get on the other tack, and they will not scruple a moment to knock their best friend on the head."

This was not a pleasant piece of information, but it did not greatly damp our spirits. We had all recovered from the effects of our exposure on the raft, but were getting somewhat weary of our long detention on board the prows. That Smith was right in the description of our hosts, we had soon too clear evidence. It was night. We were gliding calmly over the moon-lit ocean when suddenly we came upon three native craft. Smith said they were Javanese. The prows boarded, one on each side of the strangers. In an instant the Malays threw themselves on board. There was very little resistance, and they returned almost immediately, each man laden with a bale of goods. With wonderful rapidity the more valuable part of the cargo was transferred on board the prows. The chiefs prow remained at a little distance, ready to render assistance apparently if required. Esse and I were watching what was taking place. Presently we saw a figure appear at the stern of the prize. The next instant there was a plunge, and the waters closed over the man's head. Another and another followed. The prow then cast off, and a bright flame burst forth from the merchant vessel. The materials of which she was composed ignited rapidly, and in another instant she was one mass of fire; one after the other was treated in the same way. We had got half-a-mile from the scene before all the vessels taken had burned to the water's edge and sunk, leaving not a trace behind, while we sailed away with the goods which had lately filled their holds. I confess I did not feel quite as comfortable in the society of our friends after this occurrence as I had done before. We had been nearly six weeks on board, and the pirates had taken a considerable number of prizes, when Smith told us that he suspected, from the conversation he overheard, that they were about to return to their own stronghold, to which traders were wont to resort for the purchase of their goods. Our best chance of escape will be to make a bargain with one of the captains, and get him to buy us of the Rajah, we promising to repay him. Esse and I talked over the matter, and, though it did not appear very promising, we of course agreed to attempt it, if we could find no other way of escape. Two nights after this we were at sea, with the wind aft, and the water smooth, though the sky was overcast. Now and then the moon came forth, soon again, however, to be obscured. Our prow was leading. A small vessel, apparently a trader, appeared ahead, and we gave chase. She must have seen us, and made all sail to escape. We pursued eagerly. Now we saw her, now the darkness hid her from sight. On we went. The night was hot, and Esse and I, with our companions, were on the fore-part of the deck watching the chase, hoping heartily she would escape.

"She's distancing us, sir," observed Kiddle. "She's in luck, for I don't think the black fellows will have her this time."

Suddenly the moon beamed forth.

"Hillo! Why, what is that?" exclaimed Esse.

We all eagerly looked out. A little on the starboard-bow, the rays of the bright luminary fell upon the white canvas of a tall ship standing across our course.

"She's a man-of-war, or I am a Dutchman!" exclaimed Kiddle, "and a frigate too."

"Perhaps she is the Orion herself, after all," cried Esse. "Hurrah! Hurrah! Hurrah!"

CHAPTER TWENTY TWO.

Directly the crew of the prow discovered the frigate they lowered the sails, and getting out the oars, began to pull her head round in the direction of the wind's eye. At that moment, however, the chase had got close to the frigate.

"She is telling her what sort of gentry we are, and depend upon it she will be after us directly," said Kiddle.

He was right, apparently, for immediately the frigate's head sails were seen shivering in the breeze, and slowly coming about, she stood towards us on the other tack. The other prows discovered her at the same moment that we did, and were now pulling away as fast as their crews could urge them through the water. The frigate, as she approached, began firing from her foremost guns. Had one of her shots struck us between wind and water, it would have sent us to the bottom. As to the prows escaping, it seemed scarcely possible. Still the Malays held on, tugging desperately at their oars. While some of the crew were rowing, the rest were employed in examining the priming of their muskets and feeling the edge of their swords, while a low conversation was carried on among them.

"I do not quite like what they are saying, sir," said Smith to me. "As far as I can make out, they are vowing to Allah, that if the frigate comes up with them they will knock us all on the head and blow themselves up. They are in earnest, I am afraid, for I know their people have done the same sort of thing before now."

"Tell them," I said, "that as they have treated us so well, that if they will haul down their colours we will use our influence with the captain of the ship to have them set at liberty. Tell them we think she is the ship we belong to, and that if they are wise men they will follow our advice."

Smith, knowing pretty well that our lives depended upon the way he might put the matter to the old chief, began to address him slowly. Gradually he grew more energetic and warm. While he was speaking a shot came flying close by us, carrying away the greater number of the oars on one side. Escape now seemed impossible. Again we urged our advice. The chief seemed unwilling to follow it.

"Ask him if he hasn't got a wife or two and a few young children at home who would like to see him again," said Brady to Smith. "Tell him at all events we have, and if he's a wise man that he will live himself and let us live. Faith, it's a little exaggeration as far as some of us are concerned, but if it excites the old gentleman's commiseration, sure Father O'Rouke would absolve me for that as well as a few other lies I have had to tell in my life."

Smith interpreted these remarks. The Rajah spoke to his crew. Directly afterwards the uninjured oars were thrown in.

"We have got your promise, then, young officer, that my people and I shall be uninjured, and shall be allowed to go free?" said the chief.

"Yes," I answered, "I fully believe if that frigate is the one to which we belong, that the captain will carry out my promises."

On this the chief briefly addressed his crew.

The frigate, understanding apparently that we had given in, ceased firing, and directly afterwards hove to. There was just time to lower a boat, when again she stood on in chase of the other prows. The moon was now shining brightly, and by her light we saw a boat approaching us. In a few minutes she was alongside, and her crew, led by an officer, sprang on board. I thought I recognised Oldershaw's figure. "They have given in," I shouted out, "and we have promised that you would spare their lives and let them go free."

"Hillo! Who is that? Bless my heart, who are you?" exclaimed Oldershaw. "What! Ben Burton! Is it possible!"

We were all of us, it must be remembered, in Eastern dresses, finding them far more comfortable than those we had laid aside.

"Yes, and I am here too!" sung out Dicky Esse.

"I am heartily glad of it," exclaimed Oldershaw. "We thought you had all been knocked on the head by the savages long ago. And have any more of you escaped?"

"Yes, sir," said Toby Kiddle. "Here am I, and here's Pat Brady, and these two men of the 'Resolution,' and fortunate men they are, for they are the only ones alive out of the whole ship's company."

Oldershaw now learned from us, for the first time, of the sad loss of the frigate. We told him also how well we had been treated by the Rajah. On this Oldershaw went up and shook him by the hand, and told Smith to assure him that no harm would be done him or his people, and that the captain of the frigate would be very much obliged to him for the way he had treated us. The old chief seemed highly pleased, and ordered pipes and coffee to be brought aft, and in ten minutes we were all seated in the after part of the prow, smoking the fragrant weed and sipping the warm beverage, while the Malays were doing the honours to our men. I need not say, however, that Oldershaw told us all to keep a bright look-out, so that, in case of treachery being intended, we might not be taken by surprise. The frigate stood on, and from the rapid firing we heard, it was pretty evident that she was roughly handling the other prows. The chief shrugged his shoulders. "It was the will of Allah," he said: "if his people were killed, it was not his fault, nor was it ours, so he hoped it would not interfere with our present friendly relations." Such, at least, was something like the interpretation which Smith gave us of his remarks. At length the frigate was seen running back. As she approached, we fired a gun to draw her attention, and in a short time she was up to us, shortening sail as she approached. Another boat now came off from her, when Esse and I went on board and reported ourselves to Captain Oliver. He was walking the quarter-deck when we appeared at the gangway. "What!" he exclaimed, "you my midshipmen! I thought when I saw you that you were a couple of young Malays. Come into the cabin, and let me hear your account. I am, indeed, heartily glad to hear that you have escaped." Mr Schank expressed equal satisfaction at again seeing us, as, indeed, did all our shipmates. When he heard how well we had been treated by the old Rajah, he sent to request his presence on board, that he might thank him personally for his kindness to us. After some little delay, notice was given that the Rajah was coming on board in one of our boats. The sides were manned to do him honour, and in a short time he appeared at the gangway, no longer habited in the dingy costume in which we had seen him, but superbly dressed with a turban glittering with gems, and richly jewelled sword by his side, attended by four other persons also finely habited. Without the slightest embarrassment, he followed the captain, after a due amount of salaams had passed between them, into the cabin. He there took his seat with perfect composure, and Smith was summoned to act as interpreter. Captain Oliver again thanked him for his kindness to us, and then took occasion to express his regret that he should ever be engaged in deeds of which the English could not approve, such as robbing vessels and knocking their crews on the head, or sending them overboard. The old chief did not for a moment deny that such were his usual occupations, but observed quietly that his fathers had done the same before him, and, as it was necessary to live, he should be glad to hear if the English chief could point out any better occupation. "Surely," he remarked, "you do just the same. What are all these guns for? For what are the arms you and your people carry, but to rob and kill your enemies?" and the old gentleman chuckled, fully believing that he had checkmated the infidel chief.

"Well, well," answered Captain Oliver, "we will talk of that another time; but have you any favour to ask which it is in my power to grant, as I shall be glad to do anything to please you, to show my gratitude."

The Rajah thought a moment. "No," he said. "You have refrained from sending my vessel to the bottom when you had the power to do so, and I have no more to ask since you allow me to go free. But there is one favour. I should like again to see your dancing-man go through his wonderful performance."

Until we explained the remark, Captain Oliver was puzzled to know what his guest meant. "What do you say, Schank. We have a few men on board who can dance, besides the Irishman, have we not?"

"Yes, sir, there are several," observed Mr Schank.

"Very well, just go and make such arrangements as you can best manage on deck, and we will have our guest up when all is ready." In a short time Tom King entered the cabin.

"Please, sir," he reported, "the ball-room is prepared, and the dancers are ready."

"Very well," said the Captain, and he made a sign to our Malay friends to accompany him on deck.

A number of the crew with lanterns in their hands had been arranged round

CHAPTER TWENTY TWO. 121

the quarter-deck. On the after part, carpets and cushions had been spread, on which our guests were requested to take their seats, while between every two men with lanterns stood others, each with a blue light case in his hand. We had on board a couple of fiddlers, besides the marines' fifes and drums. All our musical powers had been mustered for the occasion.

"Strike up!" cried Mr Schank, and the fiddlers began to play, joined in by the other instruments as they did so. The circle of lantern men opened, and Pat Brady, followed by nearly a dozen other men, sprang into the centre. Pat first performed a jig for which he was celebrated. It was followed by a regular sailor's hornpipe. When this was finished, the band struck up a Scotch reel. At the same time the blue lights were ignited, and four men in kilts and plaids sprang into the circle and commenced a Highland fling, shrieking and leaping, and clapping their hands in a way that made the old Rajah almost jump off his cushions with astonishment, the glare of the blue lights increasing the wild and savage appearance of the dancers.

"Bismillah! These English are wonderful people!" exclaimed the old Rajah. "If they would but follow the prophet, and take to piracy like us, they might possess themselves of the wealth of all the world, for who could stand against them!" So delighted was the old gentleman with his entertainment, that he declined receiving any further present with the exception of a few bottles of rum, which he could not bring himself to refuse. He promised also that should any English people fall into his power, that, for the sake of us and our dancing friends, he would always treat them with kindness, and assist them in reaching any port they might desire.

We now put him on board his prow, and sent him rejoicing on his way. Possibly he might not have been so well-pleased when he came to discover that three of his fleet had been sunk by our guns, and yet he was evidently too great a philosopher to allow such a matter to weigh heavily upon his spirits. I was very thankful to be once more on board the frigate. Captain Oliver treated me and Esse with the greatest kindness, for, though we had kept up our spirits, we were rather the worse for the hardships we had gone through, and the strain on our nerves; for midshipmen have nerves, whatever may be thought to the contrary, though they are fortunately very tough and not easily put out of order. We were accordingly put into the sick list and relieved from duty for a couple of weeks. I repeated to Mr Schank the account which Mr Noalles had given me of himself. He was greatly astonished at what I told him.

"I little thought the man I knew so well when I was last in these seas was the one who had behaved so cruelly to my poor sister," he said. "However, he has gone, and peace be to his memory. I will do my utmost to discover his daughter, and I should think, as Mr Bramston must be well-known in Bombay, there can be little difficulty in doing that. I will write the first opportunity to a friend I have in Calcutta, and get him to make all the inquiries in his power." After cruising for some months among the East India Islands, we returned to Canton. We were there directed to convoy a fleet of merchantmen round to Calcutta. What with risks from pirates, from rocks and shoals, from hurricanes, from enemies' cruisers, and from the unseaworthiness of some, it is a wonder that we managed to bring the greater portion of the vessels under our charge safe to their destination. Mr

Schank's friend told him that he had inquired for Mr Bramston, and found that he had for some years been residing as a district judge in Ceylon, where, indeed, he had passed the greater portion of his time. He understood that he was alive and married, but how long he had been married he could not tell, or whether he had married a second time. This much was satisfactory.

We had now been upwards of four years on the station, and were every day expecting to be ordered home. The Admiral, however, told our Captain, that not having more frigates on the station than he required, he must keep us till we were relieved. We were just weighing anchor to proceed back to Canton, when a frigate was seen standing towards us.

She soon made her number. "The Thetis." The signal book was in instant requisition, and the answer to our question was: "Direct from England to relieve the 'Orion'." The signal midshipman threw up his hat as he read it. A shout ran along the decks. Before she had come to an anchor, our boat was alongside, and returned with a bag of letters and newspapers. We delayed our departure that we might receive her letters home in return. For a long time I had not heard from my mother. She was well, and she gave me a very good account of Mrs and the Misses Schank, and the dear Little Lady. But she said that she herself was sorely annoyed by letters from Mr Gillooly, who still persevered in his suit. "They are warm enough and devoted enough in all conscience," she observed, "so much so, indeed, that I feel sure they are written under the influence of potent tumblers of whisky. Though I never could endure a milk-sop, yet I have a still greater objection to the opposite extreme. Besides, Ben," she added, "my dear boy, however my friends may urge me, I wish to die as I have lived, faithful to the memory of your brave father."

I could not but applaud the resolution of my mother, at the same time that I felt anxious that she should do whatever would most conduce to her happiness. The officers and parties of the ships' companies having exchanged visits with each other, we bade our relief farewell, and with joyous hearts made sail for Old England.

CHAPTER TWENTY THREE.

Old England was reached at length. I need not give the particulars of the passage home. Nothing very particular occurred. Portsmouth was a very busy place in those days. Ships fitting out or paying off kept up a constant bustle. The water was alive, the streets were alive with human beings, and the inns were full of them. We were several days paying off, but at length were once more free. I was eager to go and see my mother, and the Little Lady, and our kind friends. Mr Schank, having business in Portsmouth, told me to go on before him, promising to follow in a few days.

"Give my love to my mother and sisters, and my very kind regards to your excellent mother," he said.

I thought he looked somewhat oddly as he spoke, and I have an idea that a more ruddy glow than usual came over his features; but that of course might have been fancy. Oldershaw, who lived a little to the north of Whithyford, agreed to accompany me, and Dicky Esse and Tom Twig happened to be going up to London the same day. We therefore all took our places on the coach together. Oldershaw had secured the box seat; we three took our places behind him. There was one other spare place, and we were wondering who would occupy it, when a stout, large-whiskered, middle-aged man climbed up and took the seat. By the way he stepped up, and by his general appearance, I saw at once that he was a seaman. Whether he was an officer or not I could not exactly make out. The guard's horn sounded, and off we dashed up Portsmouth High Street. I had by this time grown into a tall, well-made lad. I looked indeed, as I was, quite a young man, particularly contrasted with my companions, who, though really older, were both remarkably small for their age. We were not too old, however, to be up to all sorts of midshipmen-like pranks, and Oldershaw had some difficulty in keeping us in order. Dicky and Tom were somewhat inclined to play their tricks on our companion, and made several attempts to sell him. He took their jokes, however, in very good part, and always turned their batteries upon themselves. I was sitting on the opposite side to him.

"Take care what you are about," I whispered to Esse. "He may be a post-captain or an admiral, and you will find he is one of your examining captains when you come to pass."

"They do not travel on the top of stage coaches," answered Dicky. "Only small fry enjoy that privilege—lieutenants, mates, and midshipmen."

"Do not be too sure of that," I said. "At all events, you may find him the First-Lieutenant of the next ship you join, and he may not forget your free and easy style."

"If he is worth his salt he will not harbour revenge for what I have said or done," persisted Dicky.

However, I observed that both he and Twig were more careful than before in their way of addressing the stranger. I heard them telling him where we had been and some of the adventures we had gone through.

"Have you ever been out in those parts, sir?" asked Tom.

"Yes, and I know something about them, but it is a good many years ago, probably before any of you young gentlemen were born, or so much as thought of," answered the stranger.

"Have you been away from England lately?" asked Tom.

"For a good many years, young gentleman," answered the stranger.

"To a distant station, I suppose—to North America or the West Indies?"

"No," answered the stranger; "I have been where I hope you may never be, and where I may never be again—kept from all you love or care for on earth. I have been inside the walls of a French prison."

"I hope not, indeed," said Tom. "Parlez-vous Français, Monsieur?"

"As to that, I may understand a few words, but it is no pleasant matter to learn the lingo of one's enemies, and I felt something like an old master who was shut up with me, and declared he would never prove such a traitor to his country as to learn one single French word all the time he was in prison."

In a very short time Dicky and Tom got back to their chaffing mood. I was sorry not to have some conversation with the stranger. The latter, however, did not seem inclined to exchange jokes with them and became silent, every now and then, however, speaking a few words with Oldershaw, behind whom he sat. We separated in London, where Oldershaw took us to a respectable lodging-house with which he was acquainted, and early the next morning we started by the coach for Lincolnshire. Oldershaw and I occupied the only two places outside.

Just as the coach was starting, who should we see but the stranger who had come up with us from Portsmouth.

"There is one place inside if you do not mind taking it," said the guard. "Very sorry, otherwise you will have to wait for the night coach, or to-morrow morning."

The stranger stepped in and the coach drove off. I need not describe the incidents of the journey. It was dusk when we arrived at Whithyford. At length the light from the window of the little inn, at the end of the lane where I purposed getting down, appeared in sight. Begging the coachman to stop, I wished Oldershaw good-bye, and descended from my perch on the roof. My chest and bag were handed down, and the coach drove on.

"I cannot believe my eyes, Master Burton, sure it's not you!" exclaimed Mrs Fowler, the landlady of the "Wheatsheaf."

CHAPTER TWENTY THREE. 125

I assured her that I was no other than little Ben Burton, though somewhat increased in bulk during the five years I had been absent.

"And my mother?" I asked. "Is she well? And her kind friends?" The answer was satisfactory. The Misses Schank had, however, gone out to a tea party at Mr Simmon's the lawyer.

"And my mother?" I asked, "is she there too?"

"Oh! No, Lor' bless you, she never goes to such gay doings. She would be stopping to look after the old lady, who keeps up wonderfully. And I should not be surprised but what you find somebody else there. There was a strange gentleman came over from Ireland some days gone, and has been stopping in my house. He is a free and easy spoken sort of man, though I do not understand all he says, for he speaks in the Irish way, but he is a good customer at the bar, and is liberal-handed enough. However, Master Burton, I do not know as I should advise your mother to go and do it. You see if he was to ask me, it would be a different matter. I could hold my own. Besides, I am accustomed to such doings as his. When my good man that's gone, Simon Fowler, was alive, he was not happy till he had got a few quarts of beer in his inside—not to speak of gin and rum. But do you see, your dear mother is a different sort of person, and it would not do for her to take up with a gentleman with such habits."

I now began to comprehend the drift of the landlady's remarks.

"What!" I exclaimed, "is there a person such as you describe wanting to marry my mother?"

"Well, that's the plain matter of fact," answered Mrs Fowler; "and what is more he swears he will have her. He has come all the way over from Ireland, and is not going back nonplussed."

I was greatly concerned at hearing this, for although, had my mother wished to marry again, I should have been very thankful if she could have found a suitable protector, yet I was sure that such a person as Mrs Fowler described would make her miserable. There was another person I was longing to ask about, but I own, from a somewhat different feeling, I hesitated. "And Miss Emily?" I asked at length, trying to get out of the light of the candle as I spoke. "How is she?"

"Oh! She is the light of the house—the most beautifullest and brightest little creature you ever did see," answered Mrs Fowler, with enthusiasm. "Whether she's the captain's daughter, or anybody else's daughter, it does not matter to me, but I know she is a blessing to all around her."

"Thank you, Mrs Fowler, thank you," I answered, scarcely knowing what I said. "I am anxious to see my mother. Take care of my chest; I will take my bag with me." Saying this, I darted out of the house and hurried down the lane. I well knew how delighted my mother would be to see me, and I had an undefined feeling that the sooner I could be with her the better. Passing through the wicket I found the house-door partly open, and heard a voice proceeding from the back parlour. It was a somewhat loud one too:

"Oh! Mistress Burthen! Mistress Burthen! Ye will be after breaking my heart, ye will; and me waiting for you these long years, and now at last come all the way over from old Ireland to find ye as hard and obdurate as the blacksmith's anvil in the corner of Saint Patrick's street, in Ballybruree," were the first words that caught my ear. "Shure you will be afther relenting and not laving me a disconsolate widower, to go back to Ballyswiggan all alone by myself."

"Indeed, Mr Gillooly, I feel that your constancy—your pertinacity shall I call it?" and there was a slight touch of sarcasm in the voice,—it was my mother who spoke, "deserves to be rewarded; but at the same time I confess that I cannot bring myself to undertake to recompense you as you desire. All I can do is to give you my best advice, and that is to try and find some other lady who is more disposed to receive your addresses than I am."

I did not wish to be an eaves-dropper, and at the same time I scarcely liked suddenly to rush unnoticed into the room. Old Mrs Schank would, I concluded, be in the front parlour, and perhaps Emily might be with her, and I would ask her to break my arrival to my mother. Again Mr Gillooly pleaded his cause. I began to fancy, from the tone of my mother's voice and the answers she made, that she was somewhat relenting. I knew enough of the world to be aware that even sensible people sometimes marry against their convictions, and I thought it was now high time for me to interfere. Just then I heard my mother exclaim:

"Who's that? I saw someone at the window. It is impossible; yet— Oh! Mr Gillooly, you are very kind, you are very generous, but I cannot, I cannot marry you. After what I have just now seen, it is impossible!"

"It's on my knees, then, I implore you, widow Burthen!" exclaimed Mr Gillooly. "Oh! Say, would you render me a desperate man and send me forth to join the Ribbonmen, or Green Boys, or other rebels against King George? It's afther killing me ye'll be by your cruelty; and it's more than Jim Gillooly can stand, or has stood in his life, and so by the powers, Mistress Gillooly, you shall be, in spite of your prothestations and assartions, and—"

I now thought it high time to interfere, and rushing into the room, presented myself to the astonished gaze of Mr Gillooly, who was on the point of rising from his knees, with anger depicted on his countenance, and a gesture sufficient to alarm even a less timid person than my mother. She was staring with eyes open and lips apart towards the window which looked into the garden. The light from the lamp on the table fell on the face and figure of a man whom I at once recognised as my fellow-traveller from Portsmouth.

"Who are you?" exclaimed Mr Gillooly, as he saw me advancing. "That lady's son," I answered.

"Then out upon you for an impostor. That lady can have no big spalpeen of a son like you!" exclaimed Mr Gillooly, rushing towards me with uplifted fist. I could easily have escaped him by flight, but that I disdained to do, though his blow was likely to be one capable of felling me to the ground. My mother uttered a scream. At that instant the window was flung open, and in sprang the stranger. The scream arrested my assailant. He turned his head and discovered the stranger, a man of powerful frame, rushing towards him.

CHAPTER TWENTY THREE.

"Murther! murther! I'm betrayed!" shouted Mr Gillooly. "Oh! Widow, it's all your doing, and you have led me into an ambush! Murther! Murther!" and without stopping to pick up his hat or whip he rushed from the door and out through the garden and along the lane, so I concluded, as I heard his heavy footsteps growing less and less distinct as he gained a distance from the cottage.

CHAPTER TWENTY FOUR.

I left my mother, at the end of the last chapter, standing in the middle of the back parlour of Mr Schank's cottage, her Irish admirer, Mr Gillooly, scampering up the lane as fast as his two legs would carry him, the stranger who accompanied me from Portsmouth having just before, most opportunely for me, sprung through the window and saved me from the effects of that worthy's anger.

I had no disposition to follow him; indeed, I had a matter of far more interest to occupy my attention at the moment. My mother sank into a chair. I sprang forward to embrace her, and while she threw one of her arms round my neck, she pointed at the stranger, exclaiming:

"Is it real, or am I in a dream? Who are you? Say! Say! Do not mock me!"

"Polly, you are my own true loving wife, and I am your live husband—your faithful Dick Burton!" exclaimed my father, for he it was in reality, as he came forward and took my mother in his arms.

"No wonder you thought me dead, Mary, and a long yarn I have to tell you, how it all happened. And is this young gentleman Ben, our Ben?" he asked, as he put his arm round my neck and kissed me on the brow. "I know it is; yet if I had not seen him here I should not have known him. Well, to see him a quarter-deck officer, and on the road to promotion, and you, Mary, alive and well, and as young looking as ever, repays me for all I have gone through, and that's no trifle."

Now, most women under the trying circumstances I have described would have fainted away or gone into hysterics, but my mother did neither one nor the other. Perhaps we had to thank Mr Gillooly for saving her from such a result. My idea is the agitation which that worthy gentleman had put her into counteracted the effects which might have been produced, first from my sudden appearance, and then by the unlooked-for return of my father. I do not mean to say that she was not agitated, and was very nearly fainting, but she did not faint; indeed, her nerves stood the trial in a most wonderful manner. After I had been with my mother and my newly-found father for some time, I bethought me that I ought to go and pay my respects to Mrs Schank and to Miss Emily, who, my mother told me, was sitting with her; I therefore went to the drawing-room door, and, tapping, asked if I might enter.

"Come in," said a sweet voice. The owner of the sweet voice started when she saw me, for she was evidently uncertain who I could be, while the old lady peered at me through her spectacles.

Emily, however, coming forward, put out her hand.

CHAPTER TWENTY FOUR.

"How delightful! You are welcome back, Ben!" she exclaimed. "I mean Mr Burton. It is Mr Ben Burton, ma'am," she said in a higher key, and turning to the old lady.

"Ah, Ben! You are grown indeed, and you are welcome, lad. You are always welcome," she added after a minute, and made some inquiries of her son. "And you have come back in the very nick of time, for there is an Irish gentleman wants to marry your mother, and we do not like him, do we, Emily?"

"Oh! No, no," said Emily, shaking her head; "it would never do." This gave me the opportunity of saying that Mr Gillooly had taken his departure, and also that there was another very strong reason for my mother's not marrying him—the return of my father. The old lady's astonishment knew no bounds on hearing this. "And my girls are out! Dear me, they will be surprised when they come back. What a pity they should not have been here. It is a mercy your mother did not faint away altogether. And he is actually in the next room. Your father, who has been killed so many years!"

"They thought he was killed, ma'am," exclaimed Emily. "He could not have been killed or he would not be here!"

"No! To be sure! To be sure!" said the old lady. "That is very clear, and very wonderful it is; but if he had been killed it would be still more wonderful! Well, I am very glad he has come back." After a little time I went back to my father and mother, and brought him in to see Mrs Schank and the Little Lady, both of whom welcomed him cordially. I inquired after Mrs Lindars.

"She is much as usual," answered Emily, "but she looks almost as old as grandmamma. You know I call Mrs Schank grandmamma now. She really is like a grandmother to me, and the Misses Schank are like kind aunts, though I look upon your mother, Ben, quite as a mother, for one she has been to me all my life."

I was doubtful how I ought to convey her husband's message to Mrs Lindars. Indeed, I felt that it would be a very difficult task. However, it was managed. I determined first to consult my mother and the poor lady's sisters. At length they returned, and various were the notes of exclamation and astonishment with which they heard of the existence and return of my father, and still more so when they saw him.

"Well, I must say you are a very substantial, good-looking ghost," said Miss Anna Maria, in her funny, chirruping voice, "and a much better husband you will make her, I am sure, than that strange Irishman who has been haunting the village for the last week."

"Thank you, miss," said my father, looking affectionately at my mother.

"And you must stay here as long as you can, Mister Burton," said old Mrs Schank.

"Thank you again, ma'am. I shall be in no hurry to leave my wife now I have come back to her," he said, with a sailor's bow.

"But we want to know, Mr Burton, where you have been, and what you have been about," said Miss Martha Schank.

"That would take up a long time, but I will try and satisfy you ladies as soon as you are ready to hear."

"As to going to bed without some notion, we should not sleep a wink all night for thinking of it, and not be sure, after all, whether you are yourself, or your ghost, or somebody else," exclaimed the Misses Schank almost in chorus, Miss Anna Maria adding the last remark: "We heard that you were knocked overboard and killed attacking a French ship off the coast of Italy. Was that not the case?"

"It is all very true that I was knocked overboard," said my father. "But had I been killed, I do not think I should be here. The fact is, that when I fell into the water I came to myself, and not being able to reach the boats I got hold of the rudder chains of the vessel we had hoped to capture. There I hung on till the anger of the Frenchmen had somewhat cooled down, and then, finding I could hold on no longer, I sang out, and asked them to take me on board. They did so, and there being a surgeon in the ship, he dressed my wounds. They treated me pretty fairly till I got well, I must say that for them, but after that they sent me to a French prison. Unfortunately I had no money in my pocket, and was unable to buy paper to write a letter. What with the hard treatment I received, and the thoughts that my wife and child were left without anybody to look after them, I fell sick, and remained between life and death for many months. A kind French widow and her daughter took compassion on me, and by their means my life was saved. I after this wrote several times, but my letters must have been treated as were many others, and were never sent. I should, however, in time have got my freedom, but I fell in with an English officer who was going to be married, he told me, to a beautiful young lady, just when he was taken, and now she would have to wait for him for many years, or perhaps go and marry somebody else, thinking he was dead. He would, he said, give everything to make his escape, so I promised to help him, which I wished to do for his own sake. But I thought also that I might get away myself. It would be a long yarn if I was to tell you all our plans, and all the tricks we had to play to get out of prison. At last, however, we managed to get free and stand outside the walls of the town. He could talk French like a Frenchman, but I could not say a word. We were both dressed as countrymen—he of the better sort, and I, as a lout, born deaf and dumb. This did very well for some time, and whether or no the country people suspected us I cannot say, but I rather think they did, though many of them were very kind to Englishmen, and would gladly have helped them to escape if they dared. We worked our way north, travelling by unfrequented paths, or, when we had to take to the high road, going on generally at night. We got into high spirits, thinking that all would be right. This made us careless, when one day, just as we were leaving the town, a party of their abominable gendarmes pounced upon us. The captain showed great surprise, and wondered why they should lay hold of two innocent people. This was of no use, however. They soon showed him they knew who we were, and we were marched back to prison, looking very foolish, and the next morning sent off, with several other prisoners, to the place we had escaped from. There we were kept closely shut up. It was very hard and very cruel in them, just because we wanted to get our liberty. I made several other attempts, for I was determined to get free if I could. Life was worth nothing away from my wife and child. At last I succeeded with two others—an officer and another man. We reached the coast, cut out a small boat, and were making our way across the Channel when we were picked up by a man-of-war. It had come on to blow very heavy. Our boat was swamped alongside, and, as she was outward bound, we had to go away in her. I entered on board. We took several prizes, and I filled my empty pockets with gold. I was one of the prize crew of the first man-of-war we took worth sending home, and at last I once more set foot on the shores of England. As soon as I was free of the ship I came down here. There you have my history; I will tell you more particulars another day. It may serve, however, to convince you that I am no ghost, or that if I am, I am a big liar, saving your pardons, ladies, and that is what Dick Burton never was. Besides, I have an idea that my wife believes me, at all events. Don't you, Polly?"

Following my father's example, I must be somewhat brief in the remainder of my yarn. I should say, that soon after his arrival he and my mother took a cottage which happened to be vacant in the village. He fortunately had a considerable amount of prize-money and pay due to him, for which it appeared my mother had neglected to draw, and with this, in addition to what he had lately obtained, he was well able to keep house. Mrs and the Misses Schank, however, insisted upon my remaining with them, which, as may be supposed, I was very glad to do.

I spent a very happy time at Whithyford. Little Emily was my constant companion, and every day I was with her. I learned to love her more and more. At first we talked of being brother and sister, but we knew we were not, and somehow or other in time we came to leave off calling each other so. After this, at first I called her for a few days Miss Emily, but I soon dropped that again. Then I began to talk of how I was going to rise in my profession, and make heaps of prize-money, and I scarcely know, indeed, what I was going to do and be. There was Lord Collingwood, and Lord Nelson, and Lord Saint Vincent, and old Lord Camperdown, who had all been midshipmen once on a time, and were admirals and lords, and why should I not be a lord too? Emily, of course, thought that I should be, and I am not quite certain that we did not choose a title. I was to be Baron Burton of Whithyford, and I took to calling her Lady Burton, and sometimes Lady Whithyford. I do not mind confessing this now. It did no harm, and at all events made us very happy. Why should not people be happy when happiness is so easily obtained—by a little exercise of the imagination? I quite forgot to mention my mother's devout admirer, Mr Gillooly. On inquiring the next morning after our arrival of what had become of him, we found that he had been taken ill and was laid up in bed; so it was said at the "Wheatsheaf," where he remained for some time under the tender care of Mrs Fowler. When he recovered, unwilling to go back to Ireland without an English wife, which he promised he would bring, I rather think to spite some Irish fair one who had refused him, as a reward to the landlady for all her kindness, he made her an offer of his hand, which she accepted. They were married shortly afterwards. She disposed of her establishment, and, dressed in a new satin gown of the gayest colours, accompanied him back, not only as a blooming bride, but, as Anna Maria observed, a thoroughly full-blown one, to become the mistress of Ballyswiggan Hall. When Mr Schank at last came home, there was a great rejoicing, and two days afterwards the postman's knock was heard at the door, and Emily, running out, brought back a long official looking letter.

"It has come at last," he exclaimed, and his voice showed more emotion than he was wont to exhibit. "Oliver is a fine fellow; I knew he would do his best;" and holding up the letter to us all, we saw it was addressed to Commander Schank. "And now the next thing they must do is to give me a ship and post me, and then, mother, I may perhaps do something to place you and my sisters in the position you ought to occupy, and make you all comfortable to the end of your days."

"No, no, Jack! We are as well off as we wish to be. You must marry as you said you would. We would far rather see you married happily than change to the finest house in London."

"No, no, sisters," he answered, and something very like a sigh burst from his heart. "I once had a dream, but that has passed. I shall marry my ship when I get one, and I hope never to lose her while I have life."

Captain Schank was known to be too good an officer to be allowed to remain long unemployed, or I should say Captain Oliver was too zealous a friend to allow his merits to be passed by. At length another letter arrived, appointing him to the command of a fine brig sloop just off the stocks at Portsmouth. He was at once to go down and commission her, and fit her for sea.

"Ben," he said, "Captain Oliver writes me too that you will be appointed to her. You have only one year to serve, and after that he hopes you will get your commission. If the Ministry keeps in and he lives, his hopes will, I am very sure, come true. Oldershaw, as you know, is promoted, and has been appointed Second-Lieutenant of her. The First-Lieutenant is a stranger to me. I see he has been a good many years at sea as First-Lieutenant; but he may not be the worse as a First-Lieutenant on that account I hope. I must get your father to come down to Portsmouth, to help me pick up hands for the brig Oliver hopes to get him a berth on board a ship in ordinary, as some recompense to him for his long imprisonment, and for his gallant efforts to assist the Honourable Captain Burgoyne in escaping from prison.

"You should not miss the opportunity of seeing a ship fitted out. Take my advice. Make yourself practically acquainted with everything on board, from stowing the hold to rigging the topgallant masts." The next day Mr Schank started for Portsmouth, telling me to be prepared to follow him in the course of a few days.

CHAPTER TWENTY FIVE.
CONCLUSION.

The last days I spent at Whithyford ought to have been very delightful, for my kind friends vied with each other in making much of me, as of course so did my mother. My father talked of going down to Portsmouth with me, but he changed his mind.

"No, no," he said, "you know how to take care of yourself; and it is as well the old boatswain should not come and interfere with you. God bless you, my boy; go on as you have begun, and you will do well."

And Emily. I am not going to repeat all we said to each other. We were very young, and I dare say very silly. We exchanged vows, and hoped to marry when I became a commander, or perhaps, we agreed, it might not be so long; perhaps when I was a lieutenant. Many lieutenants had wives, and though, to be sure, some were not very well off, yet we hoped to be an exception to the general rule, and to have at all events enough to live upon. Thus, full of love and hope, I started away for Portsmouth. I was quickly on board the "Pearl". The First-Lieutenant, Mr Duff, was a man after Captain Schank's own heart—a thorough tar, and under him, doffing my midshipman's uniform, I was speedily engaged with a marline-spike slung round my neck, and a lump of grease in one hand, setting up the lower rigging. The brig was soon fitted for sea. Oldershaw joined her as Second-Lieutenant. My two other friends Tom Twig and Dicky Esse were glad to go to sea again with Captain Schank. I also fell in with Toby Kiddle and Pat Brady at Portsmouth. I persuaded both to join, Toby being rated as a quarter-master, and Pat as captain of the foretop.

"You see, Mister Burton," he observed, with a wink, "I can now write home to Ballybruee to tell them I have been made a captain; and sure it's the truth, and it will help to raise the family in the estimation of the neighbours, and may be they will think one captain as good as another."

I confess that I should have preferred being in a rattling frigate; and yet we had brave hearts on board the brig, and hoped at all events to do something in her. We were ordered out to the North American station, and then to proceed on to the West Indies. It used to be thought, in those days, a good thing to give ships' companies the advantage of a hot and cold climate alternately. The cold was to drive away the yellow fever, and the heat to cure us of frostbites, to which we might be subjected at Halifax or up the Saint Lawrence. We preferred, on the whole, the West Indies, for, being constantly at sea, we had not much sickness on board. We took a good many of the enemy's merchant vessels, which struck without offering much resistance; but, though they assisted to fill our pockets, we gained little honour, or glory, or a chance of promotion. We had been, indeed, a year and a half on the station without exchanging a shot with the enemy. At length, when off the east end of Jamaica, while we were on the starboard tack, a strange ship was discovered steering under easy sail on the opposite tack. What she was we could not make out. She was considerably larger than we were, but still Captain Schank determined, should she be an enemy, to attack her. About an hour before noon she passed to leeward of us, and almost within gun-shot. We made a private signal. It was not answered.

"About ship!" cried the Captain, and away we stood in chase. In about a couple of hours we were within gun-shot. Our bow gun was fired and returned by the enemy's stern chaser. She then hoisted French colours and set more sail, edging away to the southward. At length we got up abreast of her, and brought her to close action. She, however, fought well, and we soon had our braces, bowlines, and tiller-ropes shot away. The enemy, now expecting to make us an easy prize, ran us aboard.

"Boarders away!" cried Captain Schank. The Captain's wooden leg preventing him from getting on board the enemy as rapidly as he wished, Mr Duff led our men. Scarcely, however, had he reached the ship's deck when a pistol bullet through his head laid him low. I was close behind him. Oldershaw was bringing on a fresh set of boarders.

"On, lads, on!" shouted Oldershaw. We swept the enemy before us, and, though they made a stout resistance, in ten minutes we had killed, or driven below or overboard, the greater part of the crew. The remainder, who had escaped aft, threw down their arms and cried for quarter. Our prize mounted twenty-four guns, and the crew amounted to upwards of two hundred men. Two days afterwards we were entering Kingston Harbour with her in triumph. Oldershaw was appointed First-Lieutenant of the brig, and I received an order as her Second-Lieutenant. Soon after this, we were ordered to proceed, with three ships of the line and two frigates, in search of a French squadron, which had been committing depredations on the African coast, and had just been heard of in the neighbourhood of the West Indies. We were delayed by a hurricane which raged over those seas. Fortunately we were in harbour, but some of the ships which were outside suffered greatly. However, as Toby Kiddle observed, "What is sauce for the goose is sauce for the gander," and we could only hope that the enemy had suffered in the same way. At length, after cruising for some time, we, being ahead, discovered a frigate, which, from the cut of her sails, we had little doubt was French. Signalling to our consorts, we gave chase, keeping considerably ahead of all the rest. In about two hours we had got within two miles of the chase, and as we approached still nearer we commenced firing our bow guns. The French frigate, hoisting her colours, returned our fire with her stern chasers. We now shortened sail.

"If we get much nearer," said Captain Schank, "she may send us to the bottom with one of her broadsides; but at this distance we may cripple her and prevent her escaping." The nearest English frigate was by this time about three miles astern of us. Already the Frenchman had cut up our rigging a good deal, and at length one of her shots struck our bow between wind and water. It was quickly plugged, and we continued at some distance firing away, our shot every now and then striking the enemy, but what damage we had done we could not ascertain. The leading frigate was a very fast one, and was now rapidly coming up. We, I confess, were anxiously looking out for her, for, although prudence might have forbade us getting nearer the enemy, our eagerness to stop her would have made us run every risk to effect that object. At length the English frigate got within gun-shot of the enemy. She opened fire with her bow chasers. Down came the Frenchman's flag, when once more we made sail and hove to close to the prize. Captain Schank ordered me to proceed on board and take possession. I felt, I must confess, almost as surprised as a mouse would do at conquering a lion. The French captain, however, with becoming politeness though with somewhat a wry face, presented me with his sword, and we found ourselves in possession of a forty-four gun frigate, measuring upwards of one thousand tons, and a crew of three hundred and fifty men. Besides Frenchmen, there were on board several Englishmen, who formed part of the crew of an Indiaman the frigate had captured two days before. Among them were the second and third officers. The Indiaman had been overtaken at night, and the French ship had fired into her, and killed the captain and first officer and a number of the crew. The passengers who were below had happily escaped. The Indiaman's officers, thorough gentlemanly young fellows, told me that they had only lost sight of the prize the day before, that she was a slow sailer, and from the direction in which she was standing, they had little doubt in what direction we should find her. The recaptured prisoners also told us whereabouts we should fall in with the remainder of the French squadron.

We accordingly sent one of the Indiaman's officers on board the frigate, while Captain Schank received orders from the Commodore to proceed in search of the Indiaman. Scarcely had we lost sight of our squadron, which was standing in the direction the Frenchmen were supposed to be, when it came on to blow from the north-west. The wind rapidly increased till it became a downright heavy gale. Our brig, however, was a fine sea-boat, and under close-reefed topsails rode it out bravely. Our chief anxiety was, however, on account of the risk we ran of losing the Indiaman. Still the mate was convinced that she could not have passed to the northward of where we then were.

"She will be standing on the larboard tack, Captain Schank," he observed; "if she sees all clear she will run through the Gut of Gibraltar, or if not, will make for some port in the Bay of Biscay."

However, as the Atlantic is a broad highway, our hopes of falling in with her were far from sanguine. For three days we lay hove to, till at length the gale moderating we once more made sail and stood to the eastward. A bright look-out was kept for the sight of a sail, and from sunrise to sunset volunteers were continually going aloft, in the hopes of being the first to see the wished-for ship. Next morning, when it was my watch on deck, I heard a voice from the maintopmast head shouting:

"A dismasted ship on the weather-beam not four miles away."

I sent Esse, who was midshipman of the watch, aloft, and he corroborated Pat Brady's statement.

Sending below to call the Captain, I kept the brig away in the direction of the ship. The sea was still running very high. As daylight increased, we could see her clearly rolling in the trough of the sea, and in an utterly helpless condition. For some time the mate could not tell whether it was his own ship or not.

"Too likely," he observed, "for the Frenchman's shot had wounded some of our masts, and she very probably lost them in the late gale."

Captain Schank and all the officers were quickly on deck, as were the crew, and all eyes were turned to the wreck. As we drew near, we were left in no doubt of her being a large Indiaman; and Mr Paul, the mate, soon recognised her as the "Yarmouth Castle," to which he had belonged. The signal of distress was flying on the stump of her mizzen-mast. As we drew near, we discovered that the gale had otherwise severely handled her. Most of her boats were gone, and her bulwarks stove in, probably when the masts were carried away. As we passed a short distance to windward of her, a person ran to the side with a large board, on which was chalked, "Keep by us! Sprung a leak! Pumps choked! Captured by Frenchmen!"

"Ay, ay," shouted Captain Schank, and his voice borne down by the wind probably reached them. As we passed, several people rushed up to the man who had shown the board, and tore it out of his hands. This showed us that we must be careful when going alongside, lest the Frenchmen should attempt to beat us back. The difficulty of communicating with the ship was still very great, for the sea continued high and broken, and she rolled very much. We accordingly wore round and hove to at a little distance, intending to wait till the sea should go down.

The mate told us that there were a great many of the English crew and Lascars left on board, and he thought, should they make the attempt, they would be able to retake the ship from the Frenchmen. No attempt was made, however, and at length, the weather moderating, a boat, of which I took the command, was lowered, the brig being sufficiently near at the time to fire into her, should the French prize crew offer any resistance.

What was taking place on board the Indiaman we could not see, but just as we got alongside several people appeared and hove ropes to us, and assisted me with four of my men to get on board. I observed, as I reached the deck, that a scuffle was taking place forward, and I then found that the passengers and some of the crew had suddenly attacked the Frenchmen, who, it appeared, had intended manning their guns in the hopes of beating off the brig. Our appearance quickly gave an easy victory to our friends. The superior officers of the Indiaman had all been taken out of her. The carpenter, however, was on board, and told me he hoped, if the pumps could be cleared and properly worked, that the leak could be kept under. A richly-laden Indiaman was indeed a prize worth recovering. The passengers had nearly all remained on board, and expressed their gratitude for the timely succour which had been afforded them. The Frenchmen, finding that all hope of carrying off their prize was gone, yielded themselves prisoners; their commanding officer, who had, with his men, been driven forward, delivering up his sword to me. I sent

CHAPTER TWENTY FIVE.

the boat with Dicky Esse back to tell Captain Schank that I thought, with some thirty of our hands in addition to the ship's crew whom we had on board, to be able to keep the pumps going, and to rig jury-masts by which the ship might be safely carried to England. Among the passengers a gentleman was pointed out to me who had been very active in retaking the ship from the hands of the Frenchmen. I inquired his name. "Mr Bramston," was the answer.

"How strange," I thought: "and is Mrs Bramston on board?"

"Yes, sir, she is, but she is very ill, and has constantly kept her cabin."

"Have they any children?" I asked.

"No, none, sir," said a lady who overheard the question. "Poor lady, she once had a daughter, a little girl, who was lost in a very sad way, and I do not think she has ever recovered that event."

As may be supposed I could not then ask further questions, as my entire attention was required for the duty of the ship. I asked Kiddle, who accompanied me on board, what he thought of the weather.

"It's moderating, sir, and I hope we shall be able to keep the ship afloat if we get more assistance."

The sea rapidly went down, and the men I asked for were sent on board. The pumps were again speedily set going, and as the ship laboured less we began to gain upon the leak. Fortunately there was a good supply of spars on board, and I hoped, should the weather continue moderate, to be able to rig jury-masts the following day. We worked hard till nightfall, most of the Frenchmen giving their assistance at the pumps. Indeed, had we not fallen in with them, the probabilities are that the ship would have gone down; so that they owed their lives to us, although they were not well-pleased at being made prisoners. I now for the first time was able to enter the cuddy. Coming off the dark deck, I was struck by the bright light of the cabin, the tables glittering with plate and glass set for supper, well secured, as may be supposed, by the fiddles, a number of passengers, ladies and gentlemen, being collected round them. They greeted me warmly, and numerous questions were put to me as to the probability of the ship's reaching home in safety. I assured them that I hoped in the course of a week or so, if the wind was favourable, that we might find ourselves in the Chops of the Channel. "Although," I added, "you know the chances of war, but I promise you that our brig will stick by you and fight to the last for your protection."

I was not sorry to take my seat at table among them, as I had eaten nothing for some hours. The gentlemen all begged to take wine with me, and assured me they believed that, had we not fallen in with them, the ship would have gone down. When Mr Bramston addressed me, I replied that I knew his name, and asked if he came from Ceylon.

"Yes," he answered, "I have been there for many years."

I then told him that my commander, Captain Schank, had some time before written to him on an important matter, and asked whether he had received the letter.

"Yes," he answered, "just before I left India, and I will speak to you by-and-by on that matter."

After supper he took me aside, and begged to know further particulars of the death of Mr Herbert. "Though," he remarked, "that was not the name by which you knew him."

"Well," he said, after I had told him, "the less his poor daughter knows of these painful circumstances the better. I am now returning with her, and, I am thankful to say, her health has already benefited by the voyage. I trust the meeting with her mother will have a beneficial effect on her."

"I am sure it will on Mrs Lindars," I observed: "her great wish was, that should her daughter have been taken away, she might have left some children on whom she might bestow her long pent-up affection."

"Alas!" said Mr Bramston, "our one only child, a little daughter, was taken from us at an early age in a very sad way. Mrs Bramston had been very ill, and had been advised to proceed to Madras for change of air. An old naval friend offered her and me a passage, and I accordingly hurried on board, leaving our child under the charge of a friend at Colombo. I returned as soon as possible, and finding my wife yearning for her little one, I resolved to send her to her. A dhow was on the point of sailing, in which several friends had taken a passage. I committed our child and nurse to their charge. The dhow never reached her destination, and we have every reason to believe that she foundered with all on board."

"That is indeed strange!" I said aloud. I stopped, for I was afraid of raising hopes in the heart of the father which might be disappointed. He heard me.

"What do you mean?" he asked.

"When was this?" I inquired.

"In the month of July, in the year —," he said.

"That is indeed wonderful," I exclaimed, scarcely able to restrain my feelings. "I was a child at the time," I said, "but I was on board a frigate, which fell in with the wreck of a dhow. The only people alive on board were an Indian nurse and a child—a little girl. The nurse died; but the child was taken care of by my mother, and is now under the protection of the family of the commander of the brig to which I belong, Captain Schank, the officer who wrote to you on the subject of Mr Herbert's death."

"God be praised!" exclaimed Mr Bramston. "I cannot have the shadow of a doubt that the little girl who was picked up by your frigate was my daughter."

"By-the-by, I have a man with me who was on board the 'Boreas' at the time, and he can tell you even more than I can," I remarked.

Mr Bramston was eager to see him. I sent for Kiddle. He corroborated my account, adding further particulars, which left no doubt whatever on the mind of Mr Bramston that the Little Lady—my Emily—was his daughter.

"And is she a pretty child? Can you give me an idea of her size and appearance?"

"Yes, she is, sir, indeed, very pretty; but you must remember she is no longer a child; she is a young lady," I answered, feeling that my voice was very likely to betray my feelings.

"I long to see her," exclaimed Mr Bramston. "But I must break the tidings gently to her mother, or the sudden joy may be too much for her."

We were busily employed all the next day getting up jury-masts, and not till the next evening was I able to go into the cabin. I was then introduced to Mrs Bramston. I found that she was somewhat prepared for the narration I had to give her. The moment I saw her I was convinced that Emily was her daughter, for the likeness was very striking. Well, I must cut my yarn short. Having rigged jury-masts we made sail, and, the wind coming to the southward, steered a course for England. The brig kept cruising about us like a vigilant sheep-dog, ready to do battle with any who might interfere with his charge. At length England was reached, and getting leave, I accompanied my new-found friends to Whithyford. I will not describe the meeting of the mother and her child, and the elder child and her mother. One thing only made me unhappy. I dreaded lest Mr Bramston, who I found had made a large fortune in India, should object to his daughter marrying a poor lieutenant of no family. I could not bear suspense, and so Emily and I told him that we were engaged, and she added that she should break her heart if she were not allowed to marry me. Mr Bramston smiled.

"You are rather young to think of such matters now," he said, "but when my friend here becomes a commander, if you are still in the same mind, I promise you that neither your mother nor I will object."

In the course of two years I did become a commander. We were in the same mind and married. I stuck to my profession, however, was posted, got the command of a dashing frigate, in which I did good service to my country, and am now a KCB with my flag in prospect.

Lector House believes that a society develops through a two-fold approach of continuous learning and adaptation, which is derived from the study of classic literary works spread across the historic timeline of literature records. Therefore, we aim at reviving, repairing and redeveloping all those inaccessible or damaged but historically as well as culturally important literature across subjects so that the future generations may have an opportunity to study and learn from past works to embark upon a journey of creating a better future.

This book is a result of an effort made by Lector House towards making a contribution to the preservation and repair of original ancient works which might hold historical significance to the approach of continuous learning across subjects.

HAPPY READING & LEARNING!

LECTOR HOUSE LLP
E-MAIL: lectorpublishing@gmail.com